Love was serious business

It meant compromise, stretching beyond what was easy to give. It meant passion that came from the same strong feelings with which each pursued life. Passions colliding could mean destruction—or a melding of feelings so strong, nothing could hold against them.

"We're going to be good for each other," Erik promised.

Melanie pulled his head down and kissed his cheek, then his lips. "I know, Erik. I'm not afraid. I think I'm a little . . . awed. Finding you has been like walking into a garden after wandering in a desert. It feels as though life is growing all around me."

Erik caught her face in his hands and said hoarsely, "I love you, Melanie. Our lives begin here and now—no ugly past, only tomorrow."

ABOUT THE AUTHOR

A native of Massachusetts, Muriel Jensen now lives in Astoria, Oregon, with her husband, who is also a writer, two calico cats and a malamute named Deadline. She also has three grown children. Muriel loves investigating restaurants and dress shops—all in the interest of research!

Books by Muriel Jensen

HARLEQUIN AMERICAN ROMANCE

73–WINTER'S BOUNTY
119–LOVERS NEVER LOSE
176–THE MALLORY TOUCH
200–FANTASIES AND MEMORIES
219–LOVE AND LAVENDER
244–THE DUCK SHACK AGREEMENT
267–STRINGS
283–SIDE BY SIDE
321–A CAROL CHRISTMAS
339–EVERYTHING

MURIEL JENSEN

A WILD IRIS

Harlequin Books

TORONTO • NEW YORK • LONDON
AMSTERDAM • PARIS • SYDNEY • HAMBURG
STOCKHOLM • ATHENS • TOKYO • MILAN

To Tom and Bobbi,
thanks for all the fun

Published September 1990

ISBN 0-373-16358-4

Printed in U.S.A.

Chapter One

"Melanie Quinn!"

In the midst of adding a portion of rotini salad to a paper plate already protesting under its load of spaghetti and stuffed manicotti, Melanie put her food down on the buffet and turned.

"Dr. Forman," she said, extending her hand to Harvest Lake's most popular general practitioner. "You're looking well."

The tall, white-haired man, a longtime family friend, ignored her outstretched hand and enfolded her in a bear hug. "I deserve more than a handshake, girl. I removed your tonsils, stitched your scalp and separated you from a fish-hook embedded in your—"

"I remember." She hastily forestalled the reminder of precisely where a bad cast could place a barbed hook. "How are you? Are you still practicing?"

"I am, though just three days a week for the past few years. Nice to have young people around here. You're just staying for the summer, I hear."

Melanie smiled. Harvest Lake's grapevine had always been strong enough to support Tarzan. "I'm illustrating a field guide to Northwest flowers. I want to use our irises, the ones that grow in the clearing by the bend in the lake."

The doctor hugged her again. "Well, it's nice to see you home where you belong." Then he added surreptitiously, "I have to move on. Phyllis Radich has been trying to tell me about her gall bladder all evening, but so far I've managed to stay a step ahead of her."

"She's still a hypochondriac?"

The doctor looked heavenward in supplication. "She's raised the phobia to new levels. I think I'll see if I can manage to get myself arrested."

Melanie frowned at him. "Pardon me?"

Dr. Forman laughed and pointed to a rough plywood structure the size of a phone booth standing in the opposite corner of the church hall. Nailed diagonally across laths that served as bars was a sign that read Jail.

As they watched, a laughing, white-haired man was pushed into the makeshift construction by a younger man and a plump woman Melanie recognized as a friend of her Aunt Reba's. The door was ceremoniously bolted behind him to the teasing cheers of amused bystanders.

The doctor shouted a laugh. "That's the Jail and Bail event sponsored by the Jaycees to help the Ladies of the Lake raise money for Harvest House. You pay five dollars to have someone 'arrested,' and that person has to pay ten dollars to free himself. Or a friend can pay his bail. The fellow they just put in there's an old golf buddy of mine."

As Phyllis Radich began to close in, the doctor winked at Melanie. "I'd better go bail him out. Welcome home, Melanie."

"Darling, I brought you here to meet *young* men," Reba Quinn said quietly as she came up behind her niece. "The old codgers are my territory."

Melanie grimaced at her aunt. Reba was small and smartly dressed in white slacks and a blue and white sweater with a nautical design. Short gray hair feathered back from her face framed bright blue eyes and a remarkably unlined porcelain complexion. A wicked sense of humor and complete disregard for anyone's opinion but her own often belied her regal appearance.

"There's Gordon Breen," Reba said, "that little man with the glasses."

Melanie followed the jut of her aunt's chin and saw a pale man sitting alone at the only unfilled table in the church basement. He was eating with serious concentration from one of the two heaping plates in front of him, an arm curved protectively around both, as though he feared someone would steal them. Melanie raised an eyebrow at her aunt. "I don't think so."

"He does have four children, so he tends to be a little selfish about what's his," Reba said, "but he's a dentist. A dentist means security."

"I don't want security."

"Oh, well, then. There's your man." Reba motioned discreetly in the direction of a tall, muscular young man in the middle of the room. He was surrounded by women. The young ones were giggling, and the older ones smiled fondly at him as he gesticulated wildly, apparently telling a story. "Charm and muscle. Deadly combination."

Melanie shook her head, "Reba..."

"Well, sweetie, what else is there?" Reba shrugged impatiently at her own question. "Well, passion, of course. But if there was a man around here with passion, I'd keep him for myself."

Melanie picked up her plate. "Have you found us a table? One that doesn't include a dentist or a quarterback?"

"You know, Melanie, you lack a sense of humor." Reba led Melanie to a table behind the one occupied by the dentist. A family of four now sat across from him, and he glanced up with hostility, the protective curve of his arm around his food becoming tighter.

"You remind me of your father," Reba went on, sitting opposite Melanie. "He took life very seriously, too."

"He was a policeman," Melanie pointed out. "I don't think you can be too frivolous in that line of work. And anyway, I take my work seriously, but I do enjoy life as well."

"Then why won't you let me introduce you to anyone?" Reba salted a scoop of potato salad. "This is the first time you've spent more than a weekend at home in ten years, and you don't do anything but work. And you've been all over the country, but you're still single at thirty-four. If you were enjoying life, you'd be married with children."

Melanie drew a steadying breath. She's known she'd be up against this badgering from her aunt when she decided to come home for the summer. Reba's matrimonial campaigns on her behalf were legendary. But the woman was all the family she had left, except for Jolene, and that relationship was iffy at best. Still, for reasons she couldn't quite define, coming home had seemed to be a good idea. The decision had quieted the loneliness she'd been feeling for the past year. She had satisfying work and good friends, but suddenly, inexplicably, that was no longer enough. She needed family.

"Reba, I don't want to be married," she said evenly but emphatically. "On the other hand," she said, smiling at her aunt, "if you would like to be, you are free to pursue it and I won't badger you about it. I'm happy to let you be you. So please let me be me."

Reba chewed a forkful of potato salad, dabbed daintily at her mouth with a rough white napkin and sighed. "All right, we'll talk about something else. Have you heard from Jolene?"

Melanie put her plastic fork down and eyed her aunt suspiciously. "You're doing this on purpose, aren't you? All my friends are in crises with their mothers, and because I don't have a mother, are you trying to manipulate the situation so that I don't miss out on those mother-daughter confrontations?''

Reba smiled, satisfied. ''Yes,'' she admitted, unashamed. ''If one refuses to live life to the fullest by having a relationship and falling in love, then conflict is the next best thing to ensure experience and maturity.''

Melanie nodded with fatalistic acceptance. Reba knew how she felt about her stepsister, and yet she always asked about her when she wrote or telephoned. ''She visited me in Denver three years ago, in northern California two years ago, and in Alaska last year. Every time she gets a vacation, she comes to see me, no matter where I'm working.''

''She cares about you,'' Reba said quietly.

Melanie gave her aunt a doubting glance as she buttered a roll. ''She's trying to make up for ruining my teens.''

''Her mother did that.''

''No. Her mother ruined my father's life,'' Melanie said. ''Jolene ruined mine. Could we talk about the weather? Or why not discuss the reason we're here tonight? You didn't tell me much about it; you just forced me into changing my clothes and coming with you. What are the charitable Ladies of the Lake involved in now?''

Reba's eyes brightened. Melanie knew that, besides teasing her niece, Reba's dearest love was the service organization to which she'd belonged for forty years.

''Harvest House is a temporary home and school for disadvantaged boys in trouble. It was established some time after you left. It's not for very bad kids, but for those who don't have enough supervision at home because of absent fathers or overworked mothers. Jerry and Maggie Finch started it about two years ago in that clearing on Burke's Meadow in the mountains across the lake. They run it on a shoestring.'' Reba drew a quick breath and went on. ''It's private and entirely non-profit, and we've been trying to provide the facility with a few extras through fund-raising events. Potlucks like this are fun and always well attended. For a five dollar admission, you can reassure yourself that your hamburger casserole *is* better than your neighbors'. We don't raise large sums, but we like to think that because of our contributions the boys can enjoy something they wouldn't otherwise have—like the money we donated for a VCR. And the Jaycees love to support us with their 'jail.' "

Melanie looked surprised. "I went to school with Jerry Finch. I don't remember him being particularly interested in the disadvantaged."

"Well, you know your uncle and I were away from Harvest Lake for so many years while he worked for Global Oil. I didn't meet Jerry until he came back home three years ago with his new wife. She's probably turned him around. She has an art gallery in town, and she's always involved in some community project or other. He's mayor now, you know."

Melanie found that hard to believe of the grim young man who had come to Harvest Lake High in her senior year. He'd always seemed negative and withdrawn.

"Maggie! Yoo-hoo!" Reba waved both hands in the air at a tall redhead wearing a hand-painted white shirt over skintight black pants. In response to Reba's call, she waved a long, black cigarette holder like a wand. A yard of curly red hair lapped against her shoulders as she walked toward them.

"This is Melanie Quinn, my niece," Reba said, pulling Maggie down beside her on the bench. "Mel, this is Maggie Finch."

Maggie reached her free hand across the table. "I'm so pleased to meet you," she said warmly. "When Reba told me about you, I made some inquiries. Your work is excellent. I'd like to invite you to have a show at my gallery while you're here."

"Thank you." Melanie shook her hand, preparing to decline the invitation. "But, you see, I'm on commission to do..." A sharp rap against her shinbone stopped her. She looked across the table at her aunt's innocent expression.

"But certainly you could find the time, Melanie," Reba said sweetly. "I'm sure the show would be a sellout, and the money would finance you for another one of those solitary mountain treks I heard you like so much, where all you do is hunt for flowers and paint."

Melanie replied, also sweetly, "But, Reba, I only have a few small paintings with me. I'd have to send home to Denver for the bigger pieces, or I wouldn't have enough to show."

"Would that be so difficult?" she asked. "The Ladies of the Lake could sponsor the evening, with some of the proceeds going to Harvest House."

Put that way, the offer became something Melanie couldn't turn down without looking selfish in front of the mayor's wife. She smiled at Maggie. "I'd love to," she said.

"Wonderful!" Maggie's delight almost softened Melanie's annoyance over her aunt's machinations. "You're welcome to come to the gallery anytime. I'll show you the room we'll use so you can determine just how many paintings you'll need. I'll do lots of advertising and plan an elegant champagne reception."

The woman's enthusiasm made Melanie feel small for having been so reluctant to accept. "Thank you, Maggie. I'll come by one day this week."

"Wonderful." Maggie turned to Reba. "Did you remember to bring your committee's budget report? I'd like to look it over before the meeting."

"I did, but I left it in the car." Reba groaned at her own forgetfulness and began to climb out of the bench. Melanie put a hand over hers to stop her. "I'll run out and get it for you."

"Thank you, darling. The car's unlocked."

Melanie found the old blue binder containing Reba's club notes on the back seat of the red Camaro. She smiled as she retrieved the book and closed the door, wondering how many other sixty-six-year-olds drove sports cars.

The sky was dark blue with a smattering of stars that reached into the lake at the end of the block. Melanie allowed herself a moment to absorb the quiet of the small town evening and the delicious fragrance that seemed to belong to Harvest Lake alone. She'd visited many beautiful spots throughout the Northwest in pursuit of the perfect wildflower, but no other place had quite the distinctive perfume of this quiet lakeshore spot. The spring evening was redolent of pine and cedar, and the particular sweetness of clean water. The fragrance always brought back images of her childhood and the afternoons she and her father had spent fishing on the lake. She wondered if she would ever be able to remember him without an ache of loss.

The weight of the binder in her hands reminded her that she was on an errand. Melanie hurried back inside, pausing at the door when she noticed that the table she had occupied with Reba was now empty, except for their untended plates. Looking around for her aunt, she was startled when a strong warm hand closed gently over her upper arm.

"You're under arrest," a deep voice announced.

Melanie glanced up into quiet gray eyes in a smiling, angular face. She recognized the man as the one who had jailed Dr. Forman's golf buddy.

She smiled and pulled herself lightly away from him. "I don't live here, I . . ."

He pulled back very gently. "Ignorance of the law is no excuse, Miss Quinn. I have to take you in."

She lifted the book in her free hand as he led her across the room. "You don't understand. My aunt needs . . ."

"There you are." Reba appeared out of the chatting groups that had finished dinner and were milling around near an old piano. She snatched the book from Melanie's hands and patted her cheek. "Enjoy your incarceration, darling."

Melanie uttered a gasp of dismay. "Aren't you going to pay my bail?"

Reba feigned surprise. "Of course not, Melanie. I just paid to have you arrested. See you later."

"Come along quietly," the man directed as Reba disappeared into a knot of her Ladies of the Lake cronies.

Melanie looked up at him with resignation. She noticed laughter behind his eyes and a smile that sparked her own. "I haven't eaten my dinner," she complained good-naturedly, pointing in the general direction of the table where it still waited.

He looked aggrieved. "That's too bad. But last meals are only for those facing the juice."

Melanie rolled her eyes. "I should also point out that I left my purse on the table with my dinner. You can't get ten dollars out of me without it."

He shook his head pityingly. "Guess that makes you a lifer. Excuse me. Coming through. Dangerous criminal here." He pushed his way through a crowd of several men standing in conversation near the jail. Melanie recognized Dr. Forman among the amused group and pleaded with dramatic desperation, "Would you please call my lawyer?"

Melanie's "jailer" opened the door and pushed her gently inside. The cubicle was so small that when she turned to face him, they were only inches apart. He leaned a forearm on the side of the structure and grinned at her. His shoulders were broad under a dark blue T-shirt with the Harvest Lake Jaycees logo on the right side of his chest, his legs, long and lean in acid-washed jeans. He was beautiful, Melanie thought, and vaguely familiar. She studied him, trying to pinpoint where she'd seen him before. She'd recognized many of the older Harvest Lake residents when she'd arrived home, but most of her contemporaries had moved away in search of better job opportunities in Portland and Salem.

"Erik Channing," he said, accurately reading her thoughts. "I was a year ahead of you, but we were in Spanish III together."

"That's right." Smiling, Melanie extended her hand. "I got to know your father well after you went off to college. *¿Como esta?*"

His large warm hand swallowed hers. *"Muy bien. ¿Y usted?"* He laughed. "Don't answer that. I'm afraid that's the sum total of what I remember from that class. Except a few words Hector Enriquez taught me that probably shouldn't be repeated."

"Let Melanie go, Erik!" a plump, redheaded woman serving as bail bondsman called from a table a few feet away. She sat behind a money box into which she placed a bill just handed to her by Dr. Forman.

As Melanie prepared to step through the door, Erik put his arm across it. "Thanks a lot, Jake," he told the doctor wryly. "I was just getting acquainted."

Jake Forman, in the act of pocketing his wallet, looked from the grinning young man to the pretty young woman confined behind his arm. "My mistake." He laughed throatily, reopened his wallet, and dropped a five into the money box. "Guess you're rearrested, Melanie," he said, winking at her as he walked away.

Melanie frowned threateningly at her jailer. "I'm not standing here another minute without my dinner and a cup of coffee."

He shook his head apologetically. "Society discourages pampering criminals."

"Isn't there something in the law forbidding double jeopardy?"

He shrugged. "Beats me."

She folded her arms. "You never read me my rights."

He smiled, unperturbed. "That's because you don't have any."

Melanie squared her shoulders. "All right. Let's get down to the nitty-gritty." She looked around surreptitiously. "Are you open to a bribe?"

There was a small flash of humor in his eyes, as though he was enjoying some private joke. Then, he raised his right eyebrow as he, too, glanced around. "I could be," he said quietly.

"Get me my dinner, my coffee, and my purse, and I'll see that you get the biggest grape snow cone in the place."

He winced. "I didn't even like those when I was a kid."

"A box of caramel corn, then."

"No."

She peered through the bars at the booth across the aisle from the jail. A cluster of pink-cheeked ladies served customers three deep under a banner that read Almond Roca To Die For. With a determined look on her face, Melanie turned to her jailer. "A pound of almond roca, take it or leave it."

He stepped out of the small cubicle, closed the door and locked it. Then he peered between the bars at her. "Describe the purse."

"It's a small, natural straw clutch," she said.

He looked at her blankly. "In case you want to shift gears?"

She bit back a laugh. "A clutch is a purse without a strap or handle. You 'clutch' it under your arm."

"Ah." He nodded. "Be right back. Need I mention that attempted escape is punished by doubling the sentence?"

She smiled. "With my dinner and my coffee, I'll happily serve my time."

As Melanie waited, two other "prisoners" were added to the tiny cubicle, a large man with a cigar, and Phyllis Radich, the hypochondriac from whom Dr. Forman had made his escape. The woman immediately sat on the cubicle's small bench.

"I'm so nauseated," she complained, fanning herself with a business-size envelope she withdrew from her purse. "I shouldn't have eaten Mildred Feeney's fruit salad. She leaves the skins on the apples and they get me every time. I have diverticulitis, you know." She pushed a hand into her side and groaned. "Any little thing, even the seeds in berries and on dinner rolls set me off. And vegetables! Don't get me started on vegetables. I once ate a . . ."

The man with the cigar bellowed from between the bars for the bail bondsman and handed out thirty dollars. The jail door opened and the man hurried out, with Melanie following as Phyllis Radich continued to groan.

Erik, carrying her tray with all the requested items on it, approached with a frown. "What's this?" he asked.

She laughed, taking the tray from him. "A pardon."

"What about my bribe?"

"Relax," she teased. "I may be a criminal, but I'm not a welsher. Can I just please have my dinner first?"

He took her elbow and guided her to a table. "I'll have coffee with you while you eat, just to be sure you don't forget." He sat across from her and raised a hand, beckoning one of the volunteers circulating with a coffeepot.

Melanie frowned at him as she spread her napkin on her lap, and dived into her pasta. "You're not very trusting. Are you really a warden, or something?"

"Close." He held up an empty foam cup and the woman poured. "I'm the district attorney. Thank you, Mrs. Denison." He sipped, then put his cup aside and crossed his forearms on the table. His gray eyes examined her features with interest. "Prisoners like you would make the job more fun."

With some surprise Melanie realized that she hadn't been flirted with in a long time. She'd forgotten how much fun it could be. "Because I offered you a bribe?" she asked.

He shook his head. "Because you're very pretty."

She dismissed his comment with a careless toss of her head. "But you wouldn't get to look at me, would you? You'd probably do your best to have me put away for the maximum term the law allows."

"Unless you offered me a bribe."

"What would happen to that trim waistline after several pounds of almond roca?"

Melanie watched his smile form while she wondered how that thought had traveled from her brain to her lips.

"You noticed. Thank you."

"I'm an artist," she said reasonably. "I'm trained to notice good lines."

"That's right." He frowned thoughtfully. "You're an illustrator working on a book or something. The Harvest Lake *Herald* carried an article about your coming home. According to the piece, you're renowned in your field."

Melanie shook her head, a small blush coloring her cheeks. "Hardly. But I love what I do. I came home to sketch the wild iris in the forest clearing by the lake. And, frankly, I was a little homesick."

Erik sipped his coffee and smiled. "I can understand that. I spent ten years working in Los Angeles. During the first few years I swore I'd leave four or five times, but I had too much to do. Finally, the homesickness wore off until..." He paused, a vaguely troubled expression invading his open warmth. Then, he dismissed it with an inclination of his head. "...until my father got sick. That was a good enough excuse to come home."

Concerned, Melanie leaned across the table. John Channing had owned Harvest Lake Florist for as long as Melanie could remember. He'd provided the flowers for her first few tentative drawings in high school and had been kind enough to answer endless questions. He'd been a good friend. "Yes, Reba told me. How is he?"

"He had to retire, but he's fine if he doesn't overdo it. I check on him every day, but he doesn't like me hovering too close. He really lit into me for moving back here."

Melanie recalled some of the things John had told her about his son when she'd visited the flower shop. "He used to boast about you all the time. Weren't you the youngest assistant district attorney Los Angeles County ever had?"

He rolled his eyes, obviously embarrassed. "Yes. But practicing law in L.A. ages one pretty quickly."

"Are you finding it hard to adjust to small-town life after the big city?"

He shook his head. "There's a lot to be said for peace and quiet, something I didn't realize in my younger days."

"Darlings, we have the best idea!" Reba and several of her committee descended upon them, clustering around with delighted smiles. Melanie and Erik exchanged a look of trepidation.

"What's that?" Erik asked.

"Well..." Reba began. The ladies huddled a little closer. "Do you remember the cocktail party you hosted last year to benefit Harvest House?"

"Yes," he answered warily.

"We held it before the opening of our summer stock theater. It brought everyone out."

Erik nodded and the ladies began to titter. "But summer theater isn't coming to Harvest Lake this year."

Reba grinned broadly. "We have something better." She turned the grin on her niece and Melanie tried not to panic. "We have Melanie Quinn!" Reba's eyes glowed. "Imagine if you hosted a cocktail party before her show at the gallery. We'd get everyone in the county to show up, maybe even a few from out of state..." She paused for breath, apparently still not finished. "And you know what would give our publicity enough of a boost to make this practically a state-wide event?"

Melanie couldn't grasp the details, but she had a sinking feeling she could guess the gist of the plot. When she looked across the table at Erik and saw the wry humor in his eyes, she knew she was close.

"If you and Melanie, Harvest Lake's two symbols of success, will agree to cochair the event."

Chapter Two

"What do you say?" Reba asked, glowing with anticipation. The ladies waited eagerly.

Melanie saw the same reluctance she felt in accepting the proposition reflected in Erik's eyes. For a moment that surprised her. They'd just spent the last twenty minutes talking and teasing like old friends. She was reluctant because she had work to do; she'd come home to sketch the wild iris and to decide whether or not to sell her childhood home. Reba had coerced her into having the show, but she didn't need the added distraction of having to cochair it. But why should Erik Channing be hesitant? "Isn't Erik awfully busy?" she asked.

Erik leapt on her comment like a drowning man grasping at floating debris. "I really do have a full schedule."

Reba rolled her eyes. "How busy can you be in the summer in quiet little old Harvest Lake? Erik . . ." Her eyes settled on his pleadingly. "You can help us put money toward the school's bus fund, *and* make Melanie's show such a success she can retire here."

Erik shot Melanie a wry grin, but said nothing. He seemed to be waiting for her to make the final decision.

Reba turned her appeal on her niece. "The home's bus is thirty years old. We need a new one desperately." She added gravely, "The boys' lives are probably at risk every time they go out."

"I don't doubt it's a great cause, Reba," Melanie agreed, "I'm just not sure I'm—"

"You are," Reba insisted. "Trust me." She turned to Erik. "The two of you will really attract people and make this Harvest Lake's fund-raiser event of the decade!"

"Maybe even the century!" a flushed-face little lady with orange hair added excitedly. When everyone turned to look at her, she subsided in embarrassment. "Well, at least the decade."

Melanie couldn't let her personal problems prevent a group of good-hearted ladies from helping a group of underprivileged boys. "All right," she said quietly. Her reply was greeted with a collective shout from the ladies, who turned simultaneously to look at Erik.

He studied them for a moment, looked at Melanie with eyes that held resigned amusement and finally nodded. "Sure. Why not?"

He was hugged and kissed with fervor. "Come on, girls," Reba cried, waving a hand in the air in a gesture that made Melanie think of an elderly Joan of Arc rallying her troops. "Let's go tell Maggie!"

As the ladies hurried off, Melanie gave her companion a level look. "Why didn't you just refuse?" she asked candidly.

"Why didn't you?" he challenged.

Melanie sighed. "Because I can't refuse Reba anything."

Erik nodded and sipped from his cup, grimacing at the taste of cold coffee. He pushed it aside. "Apparently, we suffer from the same affliction. I have Thursdays off. We can meet at my place to plan our strategy. But I don't know much about art shows."

Melanie shrugged. "I don't much about throwing parties. So I guess we've just found the natural division of labor. You plan the party and I'll arrange the show."

Erik rubbed a thumb along his jaw. "Rather than divide the labor, maybe we could just share it—help each other with the duties we don't understand."

Melanie looked at him steadily, intrigued by the idea despite her reluctance to accept it. "I got the distinct impression you were reluctant to get involved with this project."

For a moment he looked as though he might explain, then simply shook his head. "You were mistaken," he said. "When are you free for our first meeting?"

"Afternoons," Melanie replied, accepting their partnership. "I'm usually busy with the irises in the morning."

"How about Thursday afternoon?"

At Melanie's nod, he asked, "Are you familiar with the old Scofield house?"

Melanie sat up a little straighter, her full attention snared. "Yes. Why?"

"I live there," he replied, noting her reaction. "What's the matter?"

"Nothing." She couldn't help her covetous expression as she propped an elbow on the table and leaned her chin on her fist. "It's just that it's been my lifelong dream to live there," she said dreamily. "I used to go fishing with my father and we'd anchor out there on the lake. Instead of watching my line I'd stare at the old house. Is it as wonderful inside as I've imagined?"

He smiled gently. "I don't know what you imagined, but it sounds like the way I felt the first time I saw it after coming back home. I remembered it from when I was a kid, but it didn't make much of an impression on me then. It was just old. I've put on a new roof, rewired the upstairs and added two more bathrooms. I still have years of work to put into it, but it's coming along, little by little."

Melanie leaned toward him intently. "Tell me about the room upstairs in that little gable. Does it have a window seat?"

He shook his heard regretfully, as though hating to disappoint her. "Sorry. I'm not sure what the Scofields used it for, but there was nothing in it but peeling linoleum. I put up a bookshelf on the wall that abuts the bedroom, and an admiral's lamp I found in an antique shop in New England. I don't know what to do about curtains."

"Something sheer or lace," she suggested, before she could stop herself. Then she sipped from her cup and tried to remember that it was none of her business. But she couldn't. "Or shutters, maybe. Is the fireplace stone?"

He shook his head. "Marble. I find myself seduced by the style and elegance."

"Well," she said, "it sounds wonderful."

"Don't move, ma'am!" The directive came from a tall burly man who climbed into the bench beside Erik. He smiled across the table at Melanie. "I don't know who you are, miss, but this man escaped this afternoon from the Harvest Lake Home for the Absurdly Insane. He not only slurps his soup, puts three teaspoonfuls of sugar in his coffee and wears *a Jaycees T-shirt*..." The young man covered his eyes as though the sight of Erik's shirt was more than he could stand. Then he lowered his voice and leaned toward Melanie. "He actually roots for the Dodgers. Although, he's showing remarkably good taste in having dinner with you. When I get him back to his handlers, perhaps you and I—"

"Curtis." Erik's voice cut into the man's monologue.

"What?" Curtis demanded impatiently. "I'm trying to make a little time here."

"Curtis, I'm on *my* time," Erik said with a tap of his fingertip against his watch. "What is my P.I. doing bothering me after-hours?"

Curtis smiled at Melanie. "P.I. stands for Particularly Important."

"Make that Patently Imbecilic," Erik corrected. "Melanie, since I can't get rid of him, I'd like you to meet a private investigator I often work with, Bill Curtis. Bill, this is Melanie Quinn, a former resident of Harvest Lake who's come home for the summer."

"Married?" Curtis asked of Melanie.

"Busy," she replied with a laugh. "But I am pleased to meet you. You're Fran Curtis's son, aren't you? She's a good friend of my aunt."

Curtis nodded. "Guilty. You can't be busy all the time."

"Bill, what do you want?" Erik demanded.

Curtis suddenly became serious. "I found something I thought you'd want to see," he said.

"At eight o'clock on a Friday night?"

"I... can't keep it very long," Curtis said casually.

"You mean you got it illegally," Erik guessed, already climbing out of the bench. "Bill, I keep telling you—"

"Will you relax? I didn't get it illegally."

"Then how did you get it?"

"From someone who is unaware that he's loaned it to me." Satisfied with his ironic explanation, Curtis smiled proudly at Melanie, then frowned when he met Erik's glare. "So, if you quit dawdling, I can have it back before they become aware of the... loan. Feel free to follow me whenever you're ready." He turned to smile at Melanie once more. "I hope we meet again, Miss Quinn." He pointed a thumb over his shoulder in Erik's direction. "He's no good for you. Trust me."

As Bill Curtis walked toward the door, Erik paused to look at Melanie. "I'll be in touch about the show. If you don't hear from me, it's because Bill and I are sharing a *real* prison cell somewhere."

"WHAT DO YOU THINK of Erik Channing? Isn't he gorgeous?" Reba drove along the dark, lakefront road that led to the houses where she and Melanie lived, two blocks apart. She was still riding the crest of her fund-raising coup. "You're going to make such a great team!"

Melanie, her head supported against the headrest, turned to look at her aunt. "I can't believe you had your own niece arrested."

Reba raised an eyebrow. "You can't? Darling, I thought you knew me well enough to know I'd go to any lengths to introduce you to a handsome man. And Erik's such a sweetheart."

"Your 'sweetheart' had me rearrested after Dr. Forman paid my bail."

Reba laughed. "I saw that. He must have enjoyed talking to you. And what about you? Did you enjoy talking to him?"

She had. There seemed little harm in admitting it. "I did. He bought the old Scofield place."

Reba nodded. They'd reached the driveway of Melanie's home, and Reba pulled in, turning the motor off. "He'd just moved in last year when we had the fund-raiser there."

"He's invited me to meet him there for our first meeting about the party." Lazily, Melanie unbuckled her seat belt. "I've dreamed about being inside that house since I was a little girl."

Reba's tone quieted as she asked, "Have you given more thought to selling this place?" She stared through the windshield at the simple two-story house where Melanie had grown up.

Melanie followed her gaze and sighed. "I hate to let it go, but I get back so seldom now and..." She hesitated for an instant and looked at the deep front lawn. "I never look at the lawn without seeing my father lying there."

Reba reached over to pat her hand. "I know. It just reminds me of a time when you were little, before Ray and I started following the oil, when your mother was alive and so in love with your father and we all had such good times together." She squeezed Melanie's hand a little harder. "I know things have to change. But so much has gone out of my life. I like the idea of something in Harvest Lake that draws you back to me."

Melanie reached over to hug her, then frowned at her scoldingly. "Well, even if I sold the house, you'd still be here to draw me back."

Reba looked unconvinced in the shadows of the car. "Your work is in such demand now, you're always heading off in other directions. You haven't been home in four years, and then it was only for two days. I'll bet if it wasn't for our irises, you wouldn't be here now."

"Reba, I *am* here," Melanie said gently. "Let's just enjoy the summer, okay? There's time to worry about the house, later." Melanie pushed the car door open, then turned to ask, "Do you want to come along when I visit the gallery?"

"I'd love to," Reba replied. "Let me know when, and I'll take you to lunch first."

Melanie closed the door and watched her aunt drive away. In the familiar surroundings of her childhood home, she flipped lights on, lit the burner under the kettle and turned the furnace up against the slight evening chill. Wandering into the downstairs room she'd converted to a studio, Melanie switched the light on and narrowed her eyes against the sudden glare. Around the room were photos of her father in uniform, in plain clothes when he became a detective, of her standing beside him, holding a fairly substantial bass by its lip. There were other memorabilia from his days on the force and trophies, awards, diplomas, from her days in school.

On the windowsill near her taboret was her parents' wedding photo, the big, blond Irishman, his hairline already receding at twenty-five, and the small brown-haired woman who had died at twenty-nine and was little more to Melanie than a vague impression of warmth and laughter.

Beside that photo, in a double frame, was a portrait of Melanie taken at her grade school graduation, and a photo of Jolene at about thirteen, a profusion of wavy dark hair framing an elfin face with big blue eyes that held a lost expression, and a smile that looked a little strained. Melanie had left the photos there for eighteen years because her father had always kept them there, and when she took his den over for her studio, she'd decided to change very little. But sometimes, when she was lonely, she found the photos difficult to look at, this room hard to work in.

It had been just outside that window that her father had died in her arms, the victim of a large caliber bullet and his own determination to rid Harvest Lake of a dealer in vice and corruption. She'd been only seventeen and it had been a long time before she'd been able to deal with the horror. The anguish and agony of that moment, and the grimness of the weeks that followed came back to her with fresh intensity. She'd known that would happen when she came home; it always did. But the irises were here and she had to paint them.

The memory of her father receded like a dull ache as she turned her attention to the sketch on her watercolor easel. She frowned. The iris refused to take shape. It was there, perfectly proportioned, intricately detailed, but lifeless. The iris she'd clipped this morning to bring back to the studio drooped in its glass of water, its delicate petals turning brown and curling. Melanie sat on the stool in front of her easel and took the glass in her hand, examining the sorry specimen. Irises were a particular challenge to draw because, once cut, they lasted only a day. She would try again tomorrow. Certainly, in the seven weeks left of her stay at Harvest Lake, she'd be able to produce the paintings. Of course, now she was committed to a show. That meant she'd have to send home for some of her work, and mat and frame a few smaller pieces she already had with her.

She answered the shrill whistle of the kettle, trying to focus on the details involved in the new project. The prospect of working with Erik Channing was appealing. After all, he was very appealing. During their brief encounter, she'd found him warm and amusing. There was something hidden in his eyes that gave him an air of mystery.

He'd been as reluctant to commit himself to working with her as she'd been to working with him. Yet, when she'd tried to make him admit it, he'd denied it instead and had made plans for their first meeting. Perhaps there was something in her eyes that he found mysterious, too.

Melanie tossed the iris into the trash and the water into the sink, laughing at the idea. There was nothing mysterious about her. She opened a cannister of tea and filled a metal tea egg with a fragrant Earl Grey blend. Well, whatever his reason for agreeing to cochair the project with her, it would get her into the Scofield house. Walking into the living room with a cup of steaming tea, she considered that prospect with definite anticipation.

ERIK TOSSED HIS JACKET at the brass coatrack in the corner of his office. As he sat down behind his desk, Bill Curtis handed him a manila folder. Erik opened it and began to read from the sheet of white, watermarked stationery.

The letter, dated February 7 of the current year and addressed to Jerry Finch at his Harvest Lake residence, read: "The business deal we discussed sounds workable. Acquire the product and we'll negotiate. Walter."

Erik looked behind the letter for its envelope, and finding none, he leaned back in his chair. He motioned Bill to take the chair that faced his desk. "So, Finch is putting together a deal, huh? One we can get in on from the beginning." He gave Bill a wicked grin. "Any thoughts on who Walter is?"

Bill rested his ankle on the opposite knee and looked thoughtful. "Well, there's Walker Cronkite, but I imagine he's too busy to negotiate his own deals. And, of course, there's Walter Reed, but I think he's gone to his reward, even though he's got his own hospital. Maybe that's something you should investigate. A guy has a hospital named after him and dies anyway. Doesn't seem right."

Erik closed his eyes and shook his head. He should hire Ferguson and Pratt for investigations, like all the other attorneys he knew. Or the county should spring for an in-house investigator. He'd get results quicker, with a lot less hassle. But he knew he wouldn't get the detail Curtis always came up with, and it wouldn't be delivered with such style. "You dragged me away from the potluck, Bill," Erik reminded him threateningly.

"Yeah, and a beautiful woman. You want to tell me about that?" Curtis leaned forward, anxious for details.

"Just met the lady. Nothing to tell. Give me your best guess about Walter."

"Okay." Bill propped his feet on the corner of Erik's desk and crossed his ankles. "Walter Abernathy."

Erik frowned, a meditative expression on his face. "Walter Abernathy. The Seattle restaurateur?"

"The same. He has places in Portland, San Francisco and L.A., and is one of three partners in a casino in Vegas."

"What kind of business do you suppose they discussed?"

Bill shrugged. "Got me. I just thought, with your suspicions about Finch, you'd be interested in some evidence of a possibly unsavory connection."

"Mmm." Erik scanned the letter again. "Harvest Lake's mayor dealing with a shady restaurateur with ties to Vegas." He closed the file and pushed it toward Curtis. "It might be interesting to track down the person behind the new gas station for which our illustrious mayor pushed through a zoning change."

Bill took the file. "Ned Miller owns the oil company."

"Locally, yes, but who has the state franchise?"

Bill stood up. "I'll get right on it."

Erik got to his feet and came around the desk to shake Curtis's hand. "Good work, guy. Do I want to know where you got the letter?"

Bill smiled. "I have a friend in Finch's office who's keeping his eyes open for me."

Erik nodded. "Well, you'd better warn your friend to watch himself, too. If he gets caught before we put Finch away, he could be in big trouble."

"Right."

Erik led the way out, flipping off the lights and pausing to lock his office door.

"Golf Thursday afternoon?" Curtis asked.

Erik shook his head with regret. "Sorry. Reba's got me locked into one of her schemes for Harvest House. I'm meeting with Melanie Quinn on Thursday to lay the groundwork."

Curtis raised an eyebrow. "For yourself or the project?"

"The project," he replied. "She's my cochairman. When she's not working with me, she's going to be busy in a field of irises, so don't go planning ahead."

Curtis emitted a little sigh of pleasure. "I could die a happy man in a field of irises."

Erik pushed his friend toward the stairs. "She's not your type, Bill."

"Why not?"

"She's sane . . . and she appears to have taste."

Undaunted, Curtis asked, "Does she have a sister?"

"She does, actually." They walked the two flights of stairs to the lobby of the courthouse. "She's visited Reba a few times. Her name's Joanne, or something." He smiled at Curtis as he pushed open the big glass door to the street. "She's a little . . . funny. She's a part-time actress. Last time I saw her, her hair reminded me of Vampira's and she chattered like a magpie. I think she lives in New York."

Curtis sighed with an air of exaggerated despondency. "I've got to find a woman, Erik. I mean, I'm not getting any younger, you know? I don't know what I'm doing wrong. I'm such a nice guy. I bathe regularly. I even floss."

"You do?" Erik asked.

Curtis turned to him and said seriously, "Between my toes. Every day."

Erik put a comforting arm around his shoulder. "If that's true, we could very well be on to the problem, Bill."

Chapter Three

Melanie lay on her stomach in the damp grass, eye to eye with a wild iris. Its companions leaned to the right with the late morning breeze, but Melanie's model remained still, as though in deference to her efforts to commit its delicate, ruffly lines to paper. After three hours spent prone in the clearing near the lake, she had a vicious ache in her shoulders, a headache from blinking away the sun's glare, and a terrible frustration. The lavender bloom with the pale yellow spine on its graceful falls refused to give up its secrets.

Melanie pushed herself up, sat back on her heels and tried to study her sketches objectively. "I'm closer," she finally said aloud. Then, gathering up her pad and pencils, she stuffed them into her canvas bag. "No I'm not," she grumbled, picking up her broad-brimmed hat and jamming it on her head as she rose to her feet. Slinging the bag over her shoulder, she headed off along the shore for the six-block walk home.

The sun, which had gained warmth and brilliance as June wore on, soothed the taut muscles in her back as she walked. The lake lapped quietly against its banks, a quiet background to the boisterous quack of the mallards who populated it. Approaching the forest of long-needled pines, which leaned closer to the lake, Melanie walked into its shaded canopy and breathed deeply. She was rewarded with the pine and garden fragrance that was so familiar to her.

The loud voices were a discordant note in the natural stillness. Melanie's head turned in their direction and she saw a small boat halfway across the lake.

"...have to do it," Melanie heard a masculine voice say, then a higher, more excited voice said, "...can't...won't..." There were other words that were indistinguishable, but the two she heard were spoken with emphasis.

Melanie moved closer to the lakeshore knowing the forest protected her from visibility. She heard the words "stupid" and "foolish" and then a little scream. The boaters were out too far to be observed clearly, but she could see the small vessel begin to rock wildly. Her heart beat faster at the ugly possibility of violence, but the shouting stopped and the boat began to move under the strong stroke of the oars. She was relieved to see that there were still two figures in the boat. Just a quarrel, she told herself, trying to shake off the disturbing feeling left by the brief scene. She went back to the path, distracted by more than her unsatisfactory sketches of the wild iris.

ERIK STUDIED THE PHOTOCOPY he'd made of Finch's letter and tried to read between the lines. The message was so carefully worded he was sure the author's intention had been to conceal the real subject from other eyes. He reread the two lines: "The business deal we discussed sounds workable. Acquire the product, and we'll negotiate." What business? What product did Finch have at hand that would bring a profit to a high roller like Abernathy? The paintings in Maggie's gallery? He doubted that. She showed local artists, and though their talents were formidable, their asking prices were not.

He also wondered who in Finch's office had passed Bill Curtis the note. Some city employee who hadn't gotten the vacation time he wanted? Or some conscientious civil servant who had reason to suspect Finch of wrongdoing? Could the D.A.'s office build a case that may be based on a grudge? Sure, he told himself, and the evidence would be there.

He'd been suspicious for months that something untoward was going on in the mayor's office. In subtle quiet ways Jerry Finch went to bat for what seemed, at first glance, to be unrelated matters appearing before the city council. A zoning change, a right-of-way, highway access at a dangerous intersection. When Erik had personally checked out who stood behind the various projects and found the same man involved in all three, he'd put Bill on the case. He was fairly certain they were onto something. But when he'd launched the quiet investigation, he hadn't counted on getting scared.

He felt the hollow coldness in the pit of his stomach that usually came with memories of the six weeks he'd spent in the hospital in Los Angeles. He slammed his drawer closed and walked across the floor of his small office to check the pocket of his suit jacket for a cigarette. Nothing. Lint and an old credit card slip. Damn. He yanked his office door open. "Glad, can I borrow a cigarette?"

A plump middle-aged woman in jeans and a blue sweatshirt with the picture of a boat on it and script that read Fish Harvest Lake continued to type without looking up. "You mean a cancer stick?"

Erik sighed. "Don't start with me, Gladys."

"You quit," his secretary reminded him, still typing.

"I'll give you a raise," he promised rashly.

"You can't do that," she said, pulling a neatly typed sheet out of the roller and putting a fresh one in. "The county commission would have to vote on it. This is a nonsmoking building, remember? You'll end up in the slammer."

Erik gave the back of her chair a spin and stopped it with his foot when they were eye to eye. He put his hands on her shoulders and looked down into a face that managed to appear cherubic and unyielding at the same time. "One little weed, Gladdy, and I won't tell the commissioners you take a two-hour lunch every Thursday afternoon when I'm not here, and spend it somewhere in the back of Burgess's Barber Shop."

"How did you...?" She began in indignant surprise, the color flooding up from her neck.

"I'm the D.A., Gladys. Bringing down ruthless perpetrators is what I do. Now what about the cigarette?"

Gladys, suddenly conciliatory, frowned at him. "I smoke Virginia Slims, boss. How would it look if the sheriff walked into your office and saw you smoking a six-inch long cigarette with a blue flower on it?"

Erik straightened up and put a hand over his eyes, visibly submitting to defeat. "Do you have a mint? Chocolate? Anything?"

"There I can help you." Gladys spun herself around and reached into the bottom drawer of her desk. "Gummi bears or a Hershey bar?" she asked.

He decided in an instant that popping tiny bear-shaped candies into his mouth wouldn't look much better than smoking a cigarette with a blue flower on it. "Hershey, please."

She handed him the candy bar. "And there's fresh coffee in the pot."

Putting the chocolate bar into his shirt pocket, Erik went to the old oak table that held a coffee pot and an odd assortment of cups. He poured the strong black brew into a pottery mug with his name on it that had been a birthday gift from Gladys.

"Want me to hold your calls until you've got a grip on your character again?" Gladys asked over her shoulder. Her glasses were riding so low on her nose, they seemed to have met her grin.

He raised an eyebrow at her and headed for his office. "If you think they can wait until 1997." He closed his door on the sound of her laughter.

He put the cup and the candy bar down on his desk and went to the file cabinet. He routed through the bottom drawer where he kept personal projects until he found the folder with the mailing list for last year's Harvest House cocktail party. Settling into his chair, he opened the folder and scanned the list of names while he peeled the top half of the wrapper off the candy bar.

His mind refused to register the words. It insisted on drifting back to that afternoon three years ago in an alley off Spring Street when Pete D'Annibale's men had worked him over. That feeling was gone from the pit of his stomach, and he was able to watch the scene play through in his mind's eye with a dispassion that surprised him. That happened sometimes. The fear left him and he could remember with detachment that he'd been offered a bribe, had refused it and been beaten to a bloody pulp for his convictions. Sometimes, he could even think about that with pride.

Other times, he lost the neutrality of the spectator and remembered the incident with the vivid immediacy of the victim. He felt the chilling fear he'd known when the four men had converged on him from front and back and pushed him into the alley, the surprise he had felt when Danio had pulled a fat envelope out of his breast pocket and offered it to him, saying, "Just to be cool. To forget you ever found a connection between Mr. D'Annibale and Councilman Forsythe." He could recall vividly the relief he'd felt that they were offering him an out, then the sudden, metallic rise of bile in his throat at the realization that accepting the envelope would make him just like them and Wendell Forsythe. After he'd refused, there'd been a brief moment of utter terror when he'd been backed against the wall by the four thugs, and then pain that had seemed to go on and on, to worsen when he'd thought it couldn't get any worse, to build upon itself like some clawing demon until he'd finally slipped into black oblivion.

Sweat broke out on his forehead and he closed his eyes, trying to force another picture into his mind.

Melanie Quinn. Unbidden, unexpected, her wide brown eyes came into focus. They looked surprised, as they had when he'd "arrested" her. He saw her hair, straight, almost the color of platinum, falling past her shoulders like a veil. It had been tied back last night at the potluck, and he wondered why in his mind's eye he saw it loose. There wasn't time in his life now for a woman. He had things to do. Things to prove.

His office door burst open and a tall, thickly built man in beige work pants and a blue cotton jacket walked in and leaned the palms of large, work-roughened hands on his desk. It was a moment before Erik could put aside his thoughts and focus on his father.

"Want to join me for chili and beer tonight?" John Channing asked in the quiet voice that always came as such a surprise. He was a large, solidly built man who gave an impression of power, despite his advanced age. He looked more like a logger than a man whose entire life had been devoted to flowers. "I just bought the Sports Illustrated Bloopers video."

Erik looked up into the wrinkled-lidded blue eyes and grinned, feeling centered again. "Now if it was the SI Swimsuit video..."

John grinned back. "Bought that, too."

Erik pointed him to the chair that faced his desk. "Beans, booze and babes, huh, Dad? Should I alert the Emergency Room?"

John Channing lifted a thick shoulder. "Better than dying of emphysema."

Erik rolled his eyes. "It's permanent, whatever you die of. Anyway, you've harped on me so much, I quit smoking."

His father did not look impressed. "Really? How long's it been?"

Erik looked down at the folder as though what it contained was urgent. "Four hours. I had my last one before I left the house this morning."

John snorted. "And tried to bully and bribe one out of Gladys only minutes ago. Gaspers Anonymous would not be proud of you, son."

"She told you that?" Erik shook his head, disappointed. "Some loyalty."

"We dated in high school," John said. "Her loyalty to me is older than her loyalty to you. Anyway, wouldn't you prefer to take your last breath over a shapely posterior than over a cigarette?"

Erik had to admit that he made sense. "What time are you launching the chili?"

"Seven."

"I'll be there. But you have to promise me you'll have only one beer."

"If you promise me you won't smoke today."

The two men eyed each other across the desk. How many deals like this one had they made over the years, Erik wondered? "You can have the new bike if you bring your math grade up. I'll raise your allowance but you'll have to share more chores." It had been more barter system than any formal child rearing approach but he'd been a contented child, had even learned to be happy again after his mother died. And he'd grown into a happy adult. Then, he'd moved to Los Angeles.

Erik offered his hand across the desk. "Deal. Want me to bring the beer? Or some crackers?"

"No, thanks." John stood, zipping his jacket over a thickening paunch. "I'm making corn muffins with red peppers in them. You won't believe how good they are."

Erik stood to walk him out. "Great. We'll die together in an orgy of drink, women and indigestible food." A hand on his father's shoulder, Erik turned to Gladys as they passed her desk. "You're fired," he said.

Without glancing up from a letter she was proofreading, she replied absently, "Oh, shut up."

"SKINNY!" JOHN JUDGED as he and Erik sat side by side on the sofa, beer in hand, watching the swimsuit video. "What do you think?"

Erik watched the elegantly slim model lounging against a rock in the crashing surf, and couldn't tell if the reaction in his gut was lust, the turbulent aftermath of his father's high-test chili, or a desperate need for a cigarette. "I think she's slim."

"You can count her ribs."

"Well, your taste runs to Rosie the Riveter types who can keep the home fires burning while supplying the war effort with propellers. My generation likes them more supple, less heroic."

John leaned forward, elbows on his knees, and sighed at the screen. "There's such a wonderful variety of women. They make me think of flowers. God." He leaned back against the sofa with another sigh. "The world's one big garden and I'm getting too old to hoe."

Erik reached out to take the beer can from him. "That's a romantic notion for a practical type like you. You're not going to go into a crying jag on me, are you?"

John turned to him with a frown. "You're not getting any younger either, you know. Mid-thirties. Before you know it, you'll be my age with no one to show for it."

Erik grinned at him, downing the last of his beer. "Who says I'm not hoeing?"

"I never see you with anyone."

"I usually hoe in private."

"I'm trying to talk serious here."

The peal of the doorbell brought John to his feet with a wince. "Probably the paperboy collecting," he said, kneading an arthritic hip as he limped to the door.

Erik piled their bowls and cans onto the TV tray they'd shared and carried it into the kitchen. He tossed the cans into a plastic bag his father kept by the back door for returnables and put the bowls in the dishwasher. He was pulling a can of coffee down from the cupboard when he heard her voice. He recognized it instantly.

"Hello, John." Melanie said. There was a pause and a rustle of clothing, and Erik guessed she had hugged his father.

"Well, Melly. What a nice surprise!" His father's voice boomed with delight. "Come in, come in."

"I'm back home for a few months," Melanie went on, "and my Aunt Reba told me you haven't been well. I thought I'd check on you myself."

It was a nice voice, Erik thought. Quiet. Calm. In a harshly lit, slightly messy bachelor's kitchen, it made him think of early morning whispers, fireside confidences, secrets shared in the dark.

"Erik!" his father bellowed. "Come and meet Melanie!"

"Be right there!" he called back, giving himself a minute to get the coffee going, to shake off the strange feeling of intimacy inspired by the sound of her voice.

He walked out of the kitchen, wiping his hands on a towel, trying to act casual. The effort lasted as long as it took him to catch sight of her standing just inside the living room, her hair falling straight over the shoulders of a tailored gray jacket like a swath of moonlight through a shadow. It stopped him in his tracks.

"We took a class together in high school," she explained to his father, shifting a little nervously as she noticed Erik staring. "And we got reacquainted last night."

Erik smiled as he looked into her warm brown eyes, then walked around her to take her jacket. "How are you?"

Her quiet voice was husky. "He put me in jail, John," she complained. "Reba put him up to it."

John laughed. "That's Reba." He tried to draw her inside. "Come and sit down. You're just in time for dessert."

Melanie looked guilty, and caught the sleeve of her jacket as Erik tried to hang it up. "I didn't mean to intrude on a family evening. Really. I can come back another time."

John caught her hand and pulled her toward the sofa, while motioning Erik to hang up her jacket. "When you have a present for me tucked under your arm? Not a chance. Tell her you don't mind, Erik."

Erik, on his way to the kitchen, stopped in the doorway to oblige. "I don't mind, Melanie," he assured her. "I should probably be heading home, anyway."

"I'd like you to stay," John said quietly, fixing Erik with an expression he'd often thought of as the I'm-going-to-kill-you smile. "I have some of Reba's strawberry-rhubarb pie."

Erik gave in gracefully. "So, I'll stay. I'll get the coffee."

When Erik returned with a tray, he found Melanie watching his father open her framed watercolor of a single spear of blue gladiola. For a moment his father seemed overcome. Melanie knew him well, Erik realized, to have chosen that gift.

"You remembered," John said.

Melanie hugged him. "You have a front yard full of them. It's hard to forget they're your favorite flower. How are you, John?"

He immediately removed a Charlie Russell print from the wall above the television and replaced it with Melanie's painting. On a wall that betrayed his preference for western art, it looked startlingly important rather than out of place. He came back to sit beside her, folding his arms to study his gift. "I'm great. How are you, girl?"

"I'm fine, too," she replied, looking up into Erik's eyes with a comfortable smile when he set a TV tray beside her. "I painted at the Butchart Gardens in Victoria last summer. I wish you could have been with me to see the acres of tulips. You'd have been in a gardener's heaven."

"Have you seen what Melanie brought me?" John pointed to the spot where he'd hung the gladiola.

Erik went across the room, then stared, his attention arrested by the excellence of the watercolor. It had a grace and elegance of line that drew the eye, and a kind of inner light that reached inside him and made him feel as though one of the flower's silky petals had brushed across his face.

Melanie watched Erik turn away from her painting, annoyed with herself for wondering what he thought of it. It shouldn't matter. She never read reviews and tried not to listen to either criticism or praise. They interfered with the naturalness and spontaneity of her work.

"It's wonderful," he said simply, sincerely.

Melanie tried to accept the compliment professionally and to ignore the little burst of pleasure it gave her. It didn't quite work and the sound of her satisfaction was obvious in her voice. "Thank you. I worked hard on it."

In the moment of silence that followed, Melanie's attention was drawn to the television and the ghostly slim woman in a bikini on the beach. She couldn't help but notice that, for a body so slender, its upper structure was quite remarkable.

"Ah . . . we . . ." John stammered.

Erik reached to the coffee table for the remote control and aimed it at the set. The screen went blank. He turned to Melanie with a sheepish grin. "Sorry," he said. "Stag party."

She smiled from father to son, caught between embarrassment and amusement. "It's nice that you've maintained . . . something in common."

Their laughter was interrupted by the sound of a key turning in the lock. Everyone's attention shifted to the front door as it opened slightly. There was the sound of humming and the rustle of paper. A familiar husky voice called seductively. "Jo-ohn? Joooohny!" Then a hand appeared around the door, waving something pink and lacy. The voice went on melodically, "Come and get it, Johnny."

Erik turned to his father and saw that the fingers of one hand covered his eyes, while a vivid blush rose from his shirt collar. He looked at Melanie, unable to explain what was going on. Her eyes were alight with laughter as she sprang to her feet, snatched her purse from the chair, then grabbed Erik's arm and headed for the kitchen at a run. "Thanks for the coffee, John!" she whispered.

The front door opened a little wider and the voice called sweetly. "Johnny. Your little buttercup is here." Melanie yanked Erik through the swinging door.

"What . . . ?" he began to demand.

"Ssh!" she cautioned, covering her mouth as a laugh threatened to erupt. "I'll explain outside."

Confused by what was happening and distracted by the soft pressure of Melanie's hand on his arm, Erik allowed himself to be pulled into the backyard. Melanie stopped at the corner of the house, finally succumbing to laughter as she leaned against the gate. "Didn't you recognize that voice?" she asked when she finally paused for breath.

Erik shook his head. "It was familiar, but—'

"Reba," Melanie said. She watched a grin grow on Erik's face.

"No kidding? What was she waving?"

Melanie laughed again. "Looked like a lacy pair of tap pants to me." When he gave her a blank look, she added tersely, "Underwear."

"Ah." He chuckled wickedly. "And he said he was too old to hoe."

Melanie frowned. "Pardon me?"

"Never mind. She's going to realize we were there. There are three pieces of pie and three cups of coffee sitting out on the table."

"I know, but at least she won't have to face us now. My aunt isn't easily embarrassed, but that was quite a performance. I'm sure she'll appreciate time to collect herself."

"You're right. This is like our video come to life. Well, should we watch them through a window, or go home?"

Melanie started up the walk leading to the street. "I'm sure they could teach us both a lot, but they've already made me feel old. I'm for going home."

Erik followed her, hands in the pockets of his cardigan sweater. "Old?" he asked.

"Old," she repeated, smiling up at him under the street light as they reached the sidewalk. "Reba has such style. How many other senior citizens do you know who drive a Camaro and tempt a man with tap pants?"

He laughed softly. "I'm sure they're on the endangered list. Are you walking?"

"Yes."

"Me, too." He took her elbow and stepped into the quiet street. The chilled skin he felt through her light blouse reminded him that her jacket had been left behind on his father's coat tree. "Wait a minute," he said, pulling her to a stop in the middle of the deserted street, while he pulled his sweater off and dropped it over her shoulders. He took a moment to adjust it, feeling her slender frame under his hand, getting a whiff of her light, floral scent.

Melanie felt the warmth of his hands through the soft wool as he touched her back and propelled her along the quiet street. "Thanks to our romantic senior citizens, you're in danger of catching pneumonia."

The timbre of his voice had lowered and she noted it with a curious slowing down of the tempo of her body.

"It's nice to know they have each other," she said. "They've both been alone too long. Reba was telling me just last night how lonely she gets sometimes."

Curious, Erik thought. He'd just noticed last night how lonely he'd become. There was nothing he could do about it now, of course. He had personal difficulties to settle, and it looked as though the Finch case would be heating up. He'd handle that best if he was alone. But the soft-spoken woman beside him, who could take the essence of a flower and commit it to paper, made him remember that there were other ways to live that he hadn't considered in a long time.

They had reached Lakefront Street. His home was a quarter of a mile west.

"You can leave me here," Melanie said, pointing east. "I live in that cottage at the end of the block."

Erik turned in that direction. "Now what kind of a gentleman would leave a lady on the corner?" he asked.

Melanie laughed. "The same kind who'd throw her in jail?"

He groaned. "Are you ever going to forgive me for that? I was just doing my duty as a Jaycee."

The night air was cool and thick with the smells of early summer. Water lapped quietly against the shoreline and traffic buzzed a half mile to the south. Melanie felt warm and mellow and willing to make amends. "Oh, all right. And anyway, I still owe you a pound of almond roca. You left with your friend before I had a chance to get it for you."

"Would you really have bought it for me?"

"Of course," she replied, angling him a grinning glance. "Because then, you'd have to buy me something to prevent me from telling the newspaper that the D.A. had taken a bribe."

Erik laughed raucously. "You have a criminal mind, young lady. I'm surprised you're not behind bars."

"My father was a cop," she said. "I was allowed to think creatively, but forced to behave within the law."

She stopped abruptly in front of her neighbor's house when she notice a cab idling in front of her home. She had left the porch light on and in its glow saw a cabdriver loping down her steps and a tall dark-haired young man in jeans and a leather jacket knocking at her door. The cab roared off into the night as Melanie reached the foot of her porch steps.

"Someone you know?" Erik asked, squinting into the shadows.

The visitor spun around. "Oh God!" Melanie thought, swallowing the words instead of crying them out.

She turned to Erik. "Yes. Thanks for walking me home." It was probably the last peaceful time she'd have in a while. "What time on Thursday?"

"Two o'clock would be good for me." With a frown he glanced at her visitor again. "You want me to stick around?"

"No. I'll be fine." She pushed him gently on his way. "See you Thursday."

As Erik disappeared into the shadows, Melanie turned to the figure now running down the steps. Despite the buzz cut, her visitor was not a man at all, but a pretty, shapely woman, who launched herself into Melanie's arms as though they hadn't seen each other in twenty years. "Hi, sis!"

Chapter Four

"New York was getting to be such a downer for me." As Melanie flipped on the light and held the front door open for her, Jolene dragged a large blue suitcase into the middle of the living room with both hands. Then, she let it go and straightened up, turning to envelop Melanie in another hug. "Do you believe we're both back home? It is *so* good to see you."

Melanie forced herself to smile hospitably. "It's only been a year, Jo. Did you get another vacation?"

Jolene pulled away and looked around the room, shaking her head and sighing with what appeared to be satisfaction. "No, I've left New York for good." She gave Melanie the same sweet, trusting smile she used to give her seventeen years ago. Melanie was surprised to discover that it still made her want to shake Jolene and tell her to find her own way through life. "When I heard you'd come home, I decided this would be a good place to spend a few weeks while I figure out what to do with myself." She went back to Melanie and put an arm around her shoulders. "And I've got to see you once a year, or my world goes out of kilter."

Melanie reflected dryly that it was interesting to be the stabilizing force for someone who'd knocked your own life sideways. Deftly, she pulled out from under Jolene's arm and headed for the kitchen. "Well, if you're going to plot a new course in life," she said lightly, "you'll need a cup of coffee."

"Oh, wait!" Jolene called.

Melanie turned at the kitchen doorway and watched her delve in the fat side-pocket of her suitcase. She produced a round can, and, quickly covering the distance between them, handed it to her. "I knew you'd never to able to find this in Harvest Lake."

It was a South American coffee Jolene had brought with her on her last visit, knowing Melanie's preference for a good strong brew. A thoughtful gesture on Jolene's part always made Melanie resentful, a reaction as puzzling to her today as it had been all those years ago. She forced down the resentment and made herself smile. "How nice. It's too bad I don't have cookies or croissants to go with it."

Jolene dismissed that with a quick wave of both hands that made the fringe on her jacket flutter. "Doesn't matter. I'll do some shopping tomorrow and make us something." She took the can back and led the way into the kitchen. "Everything still in the same place? Can opener near the window . . . ah, yes. That's nice, isn't it—that you can come home years after you left and still find things in the same place?"

Jolene fitted the can under the serrated cutting disk and cranked the old hand tool affixed to the side of the cupboard. Melanie took cups from the shelf and watched her work, thinking how out of place her man's haircut, her pencil-leg jeans, and her leather jacket were in this fifties-era kitchen. Still, she moved about the room with an ease Melanie had never felt there. She took over the duty of coffee-making as she had once taken over the task of making breakfast for Melanie's father.

"Aunt Reba wrote me that you were coming home to work on drawings for a book." Jolene tugged off her jacket, dropped it on a corner of the counter and took a chair at the small round kitchen table, patting the opposite place, urging Melanie to sit down with her. The dark blue, three-button T-shirt she wore clung to a small, though beautifully proportioned torso. The blue was the same color as her eyes. She looked fragile, Melanie thought, pale and a little lost.

Melanie brought cream and sugar to the table as dark, fragrant liquid began to gurgle through the coffee maker. She sat opposite Jolene. "Yes. I've done everything for it but the wild iris. I remembered how perfect they are near the lake."

"How does it feel," Jolene asked, leaning intimately toward her, "to be so successful and important?"

Melanie smiled at the flattery, but dismissed it. "I'm not important, and only fairly successful."

Jolene pursed her lips. "Come on. I dated an artist in the Village this year, and I was left reading his magazines one evening while he talked to his ex-girlfriend on the phone. She was threatening to end it all in her hot tub, or something. Anyway, there was this article about you in *American Artist*. It said you're one of the best botanical illustrators in the country."

"The writer of the piece exaggerated." Melanie got up to pour the coffee. "So, what are you going to do without acting?"

Jolene frowned. "I don't know. But I got tired of cattle calls, of diction and dance classes, of waitressing all night to make ends meet while waiting for my big break. I woke up one morning and realized that if, in the past fifteen years it hadn't happened to me yet, it probably wasn't going to." She took the cup Melanie offered and added generous amounts of cream and sugar. She stirred thoughtfully while Melanie settled across from her again and sipped appreciatively from the strong brew. "There's got to be more to life, you know? I worked like crazy to try to force my life to work out the way I wanted it to. I just thought—maybe if I let it do what it wants, I'll accomplish more. Maybe I'll even be happier."

"Have you been unhappy?" Melanie asked. It had been merely a courteous question because she'd always been sure her stepsister was too superficial to be unhappy. But when Jolene looked up at Melanie, her eyes held a grim emptiness that seemed somehow worse than pain.

"Of course," Jolene replied. "Always. Except for the time I spent here."

Melanie frowned, unable for a moment to think of anything to say. Remembering Jolene's chatty letters, she finally said, "It sounded like such a glamorous, exciting life."

Jolene snickered, her expression both wistful and bitter. "It was. Being on stage was glamorous and exciting. Being seventy-third in line at a cattle call was not. Working until three o'clock in the morning and getting up after four hours of sleep trying to look young and beautiful for an audition was not. And even when you felt glamorous and things were exciting, it wasn't the same as being . . . happy. It's got to be there, you know? Or you can't find it."

That was the first thought Jolene had ever expressed with which Melanie could relate. In pursuit of her work, she'd known some beautiful, glorious moments—in the miraculous magnificence of nature, in those rare moments when she'd felt her painting was truly inspired. But that was not the same as being happy. She knew precisely what Jolene meant.

Understanding her stepsister made her feel off balance. It had never happened before.

"Do you think either of us will ever get married?" Jolene asked with disarming candor, breaking the silence. With her bobbed hair and wide eyes she looked about twelve years old. "I mean, I'm so weird and you're so . . . precise."

"Precise." Melanie repeated the word, trying to define it in relation to herself. Proper? Rigid? Particular? No description that came to mind sounded like any quality with which she wanted to be identified.

"It isn't bad," Jolene added hastily. "In fact, after my confused childhood, becoming a part of your organized life was a great relief. You had homework and chores to do, and you did them. You had to be up on time, and you were. You had to be home on time, and you were. Your father held you accountable, and you always measured up. I admired that so much. I'd never seen that until we came here." She sighed heavily and took a sip of coffee. "I don't think my mother *ever* understood the principle."

A little relieved at being made to sound less bland and more heroic, Melanie shrugged. "Well, maybe somewhere there's a weird man for you and a precise man for me. We can only hope."

Jolene laughed, rolling her cup back and forth in her hands. "Aren't you going to ask about my hair?" she asked abruptly.

Melanie looked at the inch-high stubble. "Well..." she began tactfully. "I like it better than the purple frizz you wore last summer."

Jolene laughed again, running a long-fingered hand over her head. "It was such a mess from dyeing and perming. I kept hoping for a look I couldn't seem to find—just like the career I couldn't find, I guess. So, I decided to shave my head and start all over." She looked longingly at Melanie's straight, pale hair, reaching past her shoulders. "Now, that's hair."

Melanie made a face and pushed away from the table. "It gets brassy when I'm in the sun for too long, and I have to be careful what I wear so I don't look washed-out. Why don't I help you get your bags upstairs? I still have a little work to do tonight."

"Oh, of course. I'm sorry." Jolene said, getting to her feet. "Just tell me where you want me."

"Your room's still empty, but it hasn't been aired out." Melanie led the way upstairs, holding one of the suitcase's two long straps while Jolene held the other.

"That'll be perfect. I'll take over the cooking. I don't want you to worry about a thing."

"Jo—"

"I promise not to interfere with your work. I realize you're here to do a job, and I know I have a way of...you know...getting on your nerves, but I promise not to do that. I'll stay out of your way, and just keep you fueled so you can work efficiently."

"You don't—"

"Yes, I do. Little sisters can be a pain in the neck." Melanie helped her hoist the heavy case onto the bed. Jolene hugged her again. "But it's so wonderful to be home with you again. I know I made the right move coming here."

Reminding herself of the promise she'd made to her father all those years ago to take care of her younger stepsister, Melanie asked casually, "How long will you be staying?"

Jolene sat down on the bed with a bounce. "I should have some idea of what to do with myself by the end of summer. I'm prepared to share expenses, so don't worry. And I'll handle the cooking and housework. All you have to do is get your sketches done."

End of the summer. The words repeated themselves in Melanie's mind as Jolene gave her one more exuberant hug, then pushed her out the door, urging her to go back to work and "pretend I'm not here."

Melanie walked downstairs to the kitchen, thinking that pretending Jolene wasn't there hadn't worked eighteen years ago, and it hadn't worked during her many annual visits. She felt sure it wouldn't work now. But she'd try it.

Walking into the kitchen, Melanie tripped over the purse Jolene had left near her chair and landed against the counter where Jolene's leather jacket had been flung earlier. She hung the jacket on the back of a chair and rinsed out the coffee cups, mentally consigning her productive summer to the trash can.

"CALL ME A LOOSE WOMAN and get it over with."

Alone in her studio bathed in early-morning sunlight, Melanie looked up in surprise from packing her canvas bag. The voice was familiar, but she couldn't spot its owner. "Reba?"

"Here."

Melanie went to the open window behind her easel. Her aunt stood in the grass on the other side of the screen, her arms filled with Shasta daisies. She was unsmiling, her expression grimly resigned. "You saw everything, didn't you?"

Melanie leaned both hands on the windowsill and smiled. "Well, not *everything*. Erik and I left during the tap pants part of the performance. Did you take off anything else?"

Reba buried her face in the flowers. Melanie laughed. "Come on around to the kitchen. I'll let you in."

The kitchen was sunny and bright as Melanie walked through it to the back door. "I want to explain," Reba said.

Melanie pointed her to the table and went to pour coffee. "You don't have to explain anything to anyone." She grinned over her shoulder. "You might consider, though, that the man's health is a little delicate."

Reba made a little grimace of embarrassment. "And my approach is not. But that's just why I did it. I'd run into John that morning at the market and he seemed so down. He gets that way, you know. He's still a strong, intelligent man, and his physical limitations frustrate him. Sometimes, they really depress him. We've been friends for a long time and it's recently become..." She bobbed her neatly styled gray head from side to side in search of the correct word.

"Physical," Melanie provided, putting a steaming mug of coffee in front of her.

Reba nodded. "Physical." She sighed deeply. "He's a wonderful man. I wanted to remind him that there's still a lot of life ahead of him." She sipped from the cup, then put it down and glanced at Melanie. "I didn't expect to have an audience. Was Erik horrified?"

Melanie took the chair next to her and patted her arm. "Of course not. He might even have been a little jealous. Those flowers for me?"

"No, they're to welcome Jolene to Harvest Lake."

Melanie feigned hurt feelings. "Well, be that way."

Unperturbed, Reba continued to sip her coffee. "You'll recall that I brought you peonies when you arrived home."

Melanie relented. "I do, and they were lovely. I enjoyed them for a week. I suppose you'd like to see Jolene. She made breakfast, then went upstairs to shower. I'll call her."

"No need, I heard you talking." Jolene came into the kitchen in shorts and a plain white T-shirt, smelling of something tropical. She smiled warmly at Reba as she leaned over to give her a hug. "Hi, Auntie. It's so nice to see you."

"You, too, dear." Reba handed her the flowers. "Welcome home. What in God's name have you done to your hair?"

Jolene laughed, unembarrassed by Reba's candor. "I'd ruined it with too many chemicals, so I'm starting over. How about a muffin to go with your coffee? I made some apple spice this morning."

"I'd love one."

"That ancient coffeepot my father liked to use is on the top shelf of that cupboard." Melanie pointed behind Reba.

"The innards are missing and your daisies would look pretty in it."

Melanie was surprised by the hurt in Jolene's quick glance before she turned to the cupboard. Reba was also looking at her with subtle disapproval. It took her a moment to realize she'd said "my father" and not "Dad," as though he'd been hers exclusively.

Feeling frustrated and guilty, Melanie pushed her chair back and got to her feet. "I have to get out to my irises, and I expect you two have some catching up to do. Don't plan on me for lunch, Jo. I'll be home to change, but I'm going to Erik's for a meeting."

"Right." Kneeling on the counter to reach the pot on the top shelf, Jolene held onto the cupboard and pointed to the other side of the counter. "I filled a Thermos for you to take along. Have fun."

Reba's eyes registered Jolene's thoughtful gesture, and their censure directed at Melanie deepened a little.

Melanie snatched the Thermos. "Thanks, Jo." She tried not to sound grudging. "Bye, Auntie. I'll let you know when I go to the gallery."

SITTING CROSS-LEGGED in front of the iris that was still straight and perfect on its knoll, Melanie looked into its yellow heart. "I could use your cooperation today," she said, glancing around to make sure no one was watching. The trees rustled in the morning breeze, the lake stretched out like some gold-threaded tapestry to the hills beyond and the road was deserted, little eddies of dust whirling in the trail of the breeze. "You're not the only one with problems, you know. I have an aunt who sometimes does striptease, and a stepsister I can't love, although I know she needs that from me and I feel guilty as hell." She drew a deep breath. "And this afternoon, I have a meeting with an interesting, mysterious man and I'm nervous. I've dealt ably with sophisticated presidents of publishing companies, mercurial authors and strong silent trail guides, and *he* scares me."

Withdrawing her sketchbook and pencils from her bag and slapping them on the grass, Melanie wriggled into position on her stomach and sighed at the flower, before making her first stroke. "So, don't get temperamental with me. I've got problems of my own."

ERIK OPENED THE DOOR at Melanie's knock. Her hair was tied back in a loose bun, and he made a conscious effort not to betray his disappointment that she hadn't worn it free. Then, he noted the wayward tendrils at her temples and neck and decided they had a seductive charm all their own.

In a lacy blouse and a long white cotton skirt, with the patterned shadow of a large-brimmed hat across her face, she looked like a subject on which Monet would have happily spent an afternoon. He ignored the slight stir of some unrecognizable emotion and swept a hand toward the interior of the house. "Come in. Welcome to the Scofield house."

The casual greeting Melanie had planned to offer to show him she felt cool and worldly-wise, died in her throat. The living room was magnificent. It was enormous, a perfect replica of a turn of the century room, complete with velvet draperies over ecru sheers, London townhouse-style marble fireplace and opulent oriental carpet. It was filled with Victorian sofas and chairs, and near the fireplace was an East Indian elephant table next to a comfortable chair that looked as though it was often occupied.

Melanie looked at Erik, her eyes filled with ingenuous delight. "God, it's wonderful," she said, looking around in awe. "I knew it would be like this. I mean, it probably wasn't when I used to watch it from the lake; it was pretty run-down then. But this is what I knew it could be like.

Would it be rude to ask you to show me what you've done, before we get down to business?"

"I'd be happy to show it off," he assured her. But..." He pointed to her hat, then the elaborate oak hat tree that stood against the wall. "Do you want to do something with that?"

"Oh." Laughing, Melanie removed it and handed it to him, following him as he went to place it on a brass hook. "As long as you're not expecting a guest waving panties who'll necessitate my leaving in a hurry without it. My wardrobe's getting thin."

His chuckle was quick and deep. "I'm afraid not. All I get waved at me these days are fists and court orders."

Melanie made a sympathetic sound. "Maybe it's your jailer image. A district attorney by day, a jailer by night." She shook her head at the obvious negative implication.

He smiled down at her, his light eyes darkening. "You're here. So far, jailing you hasn't worked out too badly for me. I'll show you the kitchen."

Melanie followed him, ridiculously pleased by the innuendo in his remark.

The kitchen was at the back of the house, an enormous blue and white room with a French flavor to the Spartan white countertops and the hand-painted tiles behind the porcelain sink. A philodendron trained across an archway reached greedily toward a broad shaft of light from a skylight. Copper pots and pans were suspended from a latticework rack dropped from the ceiling, and strings of garlic and red pepper hung near the stove.

"Good heavens," Melanie exclaimed, thinking it would probably be enough to inspire her to cook.

"I know." Erik went to the middle of the room, folded his arms and looked around. "It's a little overpowering at first glance, but I like it. I'm a messy cook, so I need lots of room. A housekeeper twice a week allows me the luxury of someone to clean up after me."

"I'm not much of a cook," Melanie admitted, running her fingertips along the patterned tiles that trimmed the edge of the countertop. "I've gotten used to eating out of a backpack when I'm out in the field, or ordering out when I'm working in my studio. But a kitchen like this might inspire me to make an effort."

"You're welcome to come and practice on the days Ebbie isn't here."

Melanie gave him a dry smile. "My sister's the cook. That was her on the porch the other night. For breakfast this morning, I had more to eat than I've had in the week I've been here alone."

Erik looked surprised. "That was . . . Joanne?"

"Jolene," Melanie corrected. "You know her?"

"I've seen her once or twice with Reba, but I don't really know her," he said carefully. "Her hair used to be... longer."

Melanie explained Jolene's problem with her hair and the resultant rash decision. "She's a bit eccentric."

"You didn't look thrilled to see her," Erik observed.

Melanie sighed. "She's a stepsister. Not that that has to be a problem, but, well . . . it's a long story." She smiled up at him apologetically. "And it's such a pretty day. And such a pretty house. What's through there? And there?"

There was a door at each end of the kitchen and she seemed confused about which to investigate first.

He pointed to the right. "A patio and pool." He indicated the door on the left. "A sunroom, or as our ancestors would have it, a conservatory."

"The conservatory." She headed off on her own toward the door on the left. He followed, enjoying the straight line of her shoulders, the subtle sway of her hips, wondering about her family and her past.

Melanie stopped on the threshold, awed by the elegance of the airy, high-ceilinged room. It had a stone floor and green plants were everywhere. Green Roman-striped draperies were pulled back from a wall of windows that looked out onto the lake. Along the windows, in pots on the floor, on pedestals and on shelves, were ferns, African violets, philodendron, Chinese evergreen, and a score of other plants. She stepped into the room cautiously, expecting to hear the buzz of insects, the song of birds.

In the middle of the room was a large round table covered by a cloth that matched the drapes, and placed around it were six chairs, each of a different design, though all were made of ebony, and all wore cushions covered in pale green velvet. Melanie looked over her head to see another skylight in the domed ceiling and trailing plants growing along a decorative rail that guided them full circle and up to the light.

Erik pulled a chair out for her and pressed gently on her shoulder until she sat.

"It's so beautiful," she said, awestruck. "I don't know what to say."

Erik sat across from her, watching the pleasure on her face as her eyes roamed the room that had become his favorite. With her Gibson girl hairdo and her off-the-shoulder dress, she looked like some ethereal composite of the women who might have lived here. She seemed to fit. But he ignored that thought and glanced at her with a smile. "It is nice, isn't it? We have the Scofields to thank for the pretty canopy overhead. Fortunately, it was too difficult to take with them. The other plants I'm learning about. And everything else..." He indicated the table and the chairs and a few knick-knacks scattered about. "I've just collected as I've found them. I had more of a mood in mind than a look, and, so far, it's working."

Melanie knew the mood. It was the feeling of youth, of summer. It touched her the moment she stepped into the room—sunshine, life, beauty—and the underlying promise of love. Despite all the ugly things that had happened in her life, she lived with that feeling trapped inside her. So far, there'd been no opportunity to draw it out, no place to plant it where it would take root and grow around her.

Startled, she tried to find something practical to talk about. "Flowers would be happy here," she said. "But you have only green plants."

"Flowers droop and die when you forget to water them. Green plants are a little more forgiving. And I'm not entirely domesticated yet. I still work late and forget to come home, or eat pizza and watch football all weekend and ignore the things around here that need attention." He smiled across the table at her. "Maybe it needs a Melanie Quinn painting."

She looked around with a thoughtful line between her eyes, as though seriously considering where she would put one. Then she turned to him with a sudden smile. "In lieu of the almond roca? Perhaps we could arrange that."

"I'll buy one when you have your show," he said, getting to his feet.

"Well, you can do that," she said, standing, too, carefully pushing her chair in. "But a purchase isn't the same as a gift from the artist. I'd like to know that I gave something to the Scofield house." As he led her from the room, she confided, "I used to dream of having tea on the veranda that overlooks the lake, my hand trailing in a plate of bonbons."

"We can come close to that," he said, a hand on the refrigerator door. "We can have tea on the veranda if you'll settle for the *panforte* from Marco's rather than bonbons."

She put a hand over her heart at the thought of the lake's finest Italian chef's most delicious confection. "Marco's *panforte*. I used to love that. Can I cross my ankles on the railing? That was part of the dream."

"It kills this place's image of formal elegance," he said, opening the refrigerator door, "but it has a certain hedonistic appeal that's hard to resist. Here. You take the goodies, I'll take the tea tray. There's a veranda upstairs and down. Which would you prefer?"

"Considering what we're carrying, the downstairs one," she decided, "if you promise to show me the other one later."

"Deal."

Both verandas looked over the lake and ran the length of the house. She noticed that he had replaced the old plain railing with a turned one, painted a soft gray that matched the trim and contrasted with the butter yellow of the outside of the house.

While Erik set the tea tray and the *panforte* on a low wicker table, Melanie walked the length of the porch and back again. She looked out at the lake arrayed in sparkly lamé under the afternoon sun, and took in the fragrance and the sounds that were miraculously part of her life again. Hooking an arm around one of the porch columns, she leaned out over the water and imagined she was in her father's boat, looking up at the house and dreaming.

"God, I love this lake," she said, almost to herself.

Erik braced both hands on the railing and looked down at the water. "I know. I've always felt the same way."

Still hugging the column, Melanie turned her head to look at him. "Yet, you left."

He continued to study the water. "You know how youth is. The grass is always greener somewhere else. I wanted excitement and adventure. I wanted to practice law in a big way."

Melanie noticed a slight edge to his words, as though he'd encountered something that hadn't been part of the dream. Then a loud flutter and a splash drew their attention farther out on the lake where a mallard ruffled its feathers and settled in to enjoy the afternoon. Melanie leaned over the railing to watch him. "I must be part loon, or mallard. Or maybe it's this porch overlooking the lake. I feel as though I could leap off of it and fly away."

"Where would you go?" he asked, hooking two fingers in the belt of her skirt when she leaned out even farther. "I thought we just determined that you love it here."

"I do," she concurred, as she straightened up. He removed his hand and she shifted her shoulders, shaking off the little sensation his touch had stimulated. "But wouldn't it be nice to have an aerial view of the lake and the town?"

The back of her waist had been warm through the cotton of her blouse. Erik deliberately pushed the thought away. "Probably, but in your waterfowl persona, you'd have fish for tea instead of Italian cake."

Melanie sighed and went to one of the fan-back wicker chairs on either side of the table. "Nothing's perfect, is it? Well, tell me about the people you're inviting to our party."

An hour later, most of the tea and all but two of the little squares of cake were gone. Erik told her the guest list he was preparing included many people she would remember from the days she'd lived in Harvest Lake. Mention of some of the younger residents Erik thought she might remember from high school, drew questions from Melanie on who had married whom and who had babies. Erik filled her in on all the gossip he knew, while she listened greedily. There were many of her friends Reba hadn't known or hadn't thought to mention in her monthly letters.

"Dad had the Harvest Lake *Herald* mailed to me in L.A.," Erik said. "Nothing much has changed, except that we're all a little older." The dreamy look in her eyes, as she listened to him intently, brought him back to business. "So I thought we'd invite all the collectors within a hundred miles, then everyone in the country with a hospital, a public building, an office or a condo to decorate."

Melanie smiled, the golden afternoon spent on the porch of the Scofield house making her feel mellow, as though she was operating from within a dream. She didn't care about the party at the moment. "So, you've slipped right back into your old life again. Well, different job, but same people. It must feel as though you'd never left."

Before he could stop himself, he laughed wryly. Considering what he'd experienced in Los Angeles, and how it had affected him, it struck him as funny that to someone else it might seem that nothing had really changed. He pointed to the last two tiny cakes on the plate. "Put yourself out of your misery and polish those off."

Hesitating for only a moment, she picked up a square of *panforte* and stood up to stretch. "My knowledge of California is limited to Big Sur country in the spring. The smog and congestion in L.A. must be awful."

"It is," he agreed, leaning his head against the back of the chair to watch her with a thoughtful smile. "But there's a lot more to Los Angeles than that. It's really quite a beautiful city, and you can find a Shakespearean play or a few sets of hot jazz somewhere any night of the week. The restaurants are wonderful and you can walk into a grocery store at two a.m. for almost anything you need. Big city life does have some advantages."

Melanie shook her head. She couldn't imagine a fine restaurant ever making up for exhaust obscuring the sky. "I don't think it would do anything for me."

"Denver isn't exactly small-town life." He refilled his tea cup, then hers, and stretched a long arm across the veranda to hand it to her. She took it and perched on the edge of the railing.

"It's as close as a big city can come. Nestled in the Rockies, it'll never look like Manhattan."

"You're making me nervous sitting there," he observed quietly. "I'm not sure I'm up to a rescue."

Melanie glanced over her shoulder at the water, then back at him with a grin. "Can't swim?" she teased.

"I can swim" he said, "but with all the *panforte* you've consumed, you'd probably sink before I could get to you."

"Well!" Pretending indignation, she jumped to her feet in an exaggerated huff, overbalancing as she landed. Her dainty china cup flew out of its saucer, spewing hot tea all over Erik's shoulder and down his back, then shattering on the floor. He leaped to his feet.

"Oh, Erik!" Filled with remorse, Melanie grabbed the two tiny napkins on the tray, trying to dab at his shoulder. "Pull it off!" she said, yanking at the hem of his light sweater. The fabric steamed where the tea had landed, and she groaned, trying to hold it away from his skin until he could remove it.

"Relax," he said gently. "It wasn't that hot. It just surprised me."

But she could see the red skin at the V-neck of his T-shirt when he got the sweater off. "This, too!" she ordered, tugging at the white cotton fabric tucked into his belt.

"Miss Quinn," he said, holding his hands away from his sides as she worked. "We've only just met."

Embarrassed, horrified by her clumsiness, she dropped her hands and gave him a scolding look for teasing her. "Do you have any salve or ointment?" she asked.

He sobered, pointing through the small sitting room that led onto the veranda. "Across the hall, into my office. There's a bathroom off it."

Hurriedly following his instructions, Melanie found a tube of an aloe preparation in the medicine cabinet. She turned to hurry out of the room—and found Erik standing bare-chested in the bathroom doorway.

For an instant, she was distracted from her nursing mission by the sturdy perfection of broad shoulders and a firmly muscled torso. The bathroom seemed suddenly very small, the air very thin. Then, the irregular blotch of fiercely red skin at his shoulder reminded her that he was probably in pain. She went toward him with the tube, expecting him to back out of her way. When he continued to stand, blocking the doorway, she fought the inclination to put her hand against his solar plexus and push. Instead, she held up the tube and said with a sigh, "I'm sorry. If you'll sit on the edge of the desk, I'll put some of this on your shoulder."

"I assure you that I'm fine." He remained stubbornly in place for a moment, then stepped aside and let her pass, his dark eyes filled with speculative amusement. "But I'd be a fool to pass up such a tempting invitation."

Chapter Five

Melanie worked carefully, rubbing ointment into his strong, muscled shoulder, avoiding his gaze.

Her eyes followed several wide, long red streaks over his pectoral muscles, down to his neatly tapered waist. Then with a dismayed intake of breath, she noticed the large crescent-shaped scar.

"What happened there?" she asked, running a finger gently along the pucker of skin.

Erik had locked his hands together when she had begun rubbing ointment into his shoulder. He tightened his grip on them and on himself, as her fingertips wandered over his scar. "Ah . . . an encounter in an alley," he said, "with a couple of gentlemen who resented my interference in their business."

"What was the injury?" she insisted. The scar was large and ugly and she knew instinctively that serious damage had been done to him there.

He hesitated a moment. He usually preferred not to talk about the incident. "Why?" he asked finally.

"Because I'd like to know," she replied reasonably. "I've just scalded you, after all, and we're sitting in your office with you bare-chested. I don't think you have to be shy with me."

He had to grant her that. "Ruptured spleen," he replied. "It was removed and I haven't missed it."

She knew that ruptured spleens were sometimes the result of serious accidents—or serious beatings.

She rubbed salve into the long red marks leading down from his shoulder. "What kind of business were they conducting?"

"Various types of vice," he replied. "Graft. A city councilman was in the employ of the Mafia."

Melanie's hands halted their soothing strokes. That sounded almost too close to home.

"Apparently, they were unaware of your susceptibility to bribery," she teased. When he didn't reply, she looked into his eyes, suddenly remembering the private joke she'd seen there the night of the potluck when she'd teased him about taking a bribe. "Or were they?"

"Accepting a bribe from a pretty lady is one thing," he said with a wry smile. "Taking a large sum of money to drop a case involving prostitution, kickbacks and payoffs was something else. You aren't finished yet, are you?" he asked hopefully.

She rubbed gently over his shoulder blades. "Same thing happened to my father," she said, her voice quiet. "Only with him it wasn't the Mafia, just some small-time hood thinking he'd be a big fish in Harvest Lake, with prostitution and back room gambling. When my father tried to stop him, he was shot to death on our front lawn."

Face-to-face with her in his sitting position, Erik looked into her eyes, his own dark with sympathy. "I was in college at the time. I have a vague memory of my father writing me about it. I didn't realize that was your father."

Long ago she had learned to suppress the horror, to dismiss the picture before it formed in her mind, but she saw it now in sharp detail. "We were walking side by side from the car to the house on a Friday night after watching Jolene perform in a school play. My stepsister went to a cast party afterward. I thought the small popping sounds were a car backfiring... until my father crumpled to the ground, without a sound." She capped the tube of ointment, the ugly picture still with her—and the sound of the shots. "Sometimes I can still hear myself screaming."

Erik put an arm around her waist, not drawing her closer, just letting her know she wasn't alone. "I'm sorry," he said. "I can imagine how awful that must have been for you."

Melanie forced herself to shake off the ugly image. It would also be dangerous, she suspected, to let herself linger under Erik's touch.

She pulled gently away and went into the bathroom to replace the tube. When she returned, Erik was pulling on a blue sweatshirt.

He grinned at her. "Pays to leave your clothes hanging around. Gives you something to put on when you find yourself half-naked in front of a lady—even if you do have a neat waistline."

She smiled, but wasn't quite able to dispel the heavy mood of a moment ago. "Do you want to tell me the rest?" she asked.

He looked at her for a moment, then shook his head. "No," he said.

"Why not?"

"Because you don't really want to hear it," he said with an understanding smile, "and I don't blame you. You came here to look at the house."

He was right, but there were a few things it seemed important she know. "How long were you in the hospital?" she asked.

"Melanie..."

"How long?"

He sighed. "Six weeks. Give or take a few days."

She could only imagine the extent of the damage done to his body that would require six weeks to repair. Even imagining the details made her shudder. "Your father must have been . . ." She could think of no word to describe how John must have felt.

"He didn't know," Erik said. "I told him only that I'd broken a few ribs. He'd already had one heart attack. I was sure the news wouldn't have done him any good. Now, can we please forget it? What do you think of my office?"

For the first time since she'd entered the room, Melanie looked around, still trying to shake off the dark mood. The office gave the appearance of having wall-to-wall books. A cluttered oak desk, which Erik had been sitting on, and a leather-upholstered chair occupied the middle of the large room. Melanie got the impression Sherlock Holmes would have felt comfortable here. A green-shaded brass lamp occupied one corner of his desk, and four oak file cabinets that had the warmth of real antiques, stood against the only wall that wasn't covered with bookshelves. The room smelled of paper and linseed oil.

"You need a Doctor Watson," Melanie said, then grinned up at him. "Or would that be Bill Curtis?"

Erik laughed. "I'll have to tell him you said that. Sometimes when I work here at night, I think all this room needs is a very cultured lady in a high-necked dress playing something sweetly tragic on a spinet. Do you play?"

"Heavens, no," she denied emphatically. But it certainly was a room to inspire Victorian images. His lazy smile made her want to play along. "Ladies of the period did do watercolors, though. I could paint and hum for you one evening while you work."

He was sure she had no idea how much her teasing suggestion appealed to him. He loved this house more than anything he'd ever owned, including his hillside home in Malibu. He enjoyed his solitary evenings in it, but there were times when he longed to hear a woman's voice call him from the kitchen, or children's laughter coming from upstairs.

He took her arm and led her through the living room and up the stairs. "Want to see the turret room?"

"Love to," she said.

"We'll have to go through my bedroom," he warned.

She laughed, apparently not alarmed. When he looked disappointed, she offered, "I could go into Victorian vapors, if you like."

"That's not necessary," he said with a grimace, letting her pass before him into a wide, open room that led onto the upstairs veranda. The lake sparkled beyond. "But don't you consider me even the smallest threat to your virtue?"

"Of course not," she said, stopping in the middle of the room to look over the large oak furnishings, the beige carpet and the blue and beige bedspread and curtains. No fussy Victorian decor here. Her curiosity satisfied, she looked into his eyes and explained. "You walked me home in the dark, loaned me your sweater and were willing to defend me against my sister, whom you thought was an intruder. You're a gentleman of the noblest caliber, Mr. Channing. You would never compromise a lady without her consent."

Looking into her smiling eyes and that delicious platinum hair spilling out of her topknot, it was all he could do to stop himself from asking her if she'd consider consenting now. Instead, he drew a deep breath and pointed behind her and to the left. "The little room's right there."

Melanie walked into the semicircular room. She did a full turn, studying the small prints of ducks he had told her about, as well as the books ranged under them and the admiral's lamp. She went to the window and looked out.

"The duck's still out there," she reported.

Erik moved to stand behind her and looked over her shoulder. "Sure it's the same one?"

"It doesn't matter. There should always be one visible from this window." She pointed to the spot where they stood and looked over her shoulder to smile at him. "And there should be a window seat here so you can sit and watch him."

Propelled by an urge he didn't quite understand, except that he knew it felt right, Erik asked, "If I build a window seat, will you come and watch with me from time to time?"

He was just what her life didn't need—a man who took on criminals regardless of the consequences. Her past had already had that kind of a man in it, and she knew the painful memories her father had left behind would be with her forever. She should simply say no, and that would be that.

But Melanie looked up into Erik's quiet gray eyes and smiled instead. "We'll have to have further meetings, won't we?"

He responded to her smile. "Are you suggesting that things remain strictly business between us?"

With a hand on the wall, he had her confined between his body and the bay window. She could see the outline of his sinewy shoulder under the sweatshirt he'd put on, and she had a sudden memory of how it felt under her fingertips. She folded her arms in an attempt to ward off the little charge of awareness that ran between them. "As you've already said, you're a busy D.A. with a full schedule," she reminded him, "and I'm here to sketch irises, and, so far, it isn't going very well."

Erik noted her slight withdrawal. She was probably right. She had bad memories and so did he; they wouldn't be good for each other. Still, what was practical and what was desirable were two different things. But he didn't want to debate that now. He wanted to know that he'd see her again before next Thursday afternoon.

"Have you ever seen Harvest House?" he asked abruptly.

"Ah . . . no," she replied, surprised by the conversation's sudden turn.

"I'm going on Sunday to pick up a . . . friend." He rolled his eyes and ran a hand over his face. "Actually, he's a little monster. Reba coerced me into being a pal to one of the boys there. Parents visit on Sundays, but his mother works and can't come. You don't have to spend the afternoon with us if you don't want to, but you should see what your show will be helping to support."

The way her sketches were going, she should work on Sunday, but the possibility of seeing Erik again before their cochairmanship demanded another meeting was tempting.

"If you're sure your friend won't think I'm intruding."

Erik shook his head. "He'll probably be delighted. He's not really thrilled about having to spend time with me."

Melanie found that hard to believe. She was finding herself a little *too* pleased with his company. She glanced at her watch and was shocked to discover how late it was.

"I've got to run, Erik," she said. "My drawings of irises aren't fit to decorate facial tissue boxes . . ." She carried on about the urgency of her deadline until they stood at the open front door, he listening to her, but distracted by the sun on her hair, and she twirling her hat nervously by its broad brim.

"Thanks for tea and the tour," she said.

"I'll pick you up about noon on Sunday." He walked with her down the steps. They wandered down the front path between two rows of rosebushes and stopped at the sidewalk. He smiled down at her. "I guess our next step should be to plan the menu for the party."

She glanced up at him, anxious to get away, yet strangely reluctant to leave. That feeling didn't make sense, she realized, and she attributed it to some distortion in reality that had taken place the moment she'd come home. "I'll be going to the gallery early in the week," she said, "so I'll have something to report to you by then. Meanwhile, I'll see you Sunday."

"Right." He gestured back toward the house. "Anytime you feel the need to have tea on the veranda with your hand trailing in a plate of *panforte*, you're welcome."

She laughed, then waved and walked away.

Erik waited to see if she would turn. She paused at the corner to let a car pass, then started across the street, still staring ahead. Just as he'd accepted that she wouldn't, she turned around suddenly, the white cotton skirt swirling around her legs, one side of the brim of her hat whipping back in the breeze. She smiled and waved again, and he waved back, a warmth filling him that would last for days.

"WELL. SOME BABE." Five feet tall and bony, Greg Butler stood away from Melanie to give her soft pink cotton skirt and blouse a careful appraisal. Then he glanced up at Erik with a bold grin. "I didn't think you had it in you, Channing."

Erik closed his eyes a moment, then cast Melanie an apologetic glance. "This is a lady, not a babe," he said to the boy Melanie estimated to be thirteen. "She's a botanical illustrator. Do you know what that is?"

"Do I look like a total dweeb?" Greg demanded. "It's flowers and stuff, right? She draws them?"

Erik drew a fortifying breath. "That's right. She's doing illustrations for a book about wildflowers."

"All right." Greg smiled at Melanie. "I take art classes." He waggled an eyebrow. "Want to pose for me sometime?"

Erik put a hand over Greg's mouth, smiling innocently at the couple who passed them on their way to the dorm across the courtyard. As soon as they were out of earshot, Erik dropped his hand. "Can it for this afternoon, Greg. She's with me."

The boy folded his arms. "How come we never get a babe—I mean, a lady for me?"

"If we got you a girl," Erik asked tolerantly, "what would you do with her?"

Greg replied gravely, "Things that would probably shock you, Channing."

Erik turned to Melanie with a martyred expression. "Maybe you'd rather be home watching TV?"

Melanie smiled at the boy. "I've been looking forward to lunch and a movie. If you don't mind my coming along, Greg."

"No," he said. "You're a big improvement over Skeletor here."

"Want to get your jacket?" Erik asked, ignoring the slam.

"No."

"Do it anyway. It'll be dark and cool when I bring you back."

Greg rolled his eyes. "You're such an old lady, Channing." But he started backing toward the dorm. "I'll be right back."

"Don't hurry," Erik said. When Greg stopped to look at him, obviously wondering if *he'd* been slammed, Erik looked back at him innocently.

His expression uncertain, Greg took off for the dorm at a run. Erik put an arm around Melanie's shoulders and led her around the group of buildings that housed the dormitories, the school and the administration offices. They were all single-storied brick and stone constructions, their lines only slightly softened by borders of colorful flowers.

Behind the school, a group of boys played basketball on a concrete slab. Beyond them, other boys sat with parents at picnic tables, and some had formed teams with their parents on a grassy volleyball court.

"It looks like an institution," Melanie observed, frowning.

"That's what it is," Erik replied. "It might be hard for you to think of kids living here, but they have to know that antisocial behavior takes away their right to be with their parents and buddies, and all the things that make life secure and comfortable."

She directed her frown up at him. "Spoken like a man who prosecutes criminals. These are boys."

He didn't appear to take offense, but shrugged off the mild reproach. "Spoken like a prosecutor who sees what happens when the bad boy becomes a man who's too far gone to do anything but live out his life in Leavenworth."

He was right, of course. To make amends, she slipped her arm around his waist. "Greg seems like a little devil, but surely there's a difference between mischief and criminal activity. It's hard to believe he belongs here."

Erik tried to act casual at Melanie's physical response to him. It was hard not to think about her fingertips resting at his waist. "He doesn't," he said. "He was caught with a group of kids who'd stolen a car and totaled it. He claims that once he realized what they were doing, he didn't want any part of it, but by that time there was no way out, and he ended up here."

"Sad," Melanie said with a sigh.

Erik nodded. "Yeah. But he'd better learn now that if he hangs around with kids who behave that way, he'll pay the price with them—watch it!" He pulled her head into his shoulder, turning his body to shield hers as a volleyball whizzed by their ears. A tall, lanky boy wearing glasses chased it, shouting an apology as he passed them.

Melanie emerged from his shoulder laughing, her hair tousled, her cheeks pink from the rough brush against his sweater. He put his hand to her face, rubbing his thumb gently across her cheekbone.

Melanie watched his expression change from one of merriment to sudden, rapt attention. His gray eyes locked with hers for a moment, then moved slowly over her cheek where his thumb caressed her, then to her mouth with a concentration so intense, she felt her lips part. The moment stretched achingly, then snapped at the sudden sounds of shouts and cries from across the courtyard.

Erik looked up and Melanie turned to see a group of boys waving their arms and cheering at some activity hidden from their view by the corner of the dormitory building into which Greg had disappeared. Erik caught Melanie's hand and went to investigate.

As they rounded the corner, Melanie drew in her breath at the sight of Greg locked in combat with a boy a head taller and several years older than he was. For a moment, Greg's clever maneuvers matched them evenly, then another boy, apparently a friend of his opponent, grabbed Greg from behind, pinning his arms back. The bigger boy began to advance on him, and suddenly the cheering stopped.

Erik had wanted to give it a minute before intervening, prepared to put his money on Greg despite the other boy's size. Then he saw the look in Greg's eyes, as his arms were pinned back and his opponent came at him. Something exploded in his head as he ran forward. Recollected pain superseded logical thought as he saw Greg take a fist to the gut before he could reach him.

He grabbed a fistful of gray sweatshirt and pulled the bigger boy back, pushing him roughly against the brick wall. "You need two of you for somebody half your size?" he demanded, pushing the boy back against the wall when he tried to escape. His eyes were wide with surprise, though he tried to glare. The boy holding Greg freed him and ran.

Melanie went to Greg, who stood doubled over, fighting for breath.

"Is he all right?" Erik asked.

"Greg?" Melanie leaned over to try to look into his face. He straightened then, blowing a breath and wincing.

"I'm okay," he said. Then, darting a glance at Erik, he added, "Chill out, Channing. I'm okay."

"What's going on here?" A slender, bespectacled man in tennis whites appeared at Erik's shoulder.

Erik ignored him, looking steadily at the boy he still had pinned to the wall. "If I ever hear," he threatened, "that you've touched Greg Butler again, you'll have your next match with me." Then he released him and watched him sidle away. The crowd of boys dispersed.

"And where were you?" Erik demanded of Harvest House's assistant director. "Isn't it your job to see that these kids don't kill one another?"

"Erik . . ." Melanie caught his arm, but he didn't notice.

"I was talking to parents—" the man began to explain.

Erik pointed to Greg, who stood quietly with Melanie. "While two boys twice his size were beating him up."

"Erik . . ." Melanie repeated, tugging on him.

"I assure you—" the indignant official began.

"Don't try to assure me," Erik interrupted. "Just make sure nothing like this happens again for your own job security."

The man bristled. "You have no—"

"I—" Erik began.

Melanie tugged firmly until he was forced to look at her. "Maybe we should take Greg to lunch before any more of his afternoon is wasted," she said, trying to will him to calm down. A few days ago she would never have guessed he could become this angry.

Annoyed, he turned to her, then she saw him make a conscious effort to relax. But he refused to soften toward the assistant director. With a final glare in his direction, Erik put an arm around Melanie and one around Greg and led them toward the parking lot.

"You embarrassed me, Channing," Greg complained. "A couple more minutes and I'd have creamed Dewey Johnson."

Chapter Six

Melanie put a hand over her eyes as the notorious hockey-masked Jason claimed another victim. "You didn't tell me you were planning to see *Friday the Thirteenth*," she whispered accusingly.

Erik glanced at Greg, who was seated on his other side, tossing popcorn into his mouth in time with the background music. "Letting him pick the film was definitely a mistake. I'll make it up to you, I promise."

She looked at him from behind her hand as someone on the screen screamed hideously. "Lunch at The Burger Bistro was fun, but I don't think I can take more raw hamburger."

"Eat your popcorn," he suggested. "It'll distract you."

"I finished my popcorn."

"Want to eat *my* popcorn?"

"Don't try to appease me."

"You wanted to come."

"I thought we might see something lighthearted or musical."

"With a thirteen-year-old boy? Be serious."

Someone behind them hissed, "Sshhh!"

Melanie slid down in her seat, partially hiding her face behind Erik's upper arm. He glanced down at her with an expression she couldn't quite analyze in the dark, though it was obvious he was smiling. He reached over to cover her knotted fingers, squeezing them with one strong, warm hand. The angle of his arm now shielded her eyes further and she relaxed in the corner of her chair lulled by the warmth of his comforting touch.

"DID YOU SEE THE GUTS spill out when he carved up that guy with . . . ?" Greg spoke with grisly enthusiasm as Erik drove to Melanie's along the dark, quiet streets. Despite the fight, he seemed none the worse for wear.

"Yes," Erik replied to Greg who was sitting between him and Melanie. "But Melanie would probably appreciate it if you didn't go into detail."

He turned to her curiously. "Why? It was so neat!"

"I'm a wimp," she admitted. "I hate blood and screaming."

Greg nodded as though he understood, then turned to look at Erik's profile. "How do you suppose they get the blood to splurt out like that? When he stabbed that guy, there were little drops of blood all over—"

"Enough, Greg." Erik spoke firmly, sending him a withering glance. Melanie thought he looked as though he was holding back laughter. "We'll talk about it later."

Greg leaned back in his seat. "Okay, okay. Geez, you see something great and you can't even talk about it." He looked moodily out the window at the moonlit lake. "Too bad this isn't Loch Ness in Scotland. At least there'd be some excitement around here."

Melanie smiled down at him, feeling responsible for dulling his excitement over the movie. "Would you like to come to my house for cake and Pepsi?"

His thick dark hair falling over one eye, Greg returned her smile. It was warm and genuine and she saw for the first time a glimpse of the real boy under the glib exterior. "Yeah." He turned to Erik. "Can we?"

Erik pulled into Melanie's driveway. "Sure, if you'd like to."

"I would, unless..." Greg looked speculatively from Erik to Melanie. "Unless you'd like to take me back to the joint in case you get lucky."

Erik barely resisted the impulse to grab him by the front of his sweater and shake him. Only the expectation of retribution in the boy's eyes prevented him. The kid was a master at the art of upsetting him in the hope of exacting a response, verbal or physical, which would prove to Greg that he was worthless and that no one cared.

Erik looked at Melanie. "Would you excuse us for a minute, please?"

She gave him an encouraging smile and opened her door. "I'll put the coffee on."

Greg folded his arms and stared through the windshield as the car door closed, confining him with Erik. His thin jaw was set.

Erik turned in his seat, resting his left arm on the steering wheel. "I'm going to chew you out," he said. "Look at me."

Greg turned to him, his expression neutral. "All you're supposed to do is entertain me."

"You're such a hard case, aren't you?" Erik asked. "Hit-and-run words, no feelings, thrilled with blood and guts."

Greg put a dramatic hand to his heart. "What can I say? I'm just an old softie."

Erik saw beyond the mask of indifference to what hid beneath it. He'd lived with fear long enough to recognize it. "You're scared."

Greg made a scornful sound. "Of Johnson? He just likes to pick on me 'cause I don't take his crap. No way. I'd have handled him if you hadn't stuck your nose in."

Ten weeks of Sunday afternoons with Greg had taught Erik to accept his ingratitude. "I wasn't talking about Johnson."

Greg looked bored. "You think I'm scared of you?"

"Of the mess you're in," Erik replied quietly. "The joint, the fact that you now have a record, and your mom's home alone with no one to help her, worrying about you."

Greg's cheeks colored and his eyes filled. He looked back at the windshield. "My mom's doing fine. In another three months, I'll be out of there."

Erik nodded. "But if you don't buff up your act, you'll be back there again in no time. Or in someplace worse."

Greg gave him a murderous look. "That's all I am, isn't it? A little punk you take places so you can feel big."

"Oh, right." Erik leaned back against his door. "Being with you is great for my ego. 'You're really a jerk, Channing', 'I'm busy tonight, Channing, I'm doing my laundry.'" Erik quoted a few of their previous exchanges, then added grimly, "'Maybe you'd rather take me to the joint in case you get lucky.'"

"I didn't mean that." Greg pursed his lips tightly, as though afraid Erik would see them tremble.

"Then you shouldn't have said it. I don't care how little you've grown up with, there's no excuse for bad manners. All your big talk only makes you look small, Greg. She's a friend, and you insulted her."

The boy looked away sullenly. "Then why don't you take me back to the joint?"

"Because I'd like to have cake and coffee with the lady," he replied evenly. "And I'd like you to join us. I'd also like you to see that you get luckier with some women by getting to know them as people, than you do with others who'll share their stuff with you."

"That's not what the guys say."

"Yeah, well." Erik reached across Greg and opened his door. "If they knew it all, they wouldn't be in the joint, would they? Let's go. And watch your mouth or Loch Ness won't be the only lake with a monster in it."

Melanie admitted them at Erik's knock, leading them to the kitchen. "Coffee will be ready in a few minutes. Cake, Erik?"

He looked uncertain. "You said you couldn't cook."

"Jolene made it," she said, making a face at him.

He gave her a look of mock relief. "Then, yes, please. Is she home?"

She pointed toward the refrigerator as she carefully removed the cover from the cake plate. "She left a note saying she went to Reba's." She smiled at the boy standing awkwardly beside Erik. "Greg, my studio's in the next room. You're welcome to look it over, if you don't touch any of the paintings."

Greg looked up at Erik, his eyes still broody from their discussion, but a trace of a smile on his lips. "What do you say, warden? Can I look?"

"Go ahead." Erik ignored the barb and resisted the impulse to repeat Melanie's warning about touching the paintings. The kid wasn't deaf, just stubborn.

As Greg disappeared around the corner, Melanie pulled cups down from the cupboard. "I hope you didn't yell at him," she said quietly. "He probably didn't even know what he was saying."

Erik grinned dryly and came to lean on the counter beside her. "If you believe that, I have some silver mine shares I could sell you. He knew exactly what he was saying. But it'll please you to know that I threatened his life very quietly."

Melanie transferred slices of cake to dessert plates. "He's such a cute kid."

"Mmm." Erik carried the plates to the table. "That's how I got suckered into this. Reba met him at a party the Ladies of the Lake had for the boys a couple of months ago. He was new at the home and lonely, she said." Erik shook his head as he fell into a chair. "I've seen him once a week since then, and occasionally twice. He's never once said please, or thank you, or even seemed to be particularly happy to be away from Harvest House."

Melanie came to sit across from him. "He likes you," she said. "I can tell. He seemed to have a great time at the movie."

"He gets a thrill out of seeing people dismembered."

Melanie gave him a reproachful look. "You like him, too. Don't try to deny it."

Erik leaned back in his chair. "Maybe I do. I guess I admire his inability to be cowed by his circumstances. And the way his eyes fill up every time he mentions his mother. I missed mine like hell, so I can identify with that."

"Where is his mother?"

"She lives in an area of Portland that isn't too choice. She was trying to make it without welfare, working at two minimum wage jobs to try to make ends meet. Greg was alone a lot and that's how he got into trouble."

Melanie went to the counter for the now-filled carafe of coffee. "That's sad," she said, filling Erik's cup. "Do you think he's learned anything from what's happened to him?"

Erik shrugged. "Even if he has, at the end of the summer he'll go back to the same bad neighborhood and into the same situation. I've tried to tell him that making an effort in school and picking his friends more carefully will be a way out for him, but I believe the other influences will be stronger than any memory of what I've told him."

"Maybe not," she said hopefully.

He shrugged again, unconvinced.

Melanie pushed away from the table, hating to consider that there might be nothing brighter in Greg's future. "I'll go get him."

She found him perched on her stool, staring at the half-finished iris on her easel. He pointed to several other drawings and paintings standing around the room. "Did you do these?" he asked with flattering disbelief.

She put an arm around his thin shoulders, unable to stop herself. "Yes. Do you like them?"

He stared in wonder. "They're beautiful. It must make you feel great to know you painted them. Mr. Granger, one of the counselors at the school, teaches an art class. He's pretty good I guess, but he does kind of weird stuff, you know?" Without warning, he turned to look her full in the face. His eyes were dark and fathomless, his brow furrowed. "I'm sorry about what I said in the car. Sometimes, when I get nervous, I . . . say dumb things."

Melanie squeezed his shoulder, touched by what seemed to be genuine contrition. "Maybe if I hadn't intruded on your evening with Erik, you wouldn't have felt so nervous."

He smiled thinly. "No. It was nice to be with a lady. It's all guys at the house and I . . ." He firmed his lips and jumped off the stool, prepared to disregard the thought he'd been about to express.

Melanie sensed it was important. "You what, Greg?" she insisted.

He looked as though he were about to cry and though she knew he would have hated to give into it, she wondered if it wouldn't be a great relief for him. But he squared his thin shoulders and swallowed. "I miss my mom," he admitted. Then he sighed as though there'd been some relief in the confession.

"The important thing," she said around a lump in her throat, "is that you don't leave her again once you get home. At least until you go away to become a doctor, or something."

Melanie was rewarded with a frail smile. "I want to be an attorney. Like Erik."

About to step into the room to see what was keeping them, Erik saw Melanie with her arm around Greg, and he stopped on the threshold, afraid to shatter what appeared to be an intimate moment. He heard the boy's admission that he missed his mother. As he slipped back into the hallway, intending to resume his seat at the kitchen table before they returned, he heard, "I want to be an attorney. Like Erik." There'd been a trace of respect behind the words. If he strained his imagination, he could even hear a suggestion of affection. It was also the first time the boy had ever used his given name. Afraid he might faint dead away in the hallway, Erik hurried back to the kitchen.

"It wouldn't be such a bad place," Greg said of Harvest House about an hour later, "if there wasn't so much homework."

Melanie and Erik smiled at each other over the standard complaint of every teenager everywhere. It was on the tip of Erik's tongue to suggest that the problem might stem from his disruptive behavior during class, but he decided that his "warden" persona had probably said enough for one evening.

But Melanie leaned toward Greg and put a hand on his. "Homework's usually a lot easier if you pay attention to what happens in class. Do you do that?"

Greg slanted an accusatory look at Erik.

"I haven't said a word," Erik denied, almost as surprised as the boy by her perception.

"No one had to tell me that you probably dream time away in class." Melanie smiled at Greg, encouraging a confession. "Or that you play the clown until you get everybody else going, too."

Greg frowned at her. Erik felt a stab of sympathy for him as he watched him experience his first encounter with woman's intuition. The boy didn't know yet that even grown men were helpless against it. "Yeah," Greg said warily. "Sometimes."

"If you try to learn, instead," Melanie suggested, "I'll bet you'll have to spend less time on homework. And you'll probably become a great lawyer. And a handsome guy like you'll have lots of babes after him."

Greg struggled against the smile and lost. He looked down at his hands and laughed, embarrassed. Erik watched in wonder. Most of what he'd endured from the boy in almost three months had been variations of indifference and verbal abuse. In a little under four hours, Melanie had reduced Greg to a lump of putty. Looking into Greg's flushed face as he smiled shyly at Melanie, Erik guessed the boy was a little bit in love. He wondered with mild alarm if the same thing wasn't happening to him.

"I'd better get you back, Greg," he said, pushing away from the table.

Greg nodded reluctantly. "Thank you for the cake," he said politely.

Melanie put her arm around him as she walked them to the door. "You're welcome. Make sure Erik brings you by again."

"I will. Bye."

Erik handed him his car keys. "Let yourself in, but don't drive away."

As Greg went to the car, Erik turned to Melanie, leaning against the door frame. He looked perplexed, she thought, as though she mystified him. "Thank you," he said.

"You're welcome," she replied. "Jolene made it."

"Not for the cake. For Greg."

She shook her head, indicating that gratitude was unnecessary. "Someone should be thanking you. Caring about someone who's convinced they don't deserve it is a thankless job."

"I think this was the first outing he's really enjoyed. I think being around a woman was good for him. Maybe you'd join us again."

Of course, she thought. For Greg. "Yes, I'd like to."

"Good." He smiled and started to back away. "Good night."

Melanie watched him vault down the porch steps. As he opened the car door, illuminating the interior, Greg waved at Melanie. She waved back. So, she had promised herself that she wouldn't commit herself to one more thing this summer, but what was an occasional afternoon or evening with a friend and a troubled boy? She could handle it.

"NEXT FRIDAY NIGHT I'LL SEE if I can get permission to keep you for an overnighter. There's a doubleheader at the park." Erik pushed open the front door of Harvest House. The counselor at the desk inside waved at him. Erik waved back. "So don't do anything to get confined to the dorm between now and then."

"Yeah. That'd be cool."

Greg had been quiet all the way home. Erik put a hand on his shoulder and shook him gently. "You all right?"

"Yeah." The boy forced a smile. "Thanks for the movie. I'm sorry Melanie didn't like it. I thought it was rad."

"I'm glad you had a good time. Well..." Erik pushed the door open wider, but Greg still made no effort to go inside. The boy continued to look at him as though there was something he wanted to say. Erik let the door close and waited.

"I'm afraid you won't come back," Greg finally admitted.

"Didn't I just say—?"

"I know." Greg swallowed audibly. "You always do come back, but I'm always sure you won't."

"I'll come back," Erik said firmly.

"Why?"

Greg would know if he wasn't being honest, or if he gave him some line out of a psychology book. He folded his arms and looked down at him levelly. "You're not always a lot of laughs for me, Butler. But I know there's a kid in there that I like." He rapped a forefinger against the boy's chest. "You don't let me see him very often, but when you do, I like him. I like spending time with him—for the hell of it, and not because it makes me feel big."

Greg stared back at him, then looked down at the ground. "I'm sorry about the getting lucky crack."

Erik shrugged. "It's forgotten."

Greg looked up at him and cleared his throat. "And thanks for this afternoon." He gave him a weak smile. "Johnson probably would have killed me."

Erik laughed softly. "Until his friend came into it, I was betting on you."

Greg smiled faintly. "You were pretty scary, Channing."

Erik remembered the anguish he'd felt, the pain he'd recalled when he'd seen the boy helpless against the two bullies. "I've been beaten up myself," he said softly. "I knew how you felt. There should have been someone there to make sure that didn't happen."

Greg looked at him consideringly. "Wasn't there anybody there for you?"

"No."

Greg sighed. "Life sucks, doesn't it?"

Erik had to laugh. There were times when that pretty much summed it up. "Yeah. Sometimes."

"So, I'll see you next Friday?"

Erik offered his hand. "Next Friday."

Greg took it, and though the boy's grip was strong, his hand felt touchingly small. "Right. Bye." Greg turned and walked into Harvest House.

Erik went back to his car and sat behind the wheel for a moment before turning the key in the ignition. That was a change for the better, he thought with some surprise. And he couldn't help but think Melanie had had something to do with it. Perhaps a woman's gentleness had been enough to bring out that glimpse of softness in the boy.

Between Melanie's quiet words of praise and Greg's admission that he'd come to need him, Erik was beginning to feel a like a lump of mush. Not a good image for a D.A. Not a good one at all.

"WHAT *WOULD* ONE DO with a four-foot square canvas that looks like beetles died on it in a sea of guacamole?"

Melanie put her hand over Reba's mouth as Maggie Finch bustled past them with a client possessively clutching a pedestal bowl. "Modern art is intended to generate a mood, Reba," Melanie whispered reproachfully. "It isn't representational, it's supposed to...to bring out feeling and emotion."

Reba studied the large mottled canvas for another moment. "It works. It makes me ill."

Melanie hooked her arm in Reba's and pulled her away. "If you keep talking like that, Maggie might change her mind about the show for Harvest House."

"She didn't even hear me. Where are the French Impressionables?"

"Impression*ists*," Melanie corrected, "and this is a gallery, not a museum. Here are some seascapes. You'll enjoy those." They stopped before a wall of vivid watercolors done by a local artist.

"Now, that..." Reba said, "is something I could happily look at day after day." She pointed to a large watercolor of a sailboat, its spinnaker billowing against a sunset so vivid, one could feel the dying rays of light. Melanie had to agree. She would never deny the validity of modern art, but she could never enjoy it as she could a painting like the one before her.

"There you are." Maggie suddenly appeared beside them, wearing a diaphanous top of white silk over narrow white pants. Her red hair was wound in one large braid atop her head and held in place with two combs. "I'm so sorry to have kept you waiting. Come with me and I'll show you where we'll hang the Quinns."

She led them toward the front of the gallery, into a square anteroom that was beautifully lit. She knew her stuff, Melanie thought with respect as she walked along, studying the oils and acrylics on display. But she would definitely have to empty her apartment, and call in many of the pieces currently on loan to friends.

"Can you fill it?" Maggie asked, "or would you prefer considering something smaller?"

Before Melanie could voice an opinion, Reba said, "Oh, I'm sure she'll fill this room. The more she shows, the bigger the fund will be for Harvest House's bus."

"Mrs. Finch!" A young man peered around the wall. "Mr. Finch is on the phone."

"Ah. Excuse me. Look around. I'll try not to be too long."

Melanie rested her arm on her aunt's shoulder. "Reba, we're not going to make enough to get the kids a bus. A small used one must be as much as I make in a year."

Reba smiled at her. "I know that. What I meant was, your evening will make a substantial donation to the fund. Eventually, we'll have enough. Now, what do you think? I have a few paintings you've given me over the years. I'll loan them to you to help fill space. This room *is* large."

"Let me think about it. I might have enough inventory at home. I'll have my work cut out matting and framing, though."

Reba pointed to a pedestal in the corner. "I'll arrange a bouquet from my garden to put there. It'll be rougher than a florist's bouquet, but that would be in keeping with your wildflower studies, wouldn't it?"

Melanie nodded, her enthusiasm growing. "Perfect."

"Then, we'll—" Reba was interrupted by Maggie's loud shout from her office, then the slam of a door. Indistinguishable conversation continued to rumble across the gallery. Reba shook her head at Melanie. "The Finches have a tempestuous relationship," she whispered. "But Maggie's crazy about him."

Melanie tried to remember details about Jerry Finch when he'd been a young man. It was hard for her to imagine anyone could be crazy about him. He'd been a loner who'd seemed motivated by disdain for his fellow students rather than by shyness. Most of their peers had disliked him because he'd made it so obvious he had little use for them.

"He must have changed a lot," Melanie concluded.

"People *do* change, Melanie." Reba elbowed her in the ribs. "You seem to delight in remaining the old stick-in-the-mud you've always been, but other people sometimes look for new thresholds to cross, new horizons to discover. Maggie's so vivacious, such a doer. Maybe he found her enthusiasm contagious."

Melanie arched an eyebrow. "Thanks, Auntie. I love you, too."

"Well, where was I?" Maggie reappeared in a rustle of silk. Her cheeks were pink, Melanie noted, as though she'd just had a sauna...or a lively argument. She pointed to a little alcove at the back of the room. "I'll set up champagne over there..."

"The Ladies of the Lake will make cookies," Reba put in.

Maggie nodded approval. "And we'll all make a profit! You approve, Melanie?"

Melanie put away thoughts of Jerry Finch and looked around at the beautiful room. "Heartily. I hope we do well for you and for Harvest House."

Maggie clasped her hands together. "I'm sure we'll all make a bundle. Don't hesitate to call me if you have any questions, or to come back at any time if you'd like to measure, or whatever." She opened a large appointment book and ruffled through the pages until she found the correct date. "All right. We're set for the tenth of August at eight in the evening."

Melanie nodded, infected by Maggie's and Reba's enthusiasm. But she couldn't dispel the feeling that she'd lost complete control of what was supposed to have been a productive, but easygoing summer in Harvest Lake.

Chapter Seven

Outside the gallery in the bright afternoon sunshine, Reba hugged Melanie. "I'm off to get groceries. Want me to drop you anywhere?"

Melanie looked up the quiet street of little shops and decided she needed a break from irises and plans for her show. "I think I'll just buy myself a few things. Impractical things. Thanks for coming with me."

Reba sighed wistfully. "There's a wonderful little bikini in the window at Rolf's. Gravity and self-indulgence prevent me from buying it, but you might want to look at it. See you."

An afternoon to herself. Melanie wandered down the warm, quiet street, enjoying the luxury. The sun was hot on her back, the day smelled sweetly of flowers and the lake, and this morning she'd made the first sketch of the iris she thought might develop into something she could send her publisher. Things were looking up.

Every shop on Kirby Drive, Harvest Lake's commercial center, could be seen in forty-five minutes. It took Melanie three hours. She loved to shop, but spending so much time in remote areas in search of specimens to sketch and paint left her little opportunity to indulge herself.

She bought a cotton shirt with bold orange stripes, a pair of pleated linen shorts, a filmy floral dress with a short skirt made of two deep ruffles, a pound of white chocolate almond bark, a bottle of "Passion." She thought twice about the lime and black bikini in Rolf's window, but decided against it. Halfway out the door she thought again, then went back and bought it for Jolene. She refused to analyze why she wanted to do it, or what extremes of thoughtfulness her stepsister would be driven to as a result of Melanie's small gesture.

Jolene and Bill Curtis stood laughing on the front porch, as Melanie approached.

"Hi, Mel." Jolene pushed the door open and Bill took the largest package from her, following her inside. "Bill came by looking for Erik."

Melanie smiled at him and dropped everything in the nearest chair. "Hi. I haven't seen him today. Isn't he in his office?"

Bill shook his head. "No, and they don't know where he is." He glanced at his watch. "He told them he'd be back at four. Guess I'll just have to wait. Well . . ." He smiled down at Jolene, his eyes soft with adoration. "Thanks for letting me hang around until Melanie got home."

Jolene looked back at him with a dewy smile. "Sure. I hope you find Erik."

Bill's vulnerable expression changed to one of vague concern. "Yeah, me too." Then, he smiled at Jolene and waved at Melanie. "Bye."

Jolene walked Bill out onto the porch. Through the partially open door, Melanie heard quiet conversation and soft laughter. That was a surprise, she thought. For a young woman whose preference in men had leaned toward the dark, brooding types, she appeared as smitten with Bill as he seemed with her.

Jolene reappeared, her bright blue eyes a little unfocused as she closed the door behind her. "Isn't he cute?"

Melanie smiled in agreement. "And a little nuts. Did he say what he wanted Erik for?"

"No. He said he does investigations for him, so I guess it had something to do with that. Oops! Got it!" Jolene caught a bag that fell from the top of the pyramid of packages Melanie was carrying toward the stairs.

"That one's yours, anyway. And you can carry this one." She handed her a white bag. "It's white chocolate almond bark. If you eat more than half of it, it's worth your life."

"You bought me a present?" Jolene asked, following her up the stairs. In the doorway to Melanie's room, she pulled the scraps of fabric and strings out of the bag.

Guilt prodded Melanie at the almost pitiful pleasure her stepsister was taking in the simple gesture. "I fell in love with the bathing suit, but I'm just too...mature for it. I knew it would look great on you."

Jolene's wide eyes went from the hot colors in her hand to Melanie's face. "Thanks, Mel."

Melanie waved her away and turned back to her packages on the bed. "Why don't you try it on while I put the rest of my stuff away. Oh, wait!" Her sudden shout stopped the retreating Jolene in her tracks. Melanie held a hand out, her expression mockingly severe. "The almond bark."

Jolene laughed, handed her the bag, then ran off. *"I shouldn't have done it,"* Melanie thought as she shook out the flowered dress. "Now she'll be packing me thermoses of champagne." Still, she couldn't quite ignore the satisfaction that swelled in her breast.

"Da-da!" Jolene reappeared in Melanie's bedroom doorway in the lime and black suit. She looked like a page out of the summer issue of *Elle*.

Melanie shook her head wryly. "It looks wonderful on you. Just don't ever wear it when you're with me."

Jolene wrapped her in a hug. "I love it. Thank you. I haven't had a present since..." She shrugged. "Since I lived here."

Melanie went to the closet where she hung the orange and white top. "Surely you had friends in New York."

Jolene pulled on a T-shirt over the suit. "I had acquaintances. But we competed for a lot of roles, so there was a little undercurrent of animosity there. And most guys were..." She shrugged, looking uncomfortable for a moment as she wrapped an arm around a bedpost. "...you know. Not that thoughtful. And I worked most of my free time, so it was hard to maintain a friendship. You're the only real friend I have."

Jolene looked into Melanie's eyes, then turned away to sit on the edge of the bed, still holding the post. "Maybe it's been my fault. My mother wasn't a great example of how to cultivate and keep relationships of any kind. I mean..." She stared at her knees, her cropped hair and her slim build making her look like a very insecure adolescent. "What kind of a jerk would leave Dad..." She glanced up at Melanie and amended, "...your father."

Melanie hated these discussions. Every time Jolene visited, she tried to bring up the subject of her mother Linda's, and Melanie's father's brief, painful marriage and Linda's eventual defection. Melanie usually tried to discourage this kind of conversation, but there was something different about Jolene this year. She seemed more fragile than usual, more desperate. Melanie shut her closet door.

"Your mother was selfish and self-destructive," she said, folding all the bags into the largest one. "You're not like that. Relationships are hard for all of us."

"She used people."

That was always hard for Melanie to think about. One day it had just been her and her father, happy in their quiet, secure lives. Then Linda Slade had come to town with her beautiful thirteen-year-old daughter. Everyone talked about the easy woman waitressing at the Lakeside Inn. Two months later they all said she married Grant Quinn for a meal ticket. Melanie who'd been fifteen at the time, found herself with a pesty little sister who trailed her like a puppy, and a stepmother so transparently selfish and manipulative, it amazed her that her father couldn't see through her.

"I know you've always resented the fact that she left me here when she ran away," Jolene said.

There it was—the truth Melanie had never spoken, had even tried to deny to herself for most of her life. "Of course I did," Melanie said lightly, tossing the bags in a corner and sitting near the pillows. "You were competition. Before you came, my father seemed to love my scrambled eggs." She smiled, thinking it would ease the sting from the truth. "But you knew how to make omelets and crepes. I was jealous."

Melanie and her father had always been close, and remained close, even after Linda and Jolene had arrived. But he and Jolene had some inner understanding, some . . . link Melanie had been aware of, without understanding it, something in which she had no part. That still hurt.

"I wanted him to like me," Jolene confessed, her eyes dark with memory. For the first time, Melanie considered what the girl's life must have been like before she'd come to Harvest Lake. As the daughter of a woman who moved in with any man who made it convenient to do so, she'd moved from pillar to post, without stability or security. When she thought about that, admitting the truth wasn't quite so difficult. "He did like you," she said. "He loved you."

"I wanted you to like me, too," Jolene said, her eyes pinning Melanie's when she tried to look away. "I haven't been as lucky there, have I?"

Melanie tried to laugh off the question. "How can you say that to someone who just bought you a bathing suit and is willing to share her almond bark with you?"

Jolene's eyes remained level. "You do a lot of things to try to make me think you like me—or to try to make *yourself* think you like me—I'm never sure which." Jolene dropped her eyes, shaking her head, a long sigh escaping. "Maybe I've just done too much damage to your life."

Melanie remembered Linda and the way she'd simply left for the market one afternoon and had never come back. Grant had been frantic, certain she'd been hurt or kidnapped or worse—unable to believe she'd have left of her own accord without Jolene. An investigation through his connections in the police department discovered her in Seattle, living with a man she'd known years before. Melanie's father had never been the same after that. The spark that lit his love for life had gone out. He'd been unable to understand or cope with betrayal. But that hadn't been Jolene's fault.

"Your mother did a lot of damage to my life—not you."

Jolene sighed and got to her feet. Melanie made a production of straightening the bed. She'd said all the right things, hadn't she? Why didn't Jolene believe it? Because Melanie didn't believe it herself. It was hard to sell an idea when you couldn't look your customer in the eye.

Jolene looked at her for a moment, deep blue eyes watchful, uncertain. Melanie braced herself, expecting to be challenged. Then Jolene sighed again, apparently unsure of Melanie's credibility, or afraid to examine it too closely. She smiled faintly. "Then where's my half of the almond bark?"

ERIK SAT ON A HILLSIDE covered in fir trees and goldenrod, a pair of high-powered binoculars hanging around his neck. The sun was high and warm, the breeze cool, and bees droned in the stillness. He wondered if Bill's informant had been mistaken. Harvest House lay several hundred yards below him, nothing and no one moving on the grounds in the midafternoon quiet. The boys had just left for their weekly session in town at the YMCA pool. Since the foray into town required the presence of half of the staff, and the other half had the afternoon off because of the boys' absence, it had looked like a perfect time for the shipment Bill's informant had warned him about. Unfortunately, he hadn't overheard the day, the time, or the contents expected in the delivery. He knew only that Jerry Finch had spoken furtively about it to someone on the phone—someone he'd referred to as "Walter."

Sheltered in the tall grass, Erik leaned against a fir, beginning to wonder if he'd jumped to the wrong conclusion. Then he heard a soft, feminine hum carried to him on the scented, summer air. Great! he thought, scrambling behind the tree, glancing down the hill to be sure nothing had changed at Harvest House. Just what he needed! An afternoon hiker strolling along the hill side of Harvest Lake as he sat crouched in the grass, waiting for a break in the Finch case.

He recognized Melanie's hair before he even saw her face. She rose from the other side of the meadow that topped the hill, her platinum hair flying out behind her on the breeze like a cloud. She wore jeans and boots and a baggy red sweater, a colorful scarf tied around her neck, her canvas bag hanging from her shoulder.

Erik absorbed the pleasure the sight of her brought him. For a moment he forgot Harvest House and Jerry Finch. She moved with the graceful sway of the tall grasses as she made her way across the meadow, still humming something he could identify as classical, but couldn't name.

She stopped on the rim of the meadow, not thirty feet away from him. Sitting cross-legged before a clump of goldenrod, she opened her bag and removed a sketchpad, a plastic envelope of pencils, and a white bag from which she withdrew something she put into her mouth.

Her humming now irregular as she chewed, she tossed her hair back over her shoulder and slid down onto her stomach, bracing herself on her forearms. For what seemed an eternity, she studied a particularly full and fat stem of the golden flower, now touching it gently with a fingertip, now resting her head on her hand on the grass to study its underside. Almost forgetting why he was there, Erik watched her in fascination.

Then she sat up, settled her sketchpad on her knees, and withdrew a pencil and...a ruler? Unable to believe that, he fixed the glasses on her and verified that she was holding a six-inch ruler up against the flower's stalk. He swung the glasses to her face and watched her rapt profile as she made strokes on the page. She held the ruler up again, this time against a petal, her eyes narrowing with concentration. A wide ribbon of hair slid off her shoulder and forward, hiding her features. She tossed it back. Something stirred in him.

Erik lowered the glasses, trying to pull himself together. A glance down the hill assured him that nothing had changed. The compound was quiet, empty. He'd have to let her know she wasn't alone. With any luck, she'd leave before the delivery arrived—*if* it arrived. But that was probably a futile hope. She looked too absorbed in her work.

Straightening slowly, keeping away from the ridge, he walked toward her. "Pardon me," he said, "but I believe irises are purple. That's gorse."

She looked up with a start, her brown eyes wide. Pleasure replaced surprise in them almost instantly and he felt himself melt inside. "Irises are not always purple," she corrected with a warm smile, "and it's goldenrod, not gorse. I needed a change of pace today. I saw a car in the parking lot, but didn't know it was yours. Are you bird-watching?" She pointed to his glasses.

He squatted down beside her, taking a quick glance over the hill. Still quiet. He turned back to her, his eyes going to her hair. "I sighted a silver-crested swan," he said.

She looked back at her sketchpad, but not before he saw the pleasure deepen in her eyes. "In a meadow?" she asked lightly. "Must be a rare bird, indeed." Then she gave him a side-glance filled with amused cynicism. "You talk a sweet line, Channing, but why *are* you here?"

He shrugged. "This is my county," he replied. "I've got to watch it. Why do you use a ruler? Doesn't that kind of take the poetry out of your drawing?"

She laughed, continuing to sketch. With amazing swiftness, a pyramid of petals rose on the stalk. "No, it puts accuracy into it. Botanical illustrators are not like other artists who are free to interpret what they see. We *photograph* flowers with paint. I have to be an engineer as well as a poet."

A strong breeze blew her hair forward, and he caught it back from her face, his attention arrested by the cool silkiness of it in his hand. He'd known it would feel like that. He found himself wondering what her skin would feel like, her mouth.

For a moment she stared back at him as though she, too, had an urgent question. Then she dropped her lashes, untied the scarf, and caught her hair back with it at the nape of her neck. "I should have braided it," she said.

He shook his head. "That would have been a crime."

The sound of the powerful motor of a truck broke the sylvan peace. His attention reverting swiftly back to business, Erik carefully stepped forward until he could look down onto the compound. A semi moved slowly down the road to Harvest House, the words Wholesome Foods emblazoned on its side. As the truck approached, three figures walked out of the administration building, one of them waving the driver toward the other end of the grounds. Erik recognized him as Jerry Finch.

"What is it?" Melanie moved in front of him for a closer look. Quickly, Erik pushed her down to the grass, dropping beside her. "What—?" she began, but he wrapped an arm around her, covering her mouth with his hand. "Be quiet," he ordered softly. "Don't say a word, and keep your head down. I'll explain later."

He raised his glasses and watched the truck follow the road to the storage building, Finch and his men trailing along behind it. As the truck stopped, Erik saw Finch dart a furtive look behind him, then glance around at the hills that surrounded the compound, as though some sixth sense told him he was being watched. Erik kept low, holding Melanie down.

The truck made a laborious turn and backed up to the storage building. As Finch, his two men and the driver walked around it, now out of sight, Erik grabbed Melanie's hand and, keeping low, ran back to the trees where he'd originally planned to wait. It gave him a better angle on the truck and the building. He sat Melanie down behind the tree and leaned against it, leveling the glasses on the truck.

"Are we spying?" Melanie whispered.

"Yes. Ssh!"

Melanie tried to lean her head around the tree for a better view, but Erik pulled her back. "Your hair's like a beacon. Sit still."

Tension made his voice sharp. With the truck backed into the opening of the building, he couldn't see exactly what was being unloaded. But it was certainly cause for speculation whether "food" was actually going into the storage building. He'd seen Harvest House's kitchen on a tour for families and friends, and it boasted a pantry as large as his living room. Perhaps this was the product mentioned in Walter Abernathy's note to Finch. But what was it?

The men still out of sight, Erik rose cautiously to his feet. "I'm going down for a closer look," he whispered to Melanie. "Stay right here until I come back."

Melanie rose, too, catching his shirtsleeve. She had no idea what this was all about, except that she thought she'd seen Jerry Finch in the compound before Erik had yanked her down. Erik was obviously on some sort of surveillance of Finch, whom she felt reasonably sure couldn't have changed into the paragon Reba seemed to think he was.

"There are four men down there, Erik," she cautioned.

He pulled her hand gently from his sleeve. "I can count, Melanie. I want to see what's coming off the truck."

She caught his arm again. "I'll come with you."

"You will stay here," he said firmly, freeing himself again. "Sit down and wait."

"Look, I—" She began when they heard the sound of a heavy door slamming. Erik glanced down as Finch and his men reappeared. He sank to the ground, bringing Melanie with him. For long moments there was the sound of indistinguishable conversation followed by laughter, then the roar of the truck's motor. The vehicle pulled away and Finch's men wandered back into the administration building. For a moment Finch stood in the middle of the compound doing a slow turn, his eyes raised to the rim of the hills surrounding him. Erik's pulse began to thrum, and began to beat even faster when Finch's eyes lingered for a moment precisely where he and Melanie had been standing. Then, he put his hands in the pockets of his slacks and followed his men into the building.

"Did he see us?" Melanie whispered, her head still held to the grass by Erik's hand.

"No." He let her up, keeping low and pulling her back from the ridge before straightening. "At least, I don't think so. No thanks to you."

She dusted her hands off, raising an eyebrow at his tone. "If you'd tried to get down there while they were coming out of the storage building, they would have probably seen you. I don't know what they're up to, or why you're investigating, but it might have been L.A. all over again."

He'd considered that before he even left the office that afternoon, but in order to function he'd pushed it to the back of his mind and left it there. Fear still lived with him day in, day out, but he'd be damned if it would run his job—or his life. He resented her reminder and it showed in his expression as he reached down for her bag and handed it to her.

She took it from him and caught his arm when he would have reached down for the pad and pencils. He expelled an impatient breath, but didn't pull away. "You crave my body, or something?" he asked dryly. "You keep grabbing me."

She dropped her hand, her dark eyes contrite. "I'm sorry. That was a callous thing for me to say. Because of what happened to my father, I'm . . . sensitive about people risking their lives."

Erik looked at her steadily, catching a glimpse of something in her eyes he wanted to explore. "People in general?" he asked quietly.

She returned his steady gaze, knowing she had to be honest. "People in general," she replied. "You in particular."

He smiled gently. "I'm very resilient."

Her expression changed from softness to impatience. "But you're not indestructible. Nobody is." She reached down to stuff her things into her bag, then stood with its strap dangling from her fingers. "Should you be doing this kind of thing by yourself? Can't you—"

"Wait a minute." Still smiling, Erik took the bag from her fingers and let it drop. Then, he framed her face in his hands, watched the nervous flutter of her eyelashes and the sudden flash of interest that replaced the impatience of a moment ago. She was watching him with all the unsatisfied curiosity he'd felt since their first meeting. "Let's go back to why you're concerned about me in particular."

"You're a human being," she said reasonably. "I'm a human being." Her hands rose to his waist as though she didn't know what to do with them, then fell again.

His smile deepened. "I'm a man and you're a woman."

"Very astute." She smiled dryly. "But I'd noticed that, too."

"So your concern," he pressed her, "is that of a woman for a man?"

She thought for a moment, knowing the admission would give him an advantage.

"I've reduced drug lords to jelly on the stand," he warned softly. "Don't lie to me, Mel."

"All right." She conceded with a sigh. Her hands rose to his waist again, and this time they stayed there. "I'm concerned because I care about you, Erik. Because something's happening to us that shouldn't be marred by anything ugly."

That was all he needed to hear. He lowered his head, watched her eyes darken and her lips part and covered her mouth with his.

His kiss was gentle without being cautious—tender, yet accomplished. Melanie, whose experience had been relatively limited, gave herself over to the arms that encircled her, lost in the strength she felt in them. Her hands roamed up his back, only vaguely aware of its sinewy solidity. Her attention was focused on the sure but artful exploration of his tongue, the supple lips that urged hers to answer him in kind.

Her mouth tasted of all the sweet things he had dreamed she would embody—wonder, passion, complexity. She opened for him like a trusting innocent, then taunted him with her tongue like a woman of experience and skill. Confident one moment and shy the next, she drove him from tenderness to passion and back again, and he followed without complaint.

Needing breath, he freed her mouth but not her body. Keeping her crushed against him, he closed his eyes and focused on the deep satisfaction of simply having her in his arms. Her arms clinging to him, her head buried in his shoulder as she drew in breath, compounded the sweetness.

"God!" he said in wonder.

She looped her arms around his neck and drew back to look at him. Her cheeks were pink, her eyes a little glazed. "You made your point," she said. "I'm jelly, and you didn't even need the witness stand."

"I'm putty," he said, pulling one of her hands from around his neck and kissing its open palm. "Right in here. We're even."

Melanie shook her head with reluctance. "I swore I'd never get involved with someone who risks his life for a living."

He leaned down to nibble at her ear. "In Harvest Lake, being district attorney is about as dangerous as being a meter maid. People yell at you a lot."

She hunched her shoulders, emitting a little gasp as his breath tickled. "But Jerry Finch is more than overparked, isn't he?"

"I think so," he said absently.

"What has he done?"

"Hm?"

"Erik!" Laughing, she tugged at his hair until he raised his head. "What has he...?" She stopped abruptly, her eyes darting beyond him and widening in distress.

Erik frowned and started to turn to see what had altered her expression so suddenly.

"Don't look around!" she whispered harshly. "It's Jerry Finch." She pulled his head down and kissed him soundly, her heart pounding against his in alarm. She moved her mouth to his ear and made herself giggle. "He's coming closer. Let me do the talking." She pushed him away, her mouth turned down in a pout. "Now that's enough! We came here to work and so far..." She looked beyond him again, the gesture believably natural, as she appeared to suddenly recognize the intruder. "Jerry Finch?" she asked, stepping around Erik.

Erik made himself turn slowly and look annoyed by the interruption. It was Finch, all right. He must have spotted them on the rim of the hill. No, then he'd have brought the two burly men with him. He'd seen something, wasn't sure what it was and decided to investigate. Or maybe Finch was just out for a stroll. Somehow, Erik doubted that.

Finch appeared guarded and a little suspicious as he walked toward Melanie. She stretched her hand out to him as he drew near. Same cold eyes, she thought. Like a watchful reptile. "I expected to run into you before this," she said with apparent enthusiasm over meeting an old acquaintance. "Remember me? Melanie Quinn. We were both Harvest Lake High School class of... God, I hate to think how long ago that was. You know Erik Channing, I'm sure." She stretched her hand back toward Erik and smilingly drew him forward. "You work in the same building, I think."

Erik offered his hand to Finch and forced himself to smile as he glanced at Melanie. "No, he's in city hall. My office is in the courthouse. But we do know each other."

Finch nodded, shaking his hand. "Channing. What brings the two of you to Harvest House?"

"Our cochairmanship of the party and art show to benefit Harvest House brought us to the meadow." Melanie patted the canvas bag over her shoulder. "Maggie's given me such a large space in which to show, that I need more paintings." She tilted her head, indicating the clump of goldenrod behind her. Then she glanced at Erik, her cheeks flushing with embarrassment. Erik watched in fascination, wondering if the blush was real or an act. "I was supposed to be sketching the goldenrod, but I was . . . distracted."

Erik hooked an arm around her shoulders, planting a kiss at her temple. "To think I used to be happy playing golf on my afternoons off."

Finch looked from one to the other. His suspicion appeared to soften and he smiled, but Erik doubted the authenticity of his sudden affability. "You're welcome here, of course, Melanie," he said, "but this is private property. I'd be careful where I decide to sketch if I were you. Some irate landowner might chase you off with a shotgun."

Finch's gaze swung to Erik. "Careful, Channing," he said, smile still in place. Erik saw the threat behind the smile and heard it in the seemingly innocuous warning, "You wouldn't want her to get hurt." He inclined his head. "Don't hurry off on my account. You're welcome to stay and get your sketch or . . . whatever." He turned away and called over his shoulder. "See you at the show."

Chapter Eight

Arm in arm, Erik and Melanie watched Finch walk away. They followed slowly, talking and laughing about the show, passing the bag of white chocolate back and forth, maintaining the pretense until they reached the parking lot and Reba's car that Melanie had borrowed for the afternoon. Erik pulled her toward his Volvo.

Melanie settled into her seat, turning toward him. "Do you think he believed us?"

Erik didn't, but he didn't want to frighten her. He smiled. "*I* almost believed us. You're a good actress, Melanie. Was that blush real or not?"

She frowned at him. "I want to talk about Jerry Finch. What's he done? What were you doing in the meadow?"

"I'm not sure he's done anything," Erik replied, his smile dissolving, "but the city's made a few unusual moves since he's been mayor, which make me suspect he's on the payroll of someone influential who wants a few favors."

"But what does that have to do with Harvest House?"

"Melanie, this is very confidential."

Melanie rolled her eyes. "I'm going to buy an ad on KAHH as soon as I get home, and tell the whole town about it."

Trusting her discretion, he told her what he knew. "Bill has an informant at city hall who's been passing us information. He overheard an arrangement Finch made to accept delivery of something at Harvest House. He didn't know when it was coming or what it was, but he thought it might be related to a deal Finch is putting together with a person known to dabble in all kinds of shady things. I looked into the House's schedule and discovered that all the boys and half of the staff go to the YMCA for a couple of hours on Tuesday afternoons. The rest of the staff has the afternoon off. It seemed like a good time to accept a shipment."

"Of what?"

Teasingly, he returned her wide-eyed gaze. "I don't know. Someone prevented me from getting a closer look."

She dismissed the censure. "And it was a good thing, too. Any guesses?"

He shook his head. "Just the reasonable certainty that it wasn't food, since he put it in the storage building and not the kitchen. I've got to get in there."

"Are you crazy? He—"

"Not today," he interrupted quietly. "Later, when his guard is down."

"Can't the police help you with this?"

He shook his head. "I haven't any concrete proof of wrongdoing yet, and the chief of police and Finch are buddies. I don't know if there's really a connection there, but there could be. Things have gone awfully well for Finch. He might have had help in the right places. Until I'm sure, I'm handling it alone." As Melanie frowned, he cupped her head in his hand. "Don't worry," he said gently. "I know what I'm doing. This is not Spring Street. Finch is very small-time."

Melanie had her own opinions about that. Small-time criminals still squashed people that got in their way. She'd witnessed that firsthand. But she was sure Erik knew that, too, so she kept her thoughts to herself. "Right," she said, reaching back for the door handle. "I'd better get home."

"Not before you kiss me," he said, threading his fingers into the hair slipping out of her scarf.

She tired to look severe, but the quirk of her bottom lip gave her away. "Just because we shared a kiss in the meadow," she said primly, "don't think you can—"

He grinned. "What if Finch is watching us with binoculars, from somewhere on the hill? He'll expect to see a little romance."

"That's very transparent, Erik. You can't—"

But he did. He pulled her scarf off, gathered the silver rope of hair in his left hand and pulled her toward him with his right. There was no preliminary tenderness this time, no gentle exploration. He knew now that she was what he needed and that he had a lot to give her in return. He parted her lips. She gave eagerly, then clung to him, trembling with the intensity of her feelings. She felt hot greedy passion and she felt cold sickening fear. She shouldn't let herself love Erik. But he leaned down again to kiss her warmly, gently, and she lost her grasp on logic.

He looked into her eyes, his gray gaze like the lake in winter. "There's no turning back, Mel," he said softly. "None." He let her hair rain through his fingers and pulled himself back from her with obvious reluctance.

"I've got to go back to the office," he said, putting her scarf in her hand. He grinned. "And you'd better finish that goldenrod. I'll follow you home, and I'll call you tomorrow." He leaned across her to open her door.

"All right." Wits in pieces, scarf in hand, Melanie walked toward Reba's car.

"DOESN'T MELANIE LIKE BASEBALL?" Greg asked. He and Erik sat in the bleachers at Lakeside Park watching the team sponsored by Formby Plumbing make mincemeat out of their opponents who were wearing Dawson's Boatworks shirts.

Erik groaned as Dawson's first baseman let a grounder get by him. "I invited her," he replied, craning his neck to see whether or not the batter would get to second. He did. Disgusted, he turned his attention back to Greg. "She and her sister were having dinner with Reba. You like her?"

Greg looked surprised by the question. "Yeah. You guys . . . you know . . . getting it on?"

Erik frowned. "No, we're not getting it on. We're friends. I thought we had this discussion the other night."

"But that's not what it's all about, is it?"

"What what's all about?"

"Well. I mean, even ladies . . . have sex."

Wondering how he'd gotten into this discussion, Erik shook his head. "Not indiscriminately, no."

"What does that mean?"

"It means they don't go to bed with just anybody."

"You mean you're not good enough for her." Erik heard the tease in Greg's voice before he even looked at him. The boy was grinning, but without malice. He was afraid to think he might be getting somewhere with this kid.

Greg punched his arm, laughing. "Gotcha, Channing."

"I mean," he explained wryly, "that sex is best when it means something important. When you've gotten to know each other and care about each other so much that the next step is the love of each other's bodies."

Greg appeared to absorb that information for a moment. He looked up at Erik again. "It's gonna happen for you. She looks at you like that."

Erik raised an eyebrow. "Like what?"

"Not like some moon-eyed wimpy girl." Greg imitated his idea of an innocent simpering face. Erik laughed loudly. "But she sort of smiles at you when you're not looking, like she knows some secret about you . . . and she likes it."

That was good news. Erik tried to take it with sophistication. But he couldn't. "She really does, huh?" he asked, anxious for reassurance.

Greg nodded. "I saw her do it twice the other night. Why? Hasn't she let *you* know she likes you?"

Erik remembered the kiss in the meadow, then the kiss in the car. "Yeah, it's just that sometimes things are so great that you get a little afraid you'll lose them."

"That's fear of success," Greg said with adult nonchalance. Erik raised both eyebrows. "It's true," the boy explained. "My counselor says a lot of kids like me feel that way. They get slapped around at home, or they just screw up and end up in Juvie or someplace, and they just keep going down because they think they don't deserve to go up. It's easier not to try, you know?"

Erik looked down at Greg, afraid for a moment that he'd picked up the wrong boy at Harvest House. "That's heavy stuff. Do *you* feel that way?"

Greg looked out at the field where the bottom of the ninth had already begun. But he didn't seem to see the action. "When I'm scared, I do. When I feel good..." He gave Erik a measuring glance, as though trying to decide whether or not to say what was on his mind. Then, he expelled a self-deprecating sigh and went on. "Like after you've taken me somewhere when I was sure you weren't going to show up...I think I might make it."

Emotion swelled in Erik's throat and he had to clear it before he could speak. "You'll make it, Greg. Three short months and you'll be on your way home. You had good grades. Just keep away from the losers and you'll be fine."

A night wind ran through the park, stirring banners. Around them couples huddled together and people shrugged into jackets. Greg, in a short-sleeved shirt, without the jacket Erik suggested he bring along, folded his arms across his chest and tried not to shiver.

"Cold?" Erik asked.

Greg looked up at him, his cheeks already pale and pinched. "Yes," he admitted grudgingly, then added, "and if you put an arm around me, you're dog food."

Erik pulled off his short cotton jacket.

"I'm not wearing that," Greg said firmly. "It's nerdy."

Erik plucked at the blue and rust-colored pullover Greg had admired once before. "How about the sweater?"

Greg hesitated a moment. "You're kidding."

"Make up your mind," Erik said, "before I'm frozen dog food."

"Sure."

Erik pulled off the sweater and handed it to Greg, then pulled his jacket back on. Greg cuffed the sleeves back a few times, then turned his attention to the game. Erik saw him running a hand along the soft wool of the sleeves. Caught in the act, Greg glanced at him sheepishly. "Thanks," he said.

Erik smiled, satisfied. "Sure."

"THE SHEEP FRICASSEE..." Seated behind his desk, Erik read from Bill Curtis's notes. He hesitated, frowning over the next word, trying to imagine how it related to—

"Good God!" Bill rose out of his chair to snatch the lined yellow sheets out of Erik's hands. "An illiterate D.A. Does your constituency know that?" He slapped the sheets and sat down again. "It says here, plain as day, 'The *State franchise* is held by Northwest Oil Products,'" Bill read. He hesitated over what came next, glancing at Erik with a grin. "The light's bad in here."

"The light's bad in your brain. So, does Walter Abernathy own it, and our local gas station, and our illustrious Mr. Finch?"

"No," Bill said, trying to find his place in his notes. "Here it is. It's owned by Marvin Culver."

Frowning, afraid his theory was blown, Erik asked, "Who's that?"

Bill leaned back in his chair with a satisfied smile. "One of Walter Abernathy's partners in the casino."

Erik slapped the top of his desk. "I knew it. That's the connection. You think they're blackmailing Finch, or he's just working for them?"

Bill shrugged. "Could be either. This still isn't enough to take to court, is it?"

Erik shook his head. "But it's enough to keep us interested. I want you to look into Maggie Finch's background. Might be nothing, but let's check it out, just for the hell of it."

"Right." Bill dropped the notes on Erik's desk, then leaned back and joined his hands behind his head. "And my contact at city hall is watching for an invoice, or anything that may relate to the contents of the truck."

"Good."

"Now there's something I'd like you to do for me."

"I'm paying you," Erik said.

"Besides that. I'd like us to double-date tomorrow night with Melanie and Jolene."

Erik frowned at him. "Why don't you just take Jolene?"

"Because she suggested you and Melanie join us for dinner." Bill stood up and walked to the window, his hands jammed in the pockets of his jeans. "I met her at Melanie's last week when you were out buying lumber, or something, and had all of us worried about you."

When Erik rolled his eyes, Bill went on. "God, she's cute."

"Her hair's an inch long. I saw her from a distance and thought she was a man."

Bill turned away from the window, a silly smile on his face. "Then you haven't gotten close enough. Who'd ever imagine short hair could make a woman so attractive. She likes me. I know she does." Bill sat down again, clearly nervous. "Do this for me, buddy. I want to get to know her better. She says Melanie's been working hard painting, and getting some stuff ready for the show she's having. She thinks she needs a break."

Erik had called Melanie two days ago, after the episode at the meadow. She'd sounded warm and friendly, but had resisted all his efforts to see her. She'd even sounded vague about their next meeting to work on plans for the party and show. He hadn't been sure what to make of her reluctance, except to guess that it probably related to her fear of getting involved with him because of what had happened to her father. He'd decided to bide his time, to wait for inspiration to strike and help him change her mind. Who'd have thought, he considered with amusement, that inspiration would come in the form of Bill Curtis?

"Why don't you call Melanie?" Bill prompted. "Right now. See what she says."

"With you hanging over my shoulder?"

Bill nodded eagerly. "Yeah."

Erik ran a hand over his face and reached for the phone. "All right. Maybe you'll learn something."

MELANIE REACHED ACROSS her worktable for the telephone, frowning over whether to use the white or yellow mat over her colorful bouquet of pansies. "Hello," she said.

"Hi, Mel. It's Erik."

She'd known that immediately. A ripple of pleasure ran along her skin. "Hi," she replied. "It's Monday. You're supposed to be hard at work."

"I am. I hear you are, too."

"From whom?"

"Jolene. Bill met her on the street this morning and asked her to join him at Marco's tomorrow night. Luckily for her, she had more sense than to agree to spend an evening alone with him. Oops!'' Melanie heard a loud ''whap'' on the other end of the line.

''Erik?'' Melanie asked anxiously.

''I'm fine,'' he said. ''I just happen to be wearing several recent issues of *The Law Review*. Where was I?''

Melanie shook her head at what was probably going on at the other end of the connection. ''Jolene had more sense...''

''Oh, right. So, in the interest of love—however, misguided—I think you and I should chaperon them.''

Melanie's first thought was that she didn't need another distraction. Her second thought was that she didn't care if she needed it or not. And Jolene had been mooning over Bill Curtis since she'd met him. Encouraging a relationship between them could very well work to her own advantage. A stepsister who was being courted would have little time to plague her with endless thoughtful attentions, and might even stop preparing her favorite meals and desserts. There might be a chance she could keep her summer weight gain to three pounds rather than thirty.

''All right,'' she replied. ''In the interest of love. And I don't think Jo's interest in Bill is misguided. I think he's cute.''

She heard Erik say in some disgust, ''She thinks you're cute.''

Bill's voice replied, ''A woman with taste.'' Then he added loudly. ''Thanks, Melanie!''

''Did you hear that?'' Erik asked her. ''Shall I stay home and let Bill take both of you?''

''No, you have to come along,'' she heard Bill whisper audibly. ''Somebody has to pay!''

''All right,'' he said abruptly. ''We'll pick you up at eight?''

''Fine.''

Melanie cradled the receiver, looking out at the sunny street beyond her window. She shouldn't be this delighted at the prospect of seeing Erik again, she told herself. But she was. There was no denying it, or pretending she'd agreed simply to encourage Bill and Jolene's relationship. She was looking forward to waltzing with Erik under the lanterns on Marco's pier.

Jolene appeared at Melanie's desk. "You ready for a coffee break?"

"We have more important things to think about," Melanie said. "That was Erik and Bill on the phone."

"Both of them?"

"Bill told Erik he asked you out, and you suggested the four of us go together."

"I like Bill," Jolene said, looking down at her linked fingers. "But men make me . . . nervous. I thought I might not look like such a nerd if you came along. You always smooth the way for me. I'm not sure what it is. I'll feel more calm if you're there."

For the first time, Melanie felt the poignancy in Jolene's declaration instead of feeling the stifling sense of duty with which her confessions usually left her. She didn't know how to react. "That's silly," she said. "Bill was smitten with you that first day when he came here looking for Erik. I don't think you'll have to worry about looking nerdy to him. And anyway . . ." She smiled, trying to coax a smile out of her stepsister. "He's not exactly a hard-boiled traditionalist. He's a little eccentric himself."

Jolene laughed suddenly. "He is, isn't he? What are you going to wear?"

Melanie thought, frowning. "I didn't bring that much with me for partying. I do have a little black thing that might do."

"I have a wild pair of wraparound silk pants," Jolene said, making a face. "But no blouse. The top should be loose and flowing. I guess I should go shopping for something."

"What color are the pants?" Melanie asked. "I have a white silk shirt that might do. I'm sure it's a size larger than you need, but in that style it would pass."

Jolene's blue eyes widened. "That sounds perfect. My pants are silver."

Melanie smiled. Of course. "Let's go upstairs and see if it'll work."

Jolene followed in her wake, laughing. "Doesn't this remind you of when we were kids? You were always loaning me things out of your closet. Dad gave me an allowance, but Mom was always borrowing it for something."

Borrowing was a generous term, Melanie thought. Stealing would have been a more accurate description.

"What are you going to do with your hair?" Jolene asked, her expression openly envious as Melanie delved into her closet.

"Wear it up, I guess." Melanie grinned teasingly over her shoulder. "What're you going to do with yours?"

Jolene laughed. "Very funny. Another week and it might not look so much like I've enlisted. Once I can part it, it should look less bizarre."

"The important thing," Melanie said bracingly, pulling the blouse off the rod, "is that it's growing in healthy. This is it. What do you think?"

The blouse looked wonderful. Jolene modeled the silky white shirt with her lamé pants, and though the effect was more outrageous than anything Melanie would choose to wear, her stepsister was thrilled. She hugged Melanie effusively and promised to make a *gâteau* for dessert.

"No!" Melanie pleaded.

"Nonsense." Jolene turned in front of the full-length mirror in Melanie's room. Her eyes were sparkling. "I know how much you love it.'' She hugged her again. ''And I love you. I want to make you happy while I'm here.''

And obese, Melanie thought. Once again she'd been beaten with her own stick.

COLORFUL LANTERNS WERE STRUNG the length of the pier, the spicy aroma of Italian food mingled with the fragrance of wildflowers and summer, and the night was velvety and warm. Melanie could see the shimmer of Jolene's pants against the darkness of Bill's suit, as he twirled her around the dance floor at the end of the pier.

Melanie and Erik sat at right angles to each other at their table. Erik's back was to the dance floor. He asked quietly, ''How are they doing?''

As a delaying tactic, Melanie sipped at the flute glass of champagne. When she walked into Erik's arms on the dance floor, she sensed there truly would be no turning back. ''I'm becoming more and more convinced they're made for each other,'' she said. ''They seem to be having a wonderful time.''

''If you'd quit stalling,'' he said, his gray eyes dark in the shadows cast by the globed candlelight on the table, ''we could be having a wonderful time, too.''

Melanie feigned a look of innocence. ''Aren't you having fun?''

He pushed his chair back decisively. ''With the table between us? No.'' He stood, took the glass from her and put it aside, then walked around the table to pull out her chair. He leaned over her as she rose, his suit coat brushing against her bare shoulder, his breath warm in her ear. ''I'm not waiting another moment,'' he said, gripping her elbow, ''to hold you in my arms.''

She turned to him in a quiet corner of the crowded floor, a sigh disturbing the black ruffles at the low neck of her dress. The lapping of the water beyond the edge of the pier provided a rhythmic beat to the mellow, romantic tune.

Erik drew her into his arms, afraid to delay, afraid to give her or himself time to think. This was serious, he thought with fatalistic acceptance. This was love. He wondered if she knew it, too.

Both her arms came around his neck, and she closed her eyes with a little smile of acceptance, leaning her forehead against his chin. He pulled her closer and felt her lean her weight against him. His entire body seemed to relax, as though it finally found itself in a perfect environment. His feet began to move to the music, though he felt sure that must be a result of divine intervention; his brain was too crowded with impressions to send out impulses.

Melanie couldn't breathe. She expelled a little laugh, trying to draw in a gulp of air.

"What?" Erik asked lazily.

Her small breasts rose and fell against his chest. Whatever tenuous hold he'd had on his senses was lost. "I'm choking," she said with another laugh.

"Well, I hope you've made your peace and your affairs are settled," he said, "because I'm not letting you go."

She leaned back to give him a scolding look. "It's not you, it's the dress."

She felt his hand reach for her zipper pull and tug.

"Erik!" She dropped an arm from around him and reached behind her to disengage his hand. "Pull it back up and behave yourself. I meant that Jolene's cooking is making it impossible for me to fit into my clothes."

He leaned away from her to glance down at the gentle swell of creamy flesh above the ruffle. "I like it when you spill out a little."

"I meant the waist," she said sternly, pulling his head back down to lean her cheek against his. "I feel like I have a corset on. Jolene keeps making all my favorite foods—even a few I didn't think I'd like and have learned to love."

"I'm sure you're putting up a brave struggle," he said gravely.

"Why don't you encourage Bill to elope with her?"

"Because they'd probably have kids right away and he'd want paternity leave. Then where would I be?"

"Don't you need a cook-housekeeper?"

"I have an excellent one, thank you. Been with me since I bought the house. There's an old guy across the street who gives her the eye all the time, but she's very loyal to me."

"Will you still dance with me when I weigh two hundred pounds?" she asked mournfully.

He patted her back. "Of course. Though, maybe not on the pier. And I have an antique chair or two I wouldn't let you sit . . ."

Melanie drew away, feigning a quiver of her bottom lip. He laughed, then leaned down to kiss away the tremor. Humor was swamped instantly when she responded. His suppressed memories of their kiss in the meadow erupted like champagne from a shaken bottle. He felt her eager response, the gentle sweep of her fingers in his hair, the barest stab of her tongue. She seemed to melt in his arms with a surrender that was his every wish come true.

"You two remind me of the kind of thing I see on all-night surveillance." Erik and Melanie raised their heads at Bill's dry voice. With Jolene still in his arms, he swayed to the music. "You could at least pretend to move your feet, so we aren't thrown out for lewd behavior."

"Go away," Erik said.

"Maybe we should all sit down," Bill suggested.

Erik pulled Melanie closer and closed his eyes. "I don't want to. You sit down."

Bill sighed. "You really should come, too."

"Why?" Erik demanded impatiently.

"Because the music has stopped. The band's taking a break." He indicated the clearing dance floor, then rapped his knuckles on Erik's head and asked in concern. "Your generator's dead again, isn't it?"

Melanie bit her lip to hold back her laughter, clearing her expression of amusement when Erik turned to her accusingly. She took his arm and pulled him back toward the table. "We'll have Marco bring more wine and more *panforte*, and you'll feel better. Maybe your generator will start up again."

Walking back with her toward the table, he stopped, pulling her closer as a laughing couple bumped into them on their way to the parking lot. Melanie looped her arms around his waist, her eyes laughing up into his, and the scolding died on his lips. "I have missed you so much," he said. "And it's only been a matter of days."

"I've missed you," she admitted quietly.

Unable to help himself, he leaned down to kiss her again.

"We'd better sit down," she said, grinning as she pulled him toward the table. "Or Bill will have more to say."

"Bill always has more to say. I can't imagine what Jolene sees in him."

"He's funny, kind and handsome. For many women, that's the ideal man."

"Yours, too?"

"Yes. Except that I would add 'careful' to the list."

He rolled his eyes as they approached the table, and he pulled out her chair. Bill and Jolene were in conversation with Marco near the side door of the restaurant. "A careful man doesn't fall in love."

She smiled as Erik sat beside her. "That's dangerous talk," she cautioned.

He folded his forearms on the table and leaned toward her. "Why?" he asked.

She leaned forward too, and her hair fell over one shoulder like a cascade of liquid silver. She looked into his eyes, her fragrance rising with the night breeze and surrounding him. He had to force himself to listen, to think. "Because I might believe you are in love," she said.

He put a hand over hers on the table, his eyes dark with sudden intensity. "Believe it," he said.

"We have champagne coming," Bill announced, as he sat down next to Jolene. "And spumoni and more *panforte*." He fell into his chair, looked from Melanie to Erik, and shook his head. "You know, you're going to vaporize each other with those looks. If this table catches fire, Jolene and I are out of here."

Melanie tore her gaze away from Erik and smiled at Bill. "Actually, we were talking about you."

Bill's eyes widened. "You were?"

"Yes. I told Erik I thought you were funny and handsome."

Bill turned to Jolene. "Do you think so?"

She nodded with enthusiasm. "And a little nuts. All in all, very appealing."

Bill gave Erik a superior glance. "And you said flossing between my toes would get me nowhere."

"WOULD YOU LIKE TO COME BACK to my place for a night-cap?" Erik danced lazily with Melanie to the moody music. The night air was getting chilly, and he had both arms wrapped around her. She nestled against him, her arms curled up between them. He couldn't bear the thought of saying good-night to her.

"That would be nice," she said dreamily.

"Bill." Erik called across the few feet that separated them from Bill and Jolene. They, too, were wrapped in each other's arms. But they were staring into each other's eyes with such concentration, Erik was afraid his friend hadn't heard him.

"Yeah?" Bill finally replied absently.

"Want to come back to my place for a nightcap?"

Bill continued to stare at Jolene. "It's early."

"It's almost two o'clock in the morning. I have to be up again in four hours. So do you."

"Yeah."

"Maybe we should forget the nightcap," Melanie said.

"Then we'd have to go our separate ways," Erik pointed out.

She relaxed against him once more, as the band announced the last number. "A nightcap's a good idea," she murmured.

THE FOUR SAT in Erik's living room, sipping at crystal cups of cappuccino. Drowsily, Melanie tucked her feet under her in Erik's big chair and ran a finger over the silver filigree that braceleted the cup and curled into a handle. Bill and Erik sat on the sofa, Jolene in her stockinged feet curled up in a corner of it.

"Give me one good reason," Bill said, "why the girls and I should help you with this pool party."

"Because it's going to be held at my place just two days after Melanie's party, and I could use your help. You're my friends." He looked from one to the other with a noble smile. "And because I'll make your lives miserable if you don't. I'll call in all your parking tickets, or something."

"It's for children, Bill," Jolene cajoled.

"The kids of Harvest House. Hoods in the making."

"Aunt Reba says they have a wonderful time." Jolene gave him a dirty look. "Erik held it for them last year, along with a giant barbecue."

"All right, all right," Bill grumbled. "Just don't let Greg Butler anywhere near me."

Erik frowned at him in surprise. "He liked you."

"He lifted my wallet."

"You refused to pay what he won from you in the poker game. Anyway, he gave it back."

"He cheated," Bill accused.

Erik laughed. "He did not. He just plays better than you. Even Reba plays better than you."

Bill glowered at Erik. "Harvest House would love to know you're teaching him to play poker."

"He already knew how. I just taught him a few new angles he used to good advantage on you. You have to learn to lose with more grace."

"I enjoy being a sore loser. It usually prevents me from being invited into games where—"

The conversation was suddenly halted by a loud, teeth-jarring boom! The house shook, everything that hung from the ceiling swung and everything standing on a flat surface teetered or fell. Jolene screamed, and Bill reached for her. Melanie got to her feet, and Erik stopped her rush to the window, saying firmly, "Stay there."

The boom had died away and a strong rolling "whoosh" remained. He went to the window where a churning, orange light undulated. He blinked and looked again, unable to believe his eyes.

Where his car had been was a dancing ball of flame.

Chapter Nine

"Erik!" Melanie gasped.

He looked down at her. The bright reflection of the fire highlighted the planes of her face and danced in her eyes, making the fear plainly visible. Both of her hands clenched at her mouth, and he put an arm around her, as much to steady himself as her. "God!" Bill took one look over Erik's shoulder and rushed to the phone.

"What happened?" Jolene asked in a shaky whisper.

Across the room, Bill spoke into the telephone. "Yeah, hi, Miller. This is Bill Curtis. Dispatch the troops. Somebody just blew up the D.A.'s car. No, he's fine. We were all in the house."

He hung up and joined the other three, who had moved outside to the driveway. He stood between Erik and Jolene, putting a hand on each of their shoulders. "You think our investigation is aggravating somebody?" he asked.

Melanie looked up at Erik, her heart thumping, her mouth dry with fear. "I'd say that was an understatement."

"Maybe something was just wrong with the car?" Jolene suggested faintly.

"Without some encouragement, cars don't usually blow up while standing still," Bill said. "Somebody did this."

The sound of a siren became audible. Erik's neighbors were out in their nightclothes, openmouthed. "I told you you weren't indestructible," Melanie said, her voice high and tight. "Didn't I tell you this could happen?"

"Mel..." Erik began calmly.

She swallowed. "If you'd been in the car—"

"I know." He prevented her from finishing the thought by pulling her head onto his shoulder. A murderous rage filled him as he thought about Melanie sitting beside him in the front seat, Bill and Jolene in the back. Someone had timed that very close.

"Had it been meant to kill me," he said, turning her around and leading the group back into the house, "I'd be dead. It's just a scare tactic."

Melanie stopped him in the middle of the room. "Tell me it worked?" she pleaded.

He looked back at her without reply, then kissed her cheek. "Bill's going to take you home."

"No." Melanie shook her head.

He reached to the chair for her purse and handed it to her. "Yes." He raised a hand to silence her protest. "It's not open for discussion."

"I'm not going to leave you here alone," she announced, folding her arms in an attitude of defiance, "not when your car is being flambéed on the sidewalk."

He pushed her toward Bill, who pulled Jolene toward the door. "The police are here..." Two cars, red and blue lights flashing, pulled up in front of the house, sirens swelling, then stopping suddenly to leave a chilling silence.

"Don't worry, Melanie. I'll be coming right back," Bill assured her, "to spend the night."

Erik gave him a wry look. "That won't be necessary."

"You want Melanie to worry all night?"

She hooked an arm around Bill's neck and kissed his cheek. "Thanks, Bill. I'd feel much better knowing you were staying with him." Then she turned to Erik, her eyes uncertain. "You're sure you'll be all right?"

He wrapped her in a firm hug. "I'm sure. Go home, don't worry about anything, and I'll call you in the morning."

"Promise?"

"Promise." He pushed her toward Bill.

"BILL WILL TAKE GOOD CARE of him, Melanie." Jolene stood in the doorway to Melanie's bedroom in a long, blue T-shirt. "Try not to worry."

Melanie sat in the middle of her bed, brushing her hair. She didn't want to think; she couldn't. Life should be brand new when two people fall in love. It shouldn't be filled with all the old fears each had confronted before.

Melanie stopped brushing and nodded, her shoulders sagging wearily. "I know. I just..." She put a hand over her eyes to blot out old images of her father.

She felt an arm go around her and dropped her hand to see Jolene sitting beside her. "You're thinking about your father, aren't you?"

An anger Melanie didn't understand was supplanting her fear for Erik, and she had to pull herself together to avoid directing it at Jolene. Perversely, her stepsister's use of the words, "your father," rather than "Dad" now annoyed her.

"I always feel guilty," Jolene said, "that I wasn't there when...it happened. That you had to face it all by yourself. That I never had the chance to thank him for all he did for me." She squeezed Melanie's shoulders. "I remember how brave you were through the funeral and afterward. Even though Aunt Reba came back from Saudi Arabia to take care of us, the house seemed so empty without him. I admired you for being able to go on. All I did was cry."

Melanie remembered clearly that hatred had kept her going—hatred for her father's killer, of course, but an even deeper hatred for Linda, who had hurt him so deeply his concentration had been thrown off, his reflexes blunted.

She recalled, too, that Jolene *had* cried all the time, and she'd resented having to comfort her and watch over her. But she had promised her father.

"This isn't like that," Jolene said bracingly. "Erik's sharp."

Wanting to rid her mind of images of her father lying dead on the front lawn, and Erik's car in flames, Melanie closed her eyes. "I'm really tired, Jo," she said.

"I know." Jolene gave her back a little pat and stood. "Get some sleep."

Jolene flipped the light off as she left the room, and Melanie crawled under the sheet, worried and angry. Someone had tried to kill Erik. Or to frighten him. She couldn't take that a second time, she thought grimly.

She curled into a ball, thinking of how it had felt when he closed his arms around her to dance with her. She remembered his kiss in vivid detail, how lovingly he had looked at her, how tenderly he had held her. She closed her eyes, as weariness superseded anger. Perhaps coming home this summer had been a bad move, after all.

STANDING ON THE SIDEWALK in the dark hours before dawn, Erik watched the tow truck hook up the smoldering, burned-out hulk of his car. Bill leaned a forearm on his shoulder. "You need a Caddy," he said. "A white one. Something with status and chic."

"What would you know about chic?" he asked, turning back into the house.

"I read classy magazines. Or maybe, considering the way you and Melanie have been looking at each other, you should think about a station wagon and infant seats."

"Go home."

"I promised Melanie."

Erik stopped abruptly in the middle of his living room. He saw his father sitting on the sofa, loading a 12-gauge pump shotgun.

"Dad, that would make a serious hole in the pavement," Erik said.

John patted the stock lovingly. "It'll make a hole in the son of a bitch that nuked your car."

"Dad, why don't you go home?"

"Why don't you and Bill call it a night. I'll watch till morning." Whistling, John continued his task, apparently expecting compliance.

With a defeated sigh, Erik turned to Bill. "My father seems to be rooted here for the night. You can go home."

"Not a chance. He's making corn pancakes for breakfast." Bill gave Erik a friendly shove toward the stairs. "Go to bed. I'll lock up and settle myself in the guest room." He glanced at his watch. "You can get two hours of sleep before you have to be at the office."

"Bill . . ."

"Good night." Bill turned away, heading for the kitchen.

Erik went upstairs, a little numb. Losing control of a situation usually panicked him, but tonight he thought he deserved to feel confused. He'd taken Melanie in his arms and known that he was in love. Someone had turned his car into a Molotov cocktail, and his father and his friend seemed to be taking over his life. It was a little like being on a handcar, pumping with all his strength to stay inches ahead of a runaway freight train. God, he wanted a cigarette.

SHRUGGING INTO HIS JACKET, Erik headed toward the knock on his front door.

"Wait!" Bill ordered harshly, pulling a short-barreled revolver out of his shoulder holster and flattening himself against the wall near the door. John hobbled over, to stand behind the door, his shotgun ready. Erik rolled his eyes and opened the door.

Melanie stood there in jeans and a pink cotton sweater. Her hair was caught at the nape of her neck, the platinum tail hanging over her shoulder like a hank of silver floss. Her soft, dark eyes went over him in swift concern. Then, apparently relieved by what she saw, she smiled. His heart stalled.

"Hi," she said, jangling the car keys that hung from her index finger. "I borrowed Reba's car. Thought you might need a ride to work."

Erik grinned, glancing at his friend, then at the door behind which his father stood. "Better call for backup, guys. It's Melanie. Come on in. I'll get my briefcase." As she stepped into the room, he asked over his shoulder. "Have you met the Crockett and Tubbs of Harvest Lake?"

She turned in surprise at a sound behind her, and saw Bill pocket his revolver, while John lowered his shotgun. She smiled from one to the other. "Ignore his ingratitude. It's nice to know you two are on the job." She frowned at John. "But you be careful."

Briefcase in hand, Erik rejoined Melanie.

"Wait," Bill said, reaching to the chair for his jacket. "I'm coming with you."

"No," Erik said firmly, "you're not."

Bill ignored him, putting the jacket on. "Yes, I am. I'm your shadow until we know—"

Erik caught the front of Bill's rumpled shirt and looked him in the eye. "We are going alone," he said with emphasis on the last word. "I appreciate your concern, but you're not coming to work with me."

"Son, be reasonable..." John began.

"I've been reasonable," Erik said calmly. "I let you two spend the night here, armed like some bizarre SWAT team. I let you use all my hot water, force twelve pancakes down me and give me decaffeinated coffee. Now I'm going to work." He tightened his grip on Bill's shirtfront. "And you're not coming with me!"

Hanging dramatically from Erik's fist like some six-foot tall rag doll, Bill smiled at Melanie. "I'm getting the impression he'd like to be alone with you."

Erik released Bill, looked at him sternly, then turned to his father with the same expression. "And if either of you shows up at my office today, I'll have you arrested."

John rested his weapon on his shoulder. "We're staying the night."

With a muttered curse, Erik marched out the door. Melanie blew John a kiss, winked at Bill, then pulled the door closed behind her as she followed Erik out into the sunshine.

"Don't be such a brat," she said, unlocking the passenger-side door for him before letting herself into the car. "They're just worried about you."

Erik snapped his seat belt into place with a grumpy sidelong glance. "I had twelve corn pancakes for breakfast, and decaffeinated coffee."

Melanie turned the key in the ignition. "So you said. I had a cheese and sausage omelet and enough fruit to open a stand at the farmer's co-op. You don't hear me whining about it."

Erik leaned back against the headrest and closed his eyes. "Maybe we could send Jolene to keep house for Bill and my father. I could move in with you."

Melanie laughed as she backed out of the driveway. "I'm sure that would be harder on your health than your investigation of Finch."

Erik grinned without opening his eyes. "But I would die with a smile on my face."

Melanie gave him a backhanded thump on the chest that made him sit up and stare at her. "Don't talk like that," she said, her eyes dark, her mouth set. "Not even in jest." She gave him a moment to consider the error of his ways as she turned onto the street that would take them to the courthouse.

"What did the police say?" Melanie asked.

"It was a garden-variety homemade bomb," Erik replied. "They sent what little might be identifiable to the crime lab in Salem."

"Did you tell them about Finch?"

"No."

Melanie braked at a red light and turned to demand. "Why not?"

"I've explained that," he replied patiently. "I'm going to get him, and I won't risk mishandling this so he can find a way to weasel out of it." Without warning, he reached across the seat, took her chin in his hand and leaned forward to kiss her. "Relax. I can take care of myself."

She did not appear to be reassured. "You didn't take very good care of your car."

He cast her a grim sidelong glance as the lights turned green and she accelerated. "That's not fair."

They drove in silence for several minutes, then he said cautiously, "I know this has brought back a lot of unpleasant memories for you."

She pulled into a parking spot in front of the courthouse and turned off the motor. She turned to him, her face pale. "My memories are not 'unpleasant,' Erik. They're horrible."

"Melanie." Erik pulled her into his arms, holding her close. "I'm sorry. I didn't say that very well. What I meant was, you don't have to worry about me because this job really isn't dangerous normally. In fact, it's even a little dull sometimes. And I don't want it any other way. After what happened to me in L.A., I'm not looking for excitement, believe me." He pulled her away to look into her eyes. "But

I was elected by the people of this county. I've got to do my job."

She looked at him defiantly. "Without any help?"

"Right now, yes. Finch is corrupt, and I don't much like the fact that he runs Harvest House."

Melanie frowned. "You mean you think the kids are at risk?"

He shook his head. "Not directly. The place seems to be well run because the last thing he needs is negative publicity. But Finch is dealing with some unscrupulous people. There's a potential for trouble."

She sighed, thinking of Greg. She felt as though she would burst with frustration. "I came here to paint irises!" she exclaimed. "That was all I wanted to do. The image of one pretty, artful iris I could transfer to paper. And what did I get?" She stopped, unable to answer her own question.

Erik knew he was sticking his neck out, but he had to know. "Well? What did you get?"

She narrowed her eyes at him. "An iris that will not give up its secrets, a sister who's turning me into Dumbo, and a man whose idea of a seductive come-on is 'You're under arrest.' Now I ask you . . ."

When he laughed and leaned down to kiss her, she drew back. "Don't you have to go to work?"

"I'm not leaving without a kiss," he said.

"You're pushing it, Erik." She tried to pretend that he didn't have her captive in the corner of her own car.

"I figure I don't have a lot to lose at this point."

She smiled blandly. "Your nose could be gone in a minute," she said. "Your earlobe, a corner of your chin, a good fistful of your hair."

"They're yours," he said, reaching out to cup the back of her head in his hand.

His lips closed over hers, eliciting a soft sigh of surrender. His mouth moved gently, imaginatively, opening just enough to tease her with the possibilities before he raised his head. Desire was building in his eyes. "I could go to work," he said, softly, "or we could go back to my place."

Melanie smiled faintly. "Bill and your father are at your place. And you have things to do." She pushed at his chest. "And so do I."

Reluctantly, he reached into the back for his briefcase, then opened the door. Melanie grabbed the sleeve of his jacket. He turned back to her, an eyebrow raised in question.

"Want to come over tonight and look over my paintings for the show? At about eight?"

He smiled wickedly. "Is this like being asked to look at your etchings?"

She laughed. "Not even close."

Undaunted, he waggled his eyebrows. "Shall I bring a romantic, seductive wine?"

She turned on the motor and blew him a kiss. "Sure. Whatever goes with popcorn."

Chapter Ten

Jolene was nervous. Working in her studio, Melanie watched her through the open door to the kitchen. She took dessert plates out of the cupboard, fussed with something in the refrigerator, then cleaned off the counter, putting the plates back into the cupboard again. She wore a short dress with military buttons and shoulder tabs for her first date alone with Bill.

"You look nice," Melanie said approvingly, hoping to reassure her if insecurity was the cause for her restlessness. "Are your bringing Bill back here after the concert?"

Jolene shrugged, uncharacteristically sober. "I don't know. Maybe. Anyway, there's cheesecake for you and Erik on the bottom shelf of the fridge, and the praline topping's in the white bowl right behind it."

Melanie had explained several times that Erik was expecting only popcorn, but had been forced to give in to Jolene's insistence that that would never do.

"Thanks, Jo." She grinned. "We'll try to save some for you and Bill."

Jolene came into the studio to look over her shoulder. "Do you like Bill?" she asked.

"I can't imagine anyone disliking him," Melanie replied, surprised by the question.

"Wouldn't it be fun if you married Erik and I married Bill?" Jolene hugged her arms and laughed softly. "We could have a double wedding."

The notion was so naive, so juvenile—so Jolene—that Melanie felt half impatient, half amused. But she also felt obliged to point out, "This is life, Jo, not a Rosemary Clooney--Vera Ellen movie."

"Your father would have liked him," she said softly.

Melanie dropped the frame and wire she was working with. "Will you please stop saying that?" she shouted. When Jolene looked at her in surprise, she added more calmly. "Just call him Dad, all right?"

"I know you don't like it," Jolene said quietly, "but he loved me, Melanie. He understood me."

Melanie crossed into the kitchen to pour herself a cup of coffee. She would have found some satisfaction in denying the truth of what Jolene had said, but she couldn't. "I know," she said. Then, she turned and finally voiced the fear that had plagued her all the time Jolene had lived with her and her father, and plagued her even now, as she tried to behave maturely and logically. "Sometimes, I think he loved you more than me."

Melanie half expected swift denial, or haughty confirmation. Jolene took a few steps toward her, then stopped, leaving the kitchen table between them, and offered disarming honesty, instead. "I used to wish he would, because my mother was so hungry for power. I thought that was love—holding, owning. But he adored you. He tried hard to make me feel like his daughter, but you really were his daughter."

Melanie felt her throat close as she forced herself to admit, "It's true. The two of you did have a special understanding."

The strange turbulence in Jolene's expression seemed to focus in her eyes, and they filled with tears suddenly, tears that were bright with pain. She took a step toward Melanie. "It wasn't . . ." she began, but then was cut off by the peal of the doorbell. She remained still for a moment, obviously frustrated by the interruption. Then she shook her head, wiping her eyes as she walked slowly to the door to admit Bill.

Confused by Jolene's reaction, Melanie went to wave them off. "Have fun," she called cheerfully. "We'll save the cheesecake till you guys get back."

Jolene turned to look at her over her shoulder, her eyes wide and still anguished as Bill led her away, laughingly teasing her about something. Melanie lowered her hand and watched until they drove away.

"YOU OBVIOUSLY MADE the right decision coming back to Harvest Lake." Erik knelt on one knee in front of three studies of the stately iris. One stood in frontal elegance, one in bud, and the other in full-blown, ruffly maturity. They were matted in lavender and framed alike in simple silver frames. He studied them with an eye that was no longer impartial, and saw wild, natural perfection. He straightened and hooked an arm around her neck, pulling her close. "You certainly learned its secret," he said, kissing her temple. "But I thought the paintings were for the book you're illustrating. Why are these framed for the show?"

She pointed to a package wrapped in brown paper on her drafting table. "Those are ready to go. But I had such fits getting it just right, that by the time I'd done it over and over, there were a few extras good enough to sell."

Paintings stood all around the room, a veritable garden of watercolors. She wrapped her arms around his waist with a sigh, marveling that her paintings were ready to send to her publisher, and that she was set for Harvest House's big night.

Erik held her, his eyes lazily scanning the paintings. Then, he saw one still standing on her easel though it was obviously finished. He felt the warmth of recognition. It was a watercolor of a common goldenrod. Memories of a sunny afternoon in a meadow came back to tease him. He remembered kneeling in the grass beside her while her fingers flew over the sketch. He remembered the flower itself, fat and golden in its patch of deep green grass. He remembered her profile through his binoculars—and he realized that was the way he always felt with her. As though he saw her in fine detail, but from a great distance. And he wasn't sure which one of them was keeping them apart.

"You promised me a painting for my sunroom," he said, drawing her slowly toward the easel. "Is the goldenrod for sale?"

She looked up at him, her eyes smiling. "No. It's for you."

He smiled back. "I'd like to buy it. The show's for Harvest House, after all."

She shrugged. "Then you can buy another one. That one's a gift. I didn't mat or frame it because I thought you might prefer it a particular way."

He combed her hair back with his fingers and looked into her eyes, his pulse thick. "I think I know why you're giving me the goldenrod. But I want to hear it from you."

Melanie looped her arms around his waist, finally admitting the truth to herself, as she admitted it to him. "Because I love you. Because love should be simple, like the goldenrod. Because all that gold is what what it feels like to kiss you."

Erik's gray eyes darkened to slate and his fingers tightened in her hair as he bent down to kiss her. She felt a tremor in him that conveyed itself to her, making pudding of her arms and legs. His lips were familiar, but their consuming intensity was something new, something so intimate, her mind ran ahead to where such passion could lead.

He swept her up in his arms and strode through the living room to the sofa, laying her down on the cushions, leaning over her and banishing all coherent thought. His fingers slid up under her sweater.

Melanie shuddered with pleasure as his hands trailed slowly from her waist to her rib cage, then found her lace-cupped breasts. Through the thin fabric, her nipples beaded against his hand and sensation rayed through her, melting her limbs, sending a languorous warmth to every extremity.

Reaching under his sweatshirt, she felt warm flesh and the fluttering reaction of nerves under her fingertips. She felt supple skin over taut muscle, then ran her fingers lightly up his chest, stroking over the jut of his ribs and into the tangle of hair across his pectorals. She swept down again because he had closed his eyes, and she loved having the power to make him lose concentration. Then, she felt it—the scar with a slightly ridged curve just below his pap. Her fingers followed it six or seven inches and she fell quickly back from the brink of irrationality, cold reality jarring her to awareness.

Erik, lost in the spell Melanie worked on him so effortlessly, felt the soothing, agonizing touch of her fingers up his chest. His stomach fisted, his heart fluttered, his breath failed. She trailed down again, tracing a line along his ribs....

With a jolt, he became aware of the sudden tension in her. He opened his eyes, realizing what her fingers had found. He wanted to shout his frustration—at her, at himself—but he remained silent because he saw the anguish in her eyes.

Still braced over her, he made himself smile. "You're going to say something profound like, 'We have to talk.'"

She smiled in surprise, then pulled his face down and kissed him. ''No wonder you're such a good attorney,'' she said. ''You can read the opposition's mind.''

He shifted and pulled her up until they sat in each other's arms in the corner of the sofa. ''You think of yourself as the opposition?'' he asked with a frown.

''No,'' she denied softly, quickly. ''At least, not in spirit. But making love—it'll confuse us.''

He looked into her eyes, trying desperately to read what he saw there, to understand what she meant. He couldn't. ''Maybe it'll straighten us out,'' he said. ''Show us what's really important.''

She smiled grimly with disbelief. ''No. Right now, you know exactly what you want, and I know exactly what I want. If we make love, that will blur. Either one of us may give in to the other, and regret it later. Then the other one would feel guilty.'' She shook her head, her disheveled hair falling forward.

Erik stroked it away from her face with his fingers, holding it at her nape. ''You've never told me what you want,'' he said quietly. ''Only what you can't face again.''

She looked into his eyes, her own wide and a little sad. ''I want to love someone ordinary. Someone who isn't constantly crusading for right and justice. I want to have children and pets and time to paint. Erik, I admire you for your courage. I'm even jealous that I can't be as strong as you are. But courage died in me with my father. Death—untimely, unnecessary death is painful and ugly and much stronger than I am.''

Her tension and her emotion communicated itself to him, and while he understood it, he fought to think rationally. ''I'm not going to die,'' he said firmly. ''I know what I'm doing.''

She shot him a reproachful glance, then looked away. ''If you knew what you were doing, you'd be frightened.''

He was silent for a moment, then he took the point of her chin and turned her to face him. "I *am* frightened. That's part of my point."

Melanie frowned, looking into his eyes, trying to see more deeply inside him. "I don't understand," she whispered.

Erik disentangled himself from her and stood. He had to tell her what he felt, but he needed a little distance between them. The fear inside him was so strong he was afraid she would feel it, and then their problem would be compounded.

He paced across the worn rug, his hands in his pockets. "When I woke up in the hospital after the incident in the alley, I hurt like hell, but I felt very smug." He glanced at her with a rueful expression. "I'd dealt with serious crud and come out on top. As soon as I could sit up and reach the phone, I called the *Los Angeles Times*. Together, we nailed Forsythe to the wall, sent him and D'Annibale up for twenty years, and tracked down every one of his Mafia soldiers and put them away."

He turned at the chair to pace in the other direction, detouring at the fireplace to stare down for a moment into the empty grate. He turned and leaned a shoulder against the mantel. "Then the fear set in," he said gravely. "Sure, I'd put them away, but they were big time. When everything calmed down, I began to think about that. First, it was just a shiver up my spine, a glance in the rearview mirror." He shifted his weight and shook his head, as though the reflection itself was painful. "I started leaving my car on the street instead of in the underground parking. I took work home with me, instead of staying late at the office. I had an alarm system installed. My body had healed, but everything still ached enough to make me wonder if I could be as noble a second time." He moved slowly to the chair that stood at an angle to the sofa and sat down in it with a sigh. "Then, Reba called me about my father's failing health and I moved back home." He paused, then added, "Correction. I 'ran' back home."

Melanie went to him, sitting on the ottoman near his feet, her eyes dark with sympathy. "Then let someone else investigate Finch. Certainly whoever it is you answer to will understand."

He shook his head. "I answer to the people, Melanie. I have to do it. I have to know that I can go on, even though Spring Street will haunt me for the rest of my life."

Melanie tipped her head back in frustration. "Why?" she demanded. "To prove to yourself that you're not afraid? What you do is dangerous, Erik! You have a right to be afraid."

"Yes, I do," he agreed mildly, "but I don't have the right to let the fear hedge in my life."

Melanie stood, taking three steps away from him, then turning back, her hair flaring. "Erik, I probably understand how you feel better than anyone. I was afraid for my father and I saw what happened to him. I live with the memory every day, but I'll be damned if I'll risk enduring that a second time just to prove to myself that I can take it."

He stood also, his eyes gentle, his jaw set. "You live with it, but it's blocked you in, Mel. I love you. But I won't let you rule my life with your fear. Controlling my own takes everything I've got."

Melanie returned his steady gaze and tried to accept his honesty for the gift it was. He could have lied. He could have offered her the false hope that he'd become a corporation lawyer, or something equally safe. But the sadness the truth brought her made it difficult to look on the bright side. Still, she clung to the hope that there was one.

She sighed and folded her arms. "I prefer to think of this as an impasse, rather than an ending."

He studied her a long moment, a stormy sadness in his eyes. Then, he smiled grimly and opened his arms. She walked into them without hesitation and he enfolded her, burying his face in her hair. "It's going to be all right," he said. "I promise. I've made a lot of deals in my time. We'll find a compromise."

Melanie held on, trying desperately to think of a compromise she would accept, but she couldn't. She kept that thought to herself.

She heard the crying and the shout at the same moment that Erik did. "Stay here," he said, going to the door.

Before he could reach it, Jolene burst through it, sobbing hysterically. She hesitated only long enough to look from Erik to Melanie, who stood in stunned surprise, before running to the stairs, the sound of her sobs trailing behind her.

"Jolene, wait!" Bill cleared the threshold immediately after her, running toward the stairs as he caught a glimpse of her rounding the landing. "Jo, I don't...I didn't..." He moaned, his hands held away from him in a gesture of helplessness as she disappeared. He turned to Erik, then to Melanie, then to the stairs, raising a trembling hand to his forehead.

"What happened?" Melanie ran toward Bill, Erik following.

"Nothing," Bill replied anxiously, "At least...I don't know. We were...we were..." He swallowed, his eyes going to the stairs again.

"Come and sit down." Erik pushed him toward the sofa, his eyes dark with concern. "Was it Finch?"

At first, Bill looked at him blankly. "What?" Then, he seemed to make sense of the question. "No. Nothing like that." He sat down and drew a deep breath as Melanie and Erik sat on the broad coffee table, facing him. "The concert was over," he began more calmly, "and we got into the car. She sat in the middle, close to me, and she was smiling." He shook his head, his eyes clouding. "I kissed her."

He looked at his companions, his dark eyes showing confusion. "I mean, we'd been arm in arm all night. She was happy, having a good time. So I kissed her." He looked to Erik for support. "You know I wouldn't..."

Erik nodded. "I know. Go on."

"Well..." He thought back, his brow furrowing. "She looked surprised and a little...I don't know...scared, I guess. But I thought...I mean, that's how I felt, too. I mean, I really like her—like, maybe this could be important. I thought she was afraid of that, like I was, so I pulled her closer and kissed her again and...and she went crazy. She started to scream and push at me like I was some..." He shook his head again, his eyes glazed and hurt. "...some fiend, or something. I stopped, but she kept screaming, 'Take me home! Take me home!' so..." He fell back against the sofa, expelling a ragged breath. "I would never have hurt her. I...guess I just misread her. God. She scared me to death."

Stunned and confused by his story, Melanie stood up and headed for the kitchen. "Relax, Bill," she said over her shoulder, "I'll get you a brandy." She remembered Jolene's strange nervousness before she'd left with Bill, and their curious conversation about her father liking Bill. As Melanie thought back to it, Jolene had seemed anxious to be with Bill, yet afraid at the same time.

She poured two glasses from a bottle that had been in the house since her father had been alive. Erik appeared beside her, looking worried. "Bill wouldn't have hurt her deliberately, Melanie," he said gravely. "I swear it. He's a nut, but he's a gentle man."

Melanie nodded, handing him one of the brandies. "I know. Give this to him. I'll go talk to Jo."

Melanie had no idea why she was shaking as she climbed the stairs. Except that she had recognized the look in Jolene's eyes when she'd run into the house. Her stepsister, too, had lived with some hidden terror, something dark and ugly that had risen up tonight to torment her. *I'm not going to know what to do,* she thought in panic as she knocked on Jolene's bedroom door. *I don't even know what to do for myself.*

There was no answer, but Melanie turned the knob and the door opened. She walked into the dark, vaguely musty-smelling room, and flipped on the light.

Jolene sat stiffly in the middle of the bed, looking strangely correct in her little military dress. She was staring at the wall, her profile puffy and tearstained. She turned to Melanie, putting a hand to her eyes. "Turn the light off," she said, her voice strained with pain and tears.

It occurred to Melanie that they'd been operating in the dark for too many years. The look of sustained pain on Jolene's face forced a kinship on her that she'd denied for too long.

"Sip this first," she said gently, sitting on the edge of the bed, facing Jolene. "It'll make you feel better."

Jolene ignored the glass she offered, shaking her head, a hand still covering her eyes. "I'll never feel better. Go away."

"Not until you tell me what happened," Melanie insisted.

Jolene's face crumpled and she shook her head again. "No. Go away."

Melanie looked at her stepsister, every muscle in her body taut with suffering, and wondered what had caused it and why she had never seen it before. To run so deeply, it had to be a long-standing pain. As a teenager, she'd thought of Jolene as pesty and dependent, and had been unable to shake that notion, even when they'd both become adults. She was finally going to see beneath that facade, she realized, and prayed that they were both up to it.

"I'm not going away," she said with quiet firmness. "I'm your sister, Jo."

Jolene dropped her hand and looked at her, tears streaming down her face. "No, you're not. You're Grant Quinn's daughter. I don't have a sister, and I don't have a father."

"You may not want them," Melanie said. "But you have them. I want to know what happened."

Jolene drew her knees up, wrapping her arms around them and hiding her face in them. "Bill kissed me," she said. "That's all."

"Didn't you want him to?"

Jolene thought about that for a minute, and her face crumpled again. She began to sob. "Yes. Even though I knew... what would happen."

Melanie took one of Jolene's hands and put the glass of brandy in it. "Take a sip," she insisted. Jolene complied, choking on it. "You knew you would scream?" Melanie asked. "Why?"

Jolene dropped her knees and sat cross-legged, her head thrown back, her eyes closed, a sob still in her throat. Then she took another sip of brandy and handed the glass back to Melanie. "Because I'm always afraid," she said.

Melanie stood up to put the glass on the dresser, then sat closer to Jolene. "Jo, you'll have to tell me more," she prodded. "I don't understand."

Jolene looked at her, her eyes so dark with despair that Melanie's heart lurched. "Don't you wonder why you've always hated me?" she asked with a cold detachment that was bone chilling.

Melanie had to swallow. "I've never hated you. I've found it difficult to love you because I considered you an intruder. But that was when I was young and selfish. You won my father over. He loved you and seemed to have... a special place in his heart for you. I was jealous of that. But I never hated you."

Jolene remained calm, removed, as though she'd retreated to some emotionless place where she was safe. "What he felt was pity. Because the lover my mother had before we came to Harvest Lake used me over and over, all the time we lived with him."

Melanie went cold, as though her blood had been frozen, or drained from her completely. She opened her mouth to speak, but thought seemed frozen, too.

"Your father found out when my mother left." She closed her eyes, apparently thinking back. "He sent for her records and and found it in a police report!"

Melanie could hardly form the question. "*Had* your mother known?"

Jolene's bottom lip began to quiver, but she bit it. "I told her the first time. Then the second. She told me she could report him and he'd be taken away, and we'd be thrown out on the street and starve. If I wanted that, she'd tell the police."

Rage rose red and hot in Melanie, blinding her, making her put a hand over her mouth to hold back a scream and the threat of being sick.

Jolene sighed, exhaustion weakening her defenses. "He was strong. If I fought he...hurt me. So I let him do it over and over. Finally my volleyball coach found bruises on me and called Children's Services." Her voice was high and irregular now, as though she was losing her battle to remain impassive. "That's why you hate me. I'm dirty. You were always so clean and so good."

Something snapped in Melanie, something that seemed to free her from the tyranny of years of childish jealousy and misunderstanding. She grabbed Jolene's arms and shook her. "No!" she shouted. "That isn't true. You were all of—

what?—twelve, thirteen? What were you supposed to do? It wasn't your fault!"

"I let him..."

"You did all that could be expected of you! You told your mother, whose job it was to protect you from injury. But she was a bitch. *He* did it to *you*, you didn't let him!"

Jolene shook her head, covering her face with both hands as she began to sob again. "That's what my therapist in New York said. That it was time for me to settle up with the past, to make my peace with you."

Melanie remembered a snatch of conversation they'd had when Jolene had first arrived. She took her sister's hands and pulled them down. "What about the artist you'd dated in the Village?" she asked quietly. "Did you like him?"

Jolene shook her head. "Hard men, selfish men don't matter. I can date them because they don't care about me." She shrugged, an anguished sob rising as she ducked her head. "It's the nice ones that I won't let get close to me, because they'll feel it. They'll know...I'm dirty."

"Oh, Jo." Melanie pulled her into her arms as her sister's sobs erupted. Tears streamed down her own cheeks and fell onto Jolene's shoulder, as she rocked her back and forth, trying to calm her, wondering how one could ever penetrate and destroy such an ugly barrier to happiness. "You've got to stop saying that. You have to stop thinking it, because it isn't true!"

"I wanted to...to be an actress," Jolene wept against her, "because I thought I could live my life being somebody else. Anyone but Linda Slade's daughter. Anyone but the girl who..."

Melanie tightened her grip on Jolene. "Don't even finish the thought. The person you are is no one to be ashamed of. Daddy loved you, Jo." Melanie pulled her away and looked into her eyes, knowing truth showed in her own because what she'd said had been fact. "No wonder he thought you were special.'' Melanie stroked her damp cheek and smiled at her. ''You survived something so awful and remained trusting and loving. I'd have died—or turned into a monster.''

Jolene looked grateful for the words of support, but doubtful of their truth.

''Jo, why didn't you tell me long ago?'' Melanie asked. ''Why didn't Dad tell me?''

Jolene's dark eyes, awash with grief, suddenly filled with the unqualified affection she'd always felt for Melanie. ''He wanted to, but I asked him not to. I didn't know if you could ever understand.''

''Jo.'' Melanie pulled her into her arms again, hating herself for never having tried to get closer. Jolene's arms wrapped around her with an almost suffocating force. Melanie realized she was a lifeline to sanity at that moment, her stepsister's last hold on understanding and the hope of a normal future. ''How did you ever think I could blame you?''

Jolene sniffed against her shoulder. ''I thought you'd think I was like . . . my mother. And I knew how much you hated her.''

She'd deserved that, Melanie thought. She'd never really separated Jolene from Linda and tried to understand her. She'd just been part of the package that had ruined her life and destroyed her father—their father.

Holding Jolene, she remembered the special understanding between her sister and her father, and finally saw it for what it had been—not a plot to exclude her from their relationship, but a plan to protect her from the ugly secret.

She decided instantly that it wasn't too late to be the big sister she'd failed to be all those years ago. She reached to the dresser for a box of tissue and stuffed several into Jolene's hand. She stood up. ''I'm glad you've been seeing someone about this,'' she said, rummaging through the drawers for a nightgown. "Tomorrow, we'll call Dr. Forman and ask him to recommend someone to help you here." She found a pink silky nightshirt and held it up. "This okay?"

Jolene nodded, dabbing at her eyes.

Melanie sat in front of her with the shirt. "I'm not a psychiatrist, but it seems to me you've got to stop taking any part of the blame in order to get over this. It was not your fault, do you hear me? No one would blame you."

Jolene stared at her crumpled tissue and sighed. "I want to believe that."

"Then do it," Melanie said firmly. "Thumb your nose at that monster and Linda. Don't let them ruin the rest of your life. You deserve to get to know Bill—to marry someone wonderful and have lots of kids."

Jolene shook her head. "Poor Bill. He must think I'm crazy. I screamed at him and . . . I think I even hit him."

"He's more worried about you than himself." Melanie put her hand on Jolene's face. "He'll understand, Jo."

Jolene looked suddenly terrified and doubtful. "Could you explain it to him? So if he doesn't understand...I won't have to see the look in his eyes."

"Of course." Melanie stood, trying to look as though she were in control. "Why don't you get to bed and get some rest, and I'll look in on you later." Jolene looked so drained and pale that she bent down to hug her again. "It's going to be okay. I'll help you; I promise."

She heard Jolene's small sigh of relief.

BILL STARED AT MELANIE, rage overriding his confusion, even, momentarily, his concern for Jolene. Erik, sitting beside him on the sofa, put an arm around his shoulders.

"I know," he said quietly. "Drawing and quartering the bastard would be so satisfying. But he's out of your reach."

"But Jolene isn't," Melanie said, patting his shoulder. "She needs you to understand. She's been seeing a therapist in New York, but she still feels a lot of the blame for what happened."

He put a hand over his eyes as though the mental image he saw was too ugly to contemplate. "Who in their right mind would expect a little girl to stand up to..."

"I know. It doesn't make sense, but I think her feelings are fairly typical of someone in her situation. I'm going to call Dr. Forman in the morning and ask him to recommend a therapist to help her while she's here. Although I suspect just having told someone will make her feel better."

"God." Bill lowered his hand, shaking his head in self-disgust. "I must have terrified her."

"Now, don't *you* start taking the blame for something that isn't your fault," Erik said.

Bill looked at Melanie. "Should I stay away?"

"I don't think so." She smiled at him, feeling her casual affection for him turning to friendship. "I think what she needs is just the opposite. A man who'll be there for her, care about her and be patient."

He nodded, pushing himself to his feet. "All right. Call me, will you, and tell me what the doctor says?"

"Of course."

Erik stood up with him. "Why don't I take you for a drink," he suggested. "I could use one myself."

Bill nodded vaguely. "Sure. I'll wait for you outside."

Melanie was suddenly reminded of the disagreement she was having with Erik just before Jolene came home. In light of her sister's dramatic return and revelation, the gravity of her own problems seemed to have diminished considerably.

Erik smiled at her, framed her face in his hands and kissed her. "Lucky she had you when the past blew up in her face."

Melanie sighed. "I should have been there for her a long time ago."

"You were both children in a difficult situation," he said gently. "You're there for her now. That's what's important. How would you feel about an intruder on our meeting next week? Reba and the ladies are taking the boys to the Maritime Museum in Astoria on Sunday, so I'm picking Greg up on my afternoon off, instead."

"I wouldn't mind at all." She stood on tiptoe to hug him, then walked him to the door. "Take care of Bill."

As Melanie opened the door, the sound of squealing tires broke the small-town silence. Erik spun toward the sound, getting between Melanie and the night. Bill was halfway out of the car before the streetlight illuminated the pleated fender of John Channing's truck.

Bill got back in his car and Erik turned to Melanie, shaking his head. "My father's been guarding me again, and didn't want me to know." He leaned down to kiss her. "Good night."

BILL TOOK A LONG DRAUGHT of dark beer, then frowned across the table at Erik. "What is that in your Bloody Mary?" He'd been silent for twenty minutes, staring moodily into his drink. His expression looked clearer now, as though he'd either made a decision or accepted a truth.

Erik looked down at the swizzle stick with which he stirred his spicy drink. "A green bean. Marinated, I think."

"How classy. You can't just have a beer like one of the guys."

Erik considered Bill's harassment a good sign and rolled with it. "And end up with a gut like yours?"

"It's muscle."

"Muscle doesn't hang over your belt."

"In your case, it pushes your ears apart. Will you eat the damn bean? It's making me nervous."

Erik laughed, biting the end off the bean. "Seen *Invasion of the Body Snatchers* too many times, huh?"

The jukebox on the other side of the smoky tavern began to play a moody tune about treachery and heartache. Erik gazed around the room at a scruffy-looking couple lost in each other, a young man with his head thrown back and his eyes closed, and a lively group at the bar celebrating the end of the working day. The noise in Guffy's Bar began to swell. He leaned toward Bill. "So, let it out. What are you thinking?"

Bill took a long pull on his beer. "That I could cheerfully dismember the son of a . . ."

"What about Jolene?"

Bill leaned against the back of his chair and folded his arms. "I was already a little bit in love with her."

Erik tried to measure his expression. "She won't need pity," he cautioned.

Bill shot him a dark glance. "Are you Floyd all of a sudden?"

"Freud," Erik corrected with a grin.

"Whatever. I know she doesn't need pity. She needs someone to love and protect her from ever being hurt like that again. I can do it."

"I know you can." Erik picked up his glass, gave the ice a little shake and sipped. "Don't you feel better now that you've admitted it? You're in love, pal."

Bill leveled a steady look at Erik. "You're not in the clear, either," he pointed out.

Erik took another long sip and shook the ice again. "No. Melanie's father was a cop. He was shot right in front of her eyes by a pimp with a grudge."

Bill studied him for a moment, then nodded. "Then, she watched your car blow up. Not at all conducive to romance."

"No." Erik leaned back, needing to put that aside for a while. "You find out anything about Maggie?"

Bill picked up his beer with its picture of Samuel Adams on it, and emptied the rest into his mug. He watched the foam rise to the lip of it, then subside, before he looked up at Erik. "Nothing. She ran a successful gallery in Portland for ten years. Was divorced three years ago from a wealthy gentleman, then moved here after meeting Finch at some Seattle society wingding." Bill delved into an inside breast pocket. "But I've got something for you. I almost forgot."

Erik accepted a sheet of photocopy paper folded in four. He opened it out and leaned toward the small candle in the middle of the table.

"From our friend in the mayor's office," Bill said. "The invoice from the mysterious delivery to Harvest House."

Erik's eyes went down the curious list. "50,000 surgical needles, 190,000 loose-leaf binders..." he read to himself. The strange litany of items went on for most of the page, ending with a tractor, a generator and a drill press. He looked up at Bill with a grimace. "Finch is starting a heavy equipment school for diabetics?"

Bill laughed, the grimness that had pervaded his mood clearing. "And people think you're dumb. Stumps me, too, but it could be a list of the products Abernathy mentioned in that note. They're from a conglomerate called Inter-Tech."

"Any connection to Abernathy and friends?"

Bill frowned. "No. At least nothing apparent. I don't get it."

Erik leaned back against his chair. "Surgical needles and tractors? If Finch is stealing things to resell, or acting as a clearinghouse for stolen goods, certainly he'd be dealing in higher priced, more marketable items."

Bill nodded thoughtfully. "Then again, this kind of stuff probably gets very little attention. I'm sure that's a priority for him."

"But, where's he getting it and how?"

"You got me. But he's nervous enough about you poking around to torch your car."

Erik raised an eyebrow. "Do we know that for sure?"

"No lab report yet, if that's what you mean. But you know it and I know it. We just can't prove it."

Erik nodded, remembering the ball of flame in front of his house, with a cold feeling in the pit of his stomach. He pushed the memory aside. "Damn it. How the hell do I prove Finch intends to do dirt with tractors and drill presses?"

Bill shook his head. "We'll just have to keep watching. He'll trip himself up. He's getting nervous."

Erik downed the last of his drink and tried not to think about what had happened when Councilman Forsythe and D'Annibale had gotten nervous.

THE MAHOGANY GRANDFATHER CLOCK struck midnight. Erik rechecked the doors and windows Bill had already checked before he'd gone to bed. He passed his father, who was settled in a corner of the sofa, his feet propped on the ottoman. He'd been reading *Riders of the Purple Sage* for the past two hours, but Erik had yet to see him turn a page.

He swatted John's foot with the folder he was taking up to bed with him. "Why don't you hit the hay, Dad?"

His father didn't look up. "Not sleepy."

"Want me to bring you a brandy before I go upstairs?"

John shot him a quick, aggrieved glance over the rim of his reading glasses. "What am I, crippled?"

With a sigh, Erik sat in his chair by the fireplace. The scent of roses wafted toward him from the large bouquet Reba had placed in a copper pot on the hearth. "What's the matter?" he asked directly.

"Nothing," John replied, his eyes never leaving the page. "Except that I'm reading and you're bothering me."

"You haven't turned the page in two hours."

"Zane Gray writes brilliantly. I like to savor each word."

Erik reached forward and snatched the book out of his father's hands. He looked into John's indignant eyes and asked again, "What's the matter?"

When Erik outstared him, John pulled his glasses off and put them on the coffee table. Then, he folded his arms over his formidable paunch. "Reba proposed to me," he said heavily.

Surprised but relieved, Erik struggled manfully to withhold a smile. "That's great, Dad."

John looked at him, his glare even more powerful without the glasses. But Erik looked back at him unwaveringly.

"Turned her down," John said.

Erik knew it wouldn't be smart to betray disappointment. "Why?" he asked calmly.

John leaned back in his chair and replied very quietly, "Sex."

Erik tried to make sense of the answer. Did he mean she didn't like it? Wouldn't do it? He remembered the little scene he and Melanie had witnessed with the panties flag and knew that could not be the source of the problem.

"You having trouble with it?" he asked tentatively.

"No!" John exploded, looking distinctly offended by the suggestion. Then, he added more softly, "At least not that way."

"What way?" Erik insisted. His father was going to blow up in a minute, he knew, but sometimes that was the only way to get a straight answer out of him.

"Am I on the stand?" John demanded, struggling out of the chair to pace arthritically in front of the coffee table. "Questions! Questions! Am I paying you to defend me?"

"I don't defend," Erik replied calmly, "I prosecute. So get to the point. What's your problem with sex?"

Moodily, his father wandered back and forth in front of him. Erik drew his feet in for his own safety. "I've never been very good at talking about this stuff,'' John said, ''even when you were a kid.''

Erik tried to ease the way for him. ''Well, it's a complicated issue. Maturity doesn't necessarily make it any more understandable, except maybe in a physical sense, and sometimes even that's tricky.''

John stopped his pacing and looked down at Erik as though that sensible insight surprised him. ''I thought all your smarts were in the courtroom,'' he said with a faint smile.

Erik shrugged. ''Problems from every phase of life pass through the courtroom. I've learned a few things. Try me.''

John sighed and sat down again. He ran a hand over his face, drummed his fingers on the arm of the sofa and finally focused on his son. ''Because of my heart,'' he said slowly, ''I'm supposed to be careful about sex. You know. Be . . . moderate.''

Erik nodded. ''That makes sense.''

John sighed. ''Well, Reba's more . . . lively than that.''

''Have you been . . .'' Erik asked cautiously, ''more lively than that?''

''Yes.''

''Have you had problems? Chest pains? Anything . . .''

''No, but I worry about it a little.''

''Does Reba know you're supposed to be careful?''

''Well . . .'' John sighed heavily. ''That's the problem. When we first got—you know—physical, she didn't want to because she knew how ill I'd been.'' He glanced guiltily at Erik. ''I assured her that it was safe, that the doctor told me I could be active as long as I didn't get acrobatic. God, we've had some great times.''

Erik was torn between concentration on the image of his father and Reba engaging in anything acrobatic, and getting serious about his father flirting with his health.

"So now, because there's a possibility of a lifetime commitment here, you'd rather not have her," Erik asked incredulously, "than admit to her that the two of you will have to slow down a little bit? I'm sorry, Dad, but that's vain and dumb."

John was momentarily offended, then he shook his head. "It isn't vanity. Well... I suppose it is a little. The thing is, I know if I explained to Reba, she'd say it wouldn't matter. But is it fair to burden her with an old hulk, if she can find somebody else who would give her what she thinks she'd be getting with me?"

"She seems to want you," Erik pointed out.

"I know three men, the president of the bank included, who'd pick her up in a minute."

Erik moved out of his chair to sit beside him. "Dad, think! She loves you. You love her. What did you tell me every time I left the house when I was growing up?"

"Don't get anybody preg—"

Erik punched his arm. "I'm serious, Dad! You said, 'A good woman is so much more than what you see. And you're a fool if you settle for just a body.' I know she'd still want to marry you if you explained, and you can find a million ways to make certain she isn't cheated of anything. Don't miss what could be the best time of your lives because you *think* you know what she wants. Tell her what you can give her, then ask her if that's what she wants."

John turned his head to look at him. "What if she doesn't want me?"

Erik saw the vulnerability in his father's face and felt his throat clench. He hadn't worn that look since Erik's mother died. He put an arm around his shoulders. "Then you can stay on as my bodyguard."

John snickered. "Damn job doesn't pay anything."

"Hey. I'm just protecting your Social Security."

John stood firm against the laugh for a full ten seconds. Then, it burst from him like the roar of a powerful motor. He slapped Erik on the back. "Go to bed and let me think."

Erik got to his feet. "You want that brandy now?"

"I'll get it myself." John began to struggle to his feet, but Erik pushed him back.

"I'll get it," he insisted.

"One of you damn well better get it!" Bill's voice shouted irritably from upstairs. "And if you're going to talk and laugh all night, bring me one, too!"

MELANIE AND REBA SAT side by side on a tweed sofa in the Harvest Lake Clinic's waiting room.

"I didn't even know we had a psychiatrist in Harvest Lake," Melanie whispered.

Reba, flipping through a five-month-old issue of *Family Circle*, replied quietly. "That's why you have an aunt, darling. Dr. Kennedy comes here from Portland once a week." Her soft, wise face hardened and she tossed the magazine aside. "I'd like to get my hands on Linda Slade. Imagine letting your child suffer through such an ordeal to protect your own comfort."

Melanie patted her hand. "Poor Jo. Thanks for taking charge and making the appointment."

Reba sighed. "She never has been one to feel sorry for herself. That was obvious, even when she was only fourteen. She was trying so hard to be like you."

"I thought she was a pest," Melanie said bleakly. "I had no idea..."

Reba put an arm around her. "None of us did. Except, it seems, your father. I think Jolene understands that your life is your life and you have to deal with it the best you can." Suddenly her bottom lip began to quiver and she reached into her purse for a hanky.

Thinking her aunt was upset about Jolene, Melanie spoke consolingly. "She'll be okay. We'll all help her."

"Of course she'll be okay. She's young." Reba sniffed. "It's us old coots I'm worried about."

"Who?"

"John and me."

"Why?"

Reba's eyes were wide and moist over the tiny square of linen. "I asked him to marry me and he said, 'No, Rebie. Getting married's not a good idea.' Just like that!" Reba spread her hands in obvious despair. "No explanation, nothing! He's been acting a little different for the past few days, but I thought he was just worried about Erik."

"Maybe that's why he doesn't want to think about marriage now," Melanie suggested.

Reba shook her head adamantly. "It's more than that. I think I've just made the ultimate mistake young girls are usually warned about. I've let myself be used and cast aside."

Melanie held Reba closer as she sobbed into her hanky. "John isn't like that. He must have some concern he doesn't want to share with you. He's old-fashioned, you know. He believes men shelter their women from problems and make sacrifices to save them from unpleasantness. Maybe it has something to do with his poor health."

Reba appeared to consider the possibility with a hopeful expression in her eyes, then dismissed it. "But he takes long walks every day, he eats things that would kill weeds and he makes love like..." She stopped suddenly, looking sheepishly at her niece. "He does it very well."

"Well, if I were you," Melanie said, rubbing a hand along her aunt's shoulder, "I'd confront him with the question. 'Why won't you marry me, John Channing?' He'll have to give you a reason. He might even be relieved that you forced a showdown,'' Melanie said. ''Maybe it's something he's afraid to share with you.''

''Afraid? He knows I love him.''

Melanie sighed philosophically. ''You know how men are. Proud. Heroic . . .'' She added with a smile, '' . . . silly.''

Reba giggled.

Jolene stepped out of the doctor's office and Melanie went to her, catching her hands. ''Okay?'' she asked.

Jolene nodded. ''Yeah, I think so. Dr. Kennedy does, too. He said my reaction to Bill was pretty normal, considering. And if I didn't scare him away...'' She sighed. ''Then we're both doing okay.''

''Great!'' Reba moved between them, and led them to the door. ''Let's go have a high-calorie, high-cholesterol lunch.''

Jolene smiled grimly. ''I'm not suicidal, Auntie.''

Reba smiled blandly. ''I know, darling. *I* am.''

Chapter Eleven

"How come you got new wheels?" Reclining in the back seat of Erik's Supra, Greg investigated the ashtrays, the air-conditioning vents and the folding armrest.

"Burnout," Erik replied, with a private smile for his apt pun. "I thought it was time for something new. Like it?"

"Not bad. Must have set you back a bundle."

"It's only money. You have any trouble with the Johnson kid?"

"No." Greg turned sideways to put his feet on the seat and recline like royalty. "He must have thought you meant what you said."

"I did." Erik glanced in the rearview mirror for the boy's reaction, but it was difficult to read. He seemed edgy today, he thought. And his decision to sit in the back was deliberately made to annoy him. "You got a problem?" Erik asked.

Greg looked out the window at a velvety green pasture where a big bay grazed lazily. "Doesn't everybody?"

Erik persisted. "I meant a particular problem."

"Yeah." Greg folded his ankles on top of the console between Erik and the passenger seat. "I'm an underprivileged kid who's small for his age, short on charm and understanding and I've got ten more weeks in the joint. You want more?"

Grudgingly admitting that the kid had won another one, Erik swung his hand to lightly swat the sole of Greg's shoe. "Put your feet down," he said. "And stop feeling sorry for yourself. You put yourself where you are. Buff up your attitude and you'll get yourself out."

Greg withdrew his feet and leaned back, looking bored. "So what are we doing this week? Movies? Bowling?"

"Fishing."

"Whoop-de-do," Greg replied in a monotone. "A laugh a minute."

"Melanie's coming."

There was a moment's pause, then Greg said with the most enthusiasm he'd shown since Erik had picked him up ten minutes ago, "Yeah? All right."

Erik leaned an elbow on his open window and rubbed his forehead. He felt a headache coming on.

Melanie and John came out to the driveway to meet them. Greg jumped out of the car to greet her and eagerly accepted her hug. "Hi, John," he called briefly, then dug into his jeans pocket, smiling beatifically at Melanie. "I was hoping you'd come today. I made you something in art class."

He produced a leather key chain, tooled and painted with the initial 'M' and a flower. Melanie hugged him again. "Thank you, Greg. I needed something for my extra car key."

Erik talked himself out of being jealous by admitting that *he'd* present Melanie with the moon if he could. Greg was just another slave to her bewitching spell.

Melanie looked up at him, clutching her gift, looking almost guilty. "The caterers we saw this morning called," she said, maneuvering herself between him and Greg. "He said he *can* get those giant strawberries to dip in chocolate. And I called Lake Linens while you went for Greg, and reserved the tablecloths."

He pulled up on the garage door. "Great. We're on schedule. Now we can forget the party for the rest of the afternoon, and just have fun."

Greg shook his head at Melanie. "He thinks we're going to have fun fishing. It's sad, isn't it?"

Melanie put her hands on her hips and fixed him with a teasingly firm expression. "I happen to be one of the best fishermen in these parts. If you're not planning to have fun, you can just stay behind and help John polish the silver for the party."

John, pulling a plastic bucket of tarnish remover from a shelf in the garage, grinned at Greg over his shoulder. "I could use the help, son."

Greg rolled his eyes. "Thanks, John. I'll try the fishing. If it gets too dull, I'll swim for it."

"I thought I'd polish on the veranda," John said casually to Erik. "To keep an eye on things."

Erik nodded, knowing there was no arguing with him. The "things" his father planned to watch were himself, Melanie and Greg, and he probably planned to polish silver with his shotgun in his lap. As John disappeared into the house, Erik led Melanie and Greg through the garage to the boathouse on the other side. A U-shaped walk surrounded a ten-foot aluminum boat bobbing at its mooring. In the boat were two poles, a net, a coffee can filled with dirt and a cooler now filled with soft drinks and cookies, but destined to carry their catch home.

Erik helped Melanie in, trying not to notice her trim backside in the snug jeans. She turned to help Greg, then settled him in the middle, taking her place in the bow as Erik leapt lightly into the stern. He yanked the cord and with a roar they left the darkness of the boathouse for the bright afternoon and the almost blinding beauty of the lake.

Melanie raised her face to the wind their speed generated, and felt emotion swell in her throat. This was just how it had been for years, except that her father had been at the throttle instead of Erik. The same neat string of homes lined one side of the lake, while forested hills rose on the other. Plump mallards watched them pass with only cursory interest, unless they got too close; then, they leapt into the sky with a furor of hoarse calls and the wild flapping of their wings.

Melanie was not surprised to see that Greg looked anything but bored. Like any boy his age, he was probably enjoying the speed she suspected Erik had put on just for his benefit. But the sensitivity that lay under his brash facade was picking up everything. His dark eyes roamed over the hills, the soft clouds in the bright blue sky, the sun-embroidered water and the ducks. He was smiling.

Over Greg's head, Melanie caught Erik's eye and grinned. Fishing had been her idea, and though she'd told Erik she thought the boy would enjoy it, she wondered now if she'd needed this, too. Jolene's therapist had sent her back home to deal with her past. Perhaps, unconsciously, she'd wondered if the same would work for her. Could she love this man, even though he had things to prove that might put his life in jeopardy? Could she be courageous enough to look loss in the face and thumb her nose at it, as she'd told her sister to do? She wasn't sure. But somewhere on this lake was the girl she'd been before life had changed her. Maybe she would find her today.

God, he loved this place, Erik thought, doing a full turn around the lake before picking a spot from which to fish. How could he have ever thought it confining and provincial? It had everything a man could possibly want—good people in a beautiful setting. Finch was an aberration here, something that didn't belong, like a bruise on a beautiful apple. But he wasn't going to think about him today.

He let his eyes rest on Melanie, her face lifted to the wind, and felt an ache in his chest. He loved her. He wanted to make love to her. But Spring Street and her father's death were barriers between them that he could find no way around—not yet, anyway. But he'd promised himself he wouldn't think about that today, either.

Greg's thin face was also raised to the wind, not with Melanie's quiet worship, but with an edge of awe and excitement to his expression. There wasn't much of this clean air where he came from, and probably few sights like these. Greg looked so...young, so different from the smart-mouthed kid he'd picked up earlier this afternoon that he could almost forgive him for his harassment.

Erik eased the throttle and headed for the middle of the lake. Melanie handed Greg the smaller pole, picked up her own, reached into the coffee can and pulled out a worm. Erik watched with a smile as she efficiently threaded the worm onto her hook and dropped her line over the side.

Greg grimaced when she offered him the can. He peered inside. "They're moving," he said in disgust.

"They're supposed to," she said. "They're alive."

When he still failed to reach into the can, she indicated the shiny metal spinner about a foot up on his line. "The little spoon-like metal things on this spinner will twirl and sparkle and attract a trout, but you have to put something on the hook for him to bite. The worm."

He nodded, apparently understanding the theory. But he didn't reach into the can.

Melanie looked into his grimace and, sympathizing, baited his hook. The world was separated into two camps, she knew. Those who could put a worm on and those who couldn't. She'd seen little old ladies who did it easily and large burly men who couldn't. It was simply one of those things.

She tossed his line over on the opposite side. "Hold the rod with your right hand, and crank the line with your left. That's it."

"What if I get something?" Greg asked, looking anxious.

"I'll help you," she said, letting out a little line as the boat putt-putted across the middle of the lake. She looked up at Erik, who watched them with a grin. "Aren't you fishing?" she asked.

He shook his head. "You two are more entertaining."

Melanie looked at Greg with a conspiratorial air. "We'll show him. He'll be sorry at dinner when he doesn't have anything to eat."

"I've laid in some steaks," Erik laughed. "Just in case."

It wasn't long before Melanie had a bite. She leaped to her feet and Erik cut the motor. "Ah!" she exclaimed with a broad smile, as a fourteen-inch rainbow trout broke the water and leapt several feet into the air. "A nice one!" Her flasher winked and the fish fought, then dived under again. Melanie reeled in her line, playing him as he struggled against her.

It was another five minutes before she leaned the fish into the short-handled net Erik held out for her. In a very businesslike manner, she dumped the trout into the boat, gave him one whap with a small, lead-weight wooden club, then put the fish into the ice-filled cooler.

With a superior lift of her eyebrow at Erik, she dusted her hands off, sat down again and baited her hook. "That was almost too easy," she said in an affected tone. "Takes the fun out of it."

Greg laughed and Erik groaned, starting the motor and beginning a slow circle. They had cold drinks and ate Reba's macaroons, quietly watching the water, content in one another's company. Greg was glowing, Erik noticed, his eyes trained on the sun-shot ripples of water.

"I got one!" the boy cried, springing to his feet, waving for Melanie. "What do I do?"

"Just hold on!" she directed, moving carefully toward him as Erik cut the motor. The fish broke the water, dancing on his tail, then dived in again, at least as long as hers had been. "He's beautiful, Greg. Reel in!"

Greg cranked on the reel, pulling on the pole as though guided by instinct. For five minutes there was pandemonium, then the trout dived again, and Melanie pushed Greg to the bow. "He's running under the boat!" she cried. "Trail your pole in the water and follow him!" She pushed Greg's arm down as she spoke, walking with him across the small space in the bow and to the other side. The trout broke the water again, flashers sparkling and she applauded, delighted that they hadn't lost him.

The trout tried the same maneuver again, but Greg was ready this time, trailing his pole in the water and dancing excitedly when the trout surfaced again. "Reel! Reel!" Melanie ordered, as the fish finally appeared to lose strength.

Erik moved cautiously toward them, net ready. "Now, Erik's going to hold the net steady and you lean the trout into it. Be careful; you can still lose him."

Greg reeled the trout to the side of the boat, pulled up on the pole and tried to do as Melanie directed. But the fish thrashed in the other direction, landing on the rim of the net and balancing there for a moment of agonizing uncertainty, before falling back into the water.

Instinctively, Greg reached out for him, overbalanced, and fell into the water with a shrill cry.

"God!" Erik pushed Melanie across the boat to balance it, as he leaned over the side and grabbed the shoulder of the boy's jacket. "You're okay, I've got you," he said. "Still got your pole?"

Spitting water, his hair plastered to his head, Greg raised his left hand out of the water, white-knuckled fist still holding the pole. *"All right!"* Erik praised, taking the pole from him and sliding it back toward Melanie, flinching as the fish gave one last thrash in his face. He hauled Greg over the side and into the boat, hugging him in relief.

"You okay?" he asked, pulling off his sodden jacket.

Already shaking, Greg nodded. "I'm . . . just cold."

Erik reached behind him for the jacket he'd discarded earlier, and wrapped it around Greg, holding it in place with his arms for a moment to lend the boy some body heat. He half expected a protest, but Greg was giggling, his eyes bright. "To think I thought fishing would be dull," he said.

Erik laughed, shouting to the bow where Melanie was ably storing Greg's trout. "Do we have enough now to feed me, too?"

She looked in mock seriousness at Greg. "What do you think, Greg? Shall we share?"

Greg looked up at Erik, a shadow suddenly falling over his expression. His dark eyes, lashes spiked from the water, had a subtle look of doubt in them that had never been there, not even in the beginning, when he'd disliked Erik and thought of him as an intrusion on his time. He looked hurt, Erik thought. As though he'd betrayed him, somehow.

"Greg?" Melanie prodded, closing the lid on the cooler.

Greg glanced at her, then back at Erik. "Sure," he said without enthusiasm. "We'll share."

"I DON'T THINK I'VE EVER HAD trout this delicious." Around the table in Erik's kitchen, John and the three fishermen ate the fruit of Melanie's and Greg's labors.

"I cooked it," Erik said, passing tartar sauce to Greg.

"You had to contribute somehow," the boy said. He wore a pair of Erik's old sweats, legs and sleeves rolled up, while everything he'd come with tumbled in the dryer. Their companions took it as a tease, but Erik heard the undercurrent of hostility.

"You do fry a mean filet, Erik," Melanie said, savoring the bite of succulent, perfectly seasoned and expertly prepared fish. The fried potatoes and carrots were the perfect accompaniment. "We should open a fish restaurant. I'll catch them and you cook them."

Erik smiled across the table at her, wondering if they'd struck upon their compromise at last. "That deserves looking into. I've got two more years on my term, but after that we can go into partnership."

She didn't get it yet, he saw. She was busy savoring her dinner. "Who gets top billing?" she asked. "Quinn or Channing?"

His father had caught on and studiously concentrated on his dinner. "We could arrange it," Erik said gently, "so there was no question of billing."

"Oh, sure," she teased. "Alphabetically. C comes before Q. Well, if I'm going to go out—"

"I think," Greg interrupted matter-of-factly, "he means Channing and Channing."

Erik turned to Greg. "Thank you. She's pretty, but not always too quick."

Melanie looked first alarmed, then embarrassed, then amused. "Very resourceful, counselor," she said, then turned her attention on Greg, ignoring the playful business scheme. "Tell me what else you've done in art class."

She involved Greg in conversation, while John served ice cream and cookies. They were both avoiding him, Erik knew—Greg, because of some private problem he couldn't even guess at, and Melanie, because of the promising but tangled relationship she couldn't seem to confront. Erik went to the refrigerator for the carton of milk and topped off Greg's glass. Then, he brought the coffeepot to the table and refilled their cups. His father looked vaguely thoughtful as he crumbled a cookie onto his ice cream, and Erik wondered if he'd ever had his conversation with Reba.

Probably not. He'd find it very difficult. Furthermore, he'd hardly left Erik's side since the incident with his car. Erik replaced the coffeepot and sat down again, listening as Melanie and Greg talked about the difficulty of drawing in perspective. That was what they all needed, he concluded, grimly philosophical. Perspective.

"GREG, ARE YOU OKAY?" Greg had changed into his own clothes and was pulling on his jacket, as Erik prepared to take him back to Harvest House. Erik watched Melanie put a hand to the boy's forehead, then down his cheek as though checking for any sign of fever. "I hope you didn't catch cold."

She was seeing that remoteness in him that had worsened as the evening wore on. He looked almost ill now, his eyes large and dark, a small pleat between them as though he was in pain. She turned to Erik in concern. "Maybe I should come with you."

He shook his head, suspecting this was something he had to deal with himself. "Keep my father company. I'll take you home when I get back."

Greg hugged Melanie, shook hands with John and followed Erik out to the car. The night was cool and as clear as the day had been, a sliver of moon and a canopy of stars overhead, as they headed out of town. Erik drove without speaking, while Greg hunched in his seat in misery. Erik pulled off the road into a lay-by right across from the sign welcoming visitors to Harvest Lake. He turned off the motor and shifted in his seat to look at his companion.

"What's the problem, Greg?" he asked without preamble. "And do us both a favor and don't act like you don't know what I'm talking about."

Greg's distress took a subtle turn toward anger, but his overwhelming emotion seemed to be that of disillusionment. "Then you shouldn't act like *you* don't know what the problem is," the boy said, then turned away to stare through the windshield.

Erik thought back. The last time they'd been together he'd taken him to the ball game, and the evening had gone fairly well. Certainly, nothing had happened to cause this degree of hostility in him. "I really don't know what it is," he said calmly. "You'll have to tell me."

"No, I won't."

Erik made himself comfortable. "We're not moving until you do."

Greg folded his arms. "Fine. I stay away from the joint a little longer and you get arrested for kidnapping. Either way, I win."

Erik rested his forearm on the steering wheel, shaking his head at Greg. "Are we ever going to get beyond this smart-mouth crap, and really talk to each other?"

Greg turned in sudden, vivid anger. "Why? So you can find out more about Harvest House? I know that's why you come for me. All this garbage about spending time together is phony! I know about your plan."

Erik tried to make sense of his accusation, but without success. "What plan?"

Greg opened his mouth to reply, but anger was swamped again by a look of betrayal and anguish, and he withdrew, shaking his head. "Nothing," he said.

The temptation to shake Greg was almost too overwhelming to control, but Erik had never seen a child look so miserable. He forced himself to remain calm. "Who told you about this plan of mine?"

Greg shook his head, refusing to look at him.

"You know," he persisted, "even the court gives the accused a chance to tell his side."

With a little sob of distress, Greg unlocked his door and pushed it open, preparing to jump out into the night. Erik caught a fistful of jacket and pulled him back. Greg punched at his arm, but Erik held fast. Then, Greg exploded into sobs, the struggling bundle Erik held dissolving into a tearful, apparently heartbroken child.

Stunned, but somehow relieved, Erik settled him back in his seat and reached across him to pull his door closed and lock it. He put a hand out to stroke his hair. "It's all right, Greg. Whatever's wrong, we can fix it. Just tell me."

Greg shook his head, looking into Erik's eyes with desperation as tears spilled down his cheeks. "He said if I told . . . he'd add six months onto my time."

"Who said that?" Erik demanded.

Greg ran the palms of both hands across his eyes. "Finch."

Anger began to simmer in Erik's gut. But he forced himself to concentrate on the boy. "He can't do that," he said firmly. He reached into the glove box for the battered box of tissues that was always there, but never used. "I would never let him do that. Tell me what he said—from the beginning."

Greg scraped a tissue across his face, then leaned back in the corner of the car. His sobs subsided, but he still looked frightened and uncertain. "He . . . called me into his office one day."

"When?"

"Wednesday."

Erik nodded. The day after the Wholesome Foods delivery. "Go on."

"Well . . . he asked me if you had talked to me about Harvest House." Greg shrugged. "I said, yeah, you talk to me about it all the time. He asked, about what, and I said, about school, and the show Melanie's having—stuff like that."

Erik's anger came to a boil, but he remained silent, encouraging Greg to continue. "Then, he got mad. And he says, 'You know more than that.' I didn't know what he was talking about, so I said, 'No, I don't.' And he says, 'Channing's your buddy, isn't he? I suppose you think you're going to get a cut.'" Greg shook his head in confusion. "I still didn't know what he was talking about, so I said, 'A cut of what?', and he says, 'A cut of the stuff he's going to steal from Harvest House.' I just looked at him like he was crazy. I didn't believe you'd ever do anything like that." He looked into Erik's eyes for confirmation.

"I wouldn't," Erik said. "Greg, I'm the district attorney. This is a small town. Too many people watch me. I couldn't get away with stealing, even if I wanted to."

Greg nodded, his brow pleating again as he thought back. "That's what I told him. Then, he asked me why I thought you picked me up every week—a loser like me. He said you did it so you'd have a chance to case the place, and to try to learn stuff from me that would help you." His voice tightened with emotion. "That kind of made sense."

Erik slapped a hand against the steering wheel, his anger boiling over. He felt more vindictive toward Jerry Finch than he'd ever felt toward the men who'd beat him up in L.A.—more determined to nail him for anything he could pin on him. There had to be a low place in hell for someone who'd use a kid's fears to his own advantage.

Greg jumped and shrank away. Erik lowered his hand, trying to pull himself together. "I'm sorry," he said quietly. "I'm not mad at you—except for falling for a line like that. I thought you believed in yourself, and I thought you were gaining a little respect for me."

Greg's face crumpled.

Erik reached across the console to pull the boy into his shoulder. Greg wrapped his arms around his neck and held on. "I'm sorry. I guess . . . I thought he knew what he was talking about. I mean . . . he runs the joint."

"I know." Erik held him close, rubbing a hand comfortingly between his shoulder blades. "Sometimes, rotten people get into places where they shouldn't be. Did he say anything else?''

Greg pulled away, sniffling. ''That if you asked me any questions or talked about Harvest House, I should tell him. That's all.''

Erik nodded. ''Okay. Look, I'm going to tell you something you've got to keep to yourself, okay? I'm conducting an investigation on Finch and I can't tell anyone about it yet.''

Greg's eyes widened, his expression brightening. ''You mean . . . *he's* done something wrong?''

''Lots of things. I've almost got him nailed and I think he knows that. That's why he's trying to find out from you what I know.''

Greg thought about that a minute, then all the doubt in his expression cleared. ''I get it. He was bluffing me out to see if I knew anything.''

Erik grinned. ''Exactly. When you go back and he asks you what we talked about, I want you to tell him I asked about the storage building.''

Greg nodded, his cagey self again. ''There's something weird in there, isn't there? Finch goes in there late at night. I've seen him.''

''Yeah.'' Erik took hold of the boy's shoulders, his expression grave. ''Now, it's very important that you act like you don't know anything, except that I asked about the storage building. Keep a low profile, don't do anything to get into trouble. Tomorrow night's the big party and Melanie's show, and two days after that, we're having the barbecue at my place, so I'll see you then. You going to be okay?''

Greg nodded, smiling. ''Yeah. Am I getting paid for this?''

Erik laughed softly. The kid he knew was back. ''Sure. What's your price?''

The boy's face became serious, his eyes intense. "When I get out—you and Melanie come to Portland and meet my mom."

Erik had to wait a moment to speak. "You got it." He straightened in his seat and reached for the ignition.

"Wait," Greg said, delving into his jacket pocket. He withdrew a tooled leather key chain like the one he'd given Melanie, except that it bore the initial "E" with a flower on it. "The flower's a little girlie," Greg explained sheepishly, "but we didn't have anything else."

"I like it." Erik removed his keys from the ignition and added the fob to the simple metal ring that held them together. He swallowed, absurdly pleased. "Tell you the truth, I was jealous of Melanie's."

Greg shrugged. "This morning, I was afraid you were a creep. But I guess the creep was me."

Erik put an arm around him and gave him a quick hug. "No. I can see where you got confused. But I'd never steal, or set you up. I swear."

"I know." Greg looked excited. "Are you setting Finch up to make a move on whatever he's got in the storage building?"

Erik pushed him back in his seat, wondering if the boy's brain ever slowed down. "The less you know about the rest of it, the better. Buckle up. We'll talk at the barbecue."

"WHAT WAS THE PROBLEM with Greg?" Melanie asked quietly. Erik had pulled up in her driveway and now seemed distracted, staring moodily through the windshield as though he'd forgotten why he was there. "Erik?"

He turned to her with an apologetic smile. "Sorry. I'm angry enough to eat sidewalk."

She turned in her seat to face him. "At Greg?"

"No." He related the story the boy had told him, leaving out the part about asking Greg to tell Finch he'd inquired about the storage building. She'd guess what he was up to, and he didn't want that yet.

Melanie listened, her eyes widening, her mouth falling open. "That black-hearted—"

"I'll get him," Erik said with dark determination. "Don't worry."

She couldn't help but be worried by Erik's resolve. A man like Finch, who would ruthlessly use a child to his own advantage, wouldn't think twice about destroying any man who got in his way.

"Will there ever be a time," she asked reasonably, "when you *can* ask for help with this?"

His reaction was to reassure her once again that he had a handle on it. But he knew how keenly she felt the danger—and the lengths to which she would go to avoid coming face-to-face with loss a second time. She would leave, and he didn't think he could bear it.

"The minute I can prove anything," Erik promised, "or pin Finch to Abernathy with evidence, I can take it to the Grand Jury and bring in the police." He smiled grimly and added, "If I can be sure the chief's not involved."

Melanie rolled her eyes and leaned her cheek against the headrest. "God, what a tangle. I'm going to get an ulcer."

"Maybe it was my cooking," Erik suggested.

"No, it's your job."

He leaned forward to nuzzle her ear. "Promise you'll marry me and the job's history as soon as my term is up. We'll travel from one flower-filled meadow to another, and you can support me with your painting."

Melanie pushed him away to look into his eyes. "Promise?"

Erik looked back at her, taken aback by her seriousness. He straightened and called her bluff. "Yes. Do you?"

She didn't hesitate. "Yes. I'll marry you."

They stared at each other, a little alarmed at how quickly playful goading had turned into a commitment.

After a moment, Melanie smiled. "Shouldn't you kiss me?"

Erik continued to stare at her. "I think I'm still in shock. Yes." He reached for her. "Come here."

The sudden, loud honking behind them signaled Bill and Jolene's return from dinner. With a groan, Erik rolled down his window.

"Necking in the driveway!" Laughing, Bill leaned down to look at them, his arm around Jolene, who also peered into the car. "How *gauche*."

"Leave them alone." Jolene slapped his chest and smiled at Melanie. "When you're finished, come on inside. I'll fix something."

With a wry glance at Melanie, Erik opened his door. "We're finished. It's just not the same with an audience. Come on, Mel."

"Want to invite your dad?" Bill asked.

Erik closed his eyes. "You mean he's here?"

"Parked halfway down the street. Must have followed you."

Erik put a hand over his eyes and groaned.

"I'll get him," Melanie laughed. "And don't you dare yell at him, or the deal's off."

"What deal?" Bill wanted to know.

Erik shot him a forbidding look as he followed Melanie down the road.

Chapter Twelve

The cocktail party preceding her show was like a movie spectacular. Though, technically, Melanie had cochaired the preparation of the event, she felt she'd really done little but consult the caterer and agree with Erik's plans.

She looked around at the silver, the crystal, the candles, the elegant canapés and expensive champagne, and realized that Erik had put much more time and effort into the preparations than he'd exacted from her.

Elegantly dressed men and women wandered throughout the house, but the party centered in the conservatory and spilled out onto the gallery suspended over the lake, where Melanie found herself trapped in a corner by an intense young man in glasses, a foulard, and a Byronic hairdo.

"You don't approach Redouté, of course," he said with a superior but apologetic little laugh. "He was by far the master of botanical illustration. But, I think your paintings have more life than those of Fantin-Latour. There's such a precious balance, don't you think, between the science and the art of your medium? What are you doing after the show?"

The direct question was such a surprise after his critique both of her work and the work of the two finest botanical illustrators of the Western world, that she simply blinked in reply.

"She's busy," Erik's voice said from behind her.

Melanie looked up in surprise as his arm draped across her shoulders. He smiled graciously at the young man. "But the young lady you came with is looking very forlorn standing by the champagne fountain."

Not at all chagrined at having been caught making time with Melanie while his date languished in the next room, the young man kissed Melanie's hand and gave her a toothy grin before disappearing.

"Who was that?" Melanie asked.

Erik shook his head. "No idea. He arrived with the Harvest Lake Community College president. A prize art student, I suppose. He'd better leave you alone if he wants to retain the use of his painting hand."

Melanie suppressed a grin as he led her inside. "How do you know I'm busy tonight?"

"Simple." He took a chocolate-dipped strawberry from the tray of a passing waiter, and popped it into her mouth. "I have a prior claim on your time."

She chewed and swallowed. "To discuss art?" she teased.

He smiled down at her, looking wickedly dangerous in his dark evening clothes. "No." He leaned down to whisper in her ear. "To create it."

IT BECAME APPARENT almost immediately that Melanie's show was an unqualified success. A petite woman in a Chanel suit stood several yards back from Melanie's Alpine meadow series, and stared with deep concentration.

"She's from Northwest Bank," Reba whispered. "She's been around the room four times and she keeps coming back to those."

While they watched, the woman beckoned Maggie over and pointed expansively along the length of the series. She took Maggie's arm and walked her across to a painting of a bouquet of apple blossoms, then to another of pansies.

Beaming, Maggie dotted the frame of each painting with a red sticker to mark it sold. It occurred to Melanie that either Maggie didn't know about her husband's activities or she was an excellent actress. She'd been gushing over her artist all evening.

A quick scan of the room made Melanie's pulse quicken with excitement. They liked her work. More than half of her paintings wore sold stickers. The gallery was filled with West Coast critics, private collectors and people off the street. The buzz was that her illustrations had both botanical precision and aesthetic heart.

The Ladies of the Lake clustered around her in their Sunday dresses. "Melanie, isn't it wonderful? The Harvest House new bus fund has gained several thousand dollars already! That man in the blue suit is from the governor's office! And that one is an attorney representing a client in Los Angeles."

Melanie looked around in wonder. Her career has been successful almost from the beginning, but this recognition and acceptance from the people she'd grown up with, as well as the buyers from out of state, was more gratifying than she'd expected.

Reba and the ladies wandered away to talk to Maggie, and Melanie expelled a long breath. Well, she thought with satisfaction, she managed to save this summer after all. Then, she looked across the room at Erik, Jolene and Bill standing in front of the illustration of the wild iris. She considered the man she loved, the sister she'd finally claimed, her new friend and the flower that had finally come to life for her. Or, did this summer save her? she wondered.

Maggie, trailing yards of yellow chiffon, was like a comet on some erratic path, crossing here, there, stopping suddenly to reverse direction. She was obviously thrilled with the show's success. As the crowd thinned and Melanie found herself alone for a precious moment, she watched her hostess and decided that no one could act that well. Maggie couldn't know what Jerry was up to.

Of course, it would have been difficult for anyone to tell, Melanie thought. He'd made an appearance tonight with Police Chief Olson, behaving with mayoral charm. He bought a rendering of a sprig of heather, had his photo taken with Melanie for the newspaper and shook hands around the room, making a special point of speaking to Erik. His skilled smoothness made her skin crawl.

ERIK SAW HIS FATHER studying Melanie's watercolor of a sprig of mountain ash, and walked up behind him. The painting had been done in the fall, he guessed, because it was a jaunty comb of orange leaves and dark berries on a nubby twig. Even in deep summer, the sight of it evoked for him the smell of woodsmoke and the sharpening fragrance of approaching winter.

"Like that?" Erik asked.

John nodded gravely, still staring. "There's such heart in her work. You let her get away, son, and you're a fool."

"Don't worry. You talk to Reba?"

John sighed and turned away from the painting, continuing his slow circuit of the room. "Not yet. But I will."

"Tonight would be a good time," Erik suggested, following him. "She keeps looking at you."

"She's so proud of Melanie." John stopped in front of the bright bouquet of pansies. "I don't want to ruin her evening. Isn't this beautiful?"

"Don't change the subject. Look, she's carrying out the pots of flowers she brought." He turned his father around until he faced the door through which Reba struggled with an arrangement of blood-red roses. "She could probably use some help."

"Then you help her," John said, trying to turn away.

"I don't have anything to tell her," Erik said, taking a nearby pot of colorful glads and handing them to his father. "You do. Follow her out." John looked back at him reluctantly, and Erik pushed him toward the door. "Go on. Take her for coffee. Tell her not to worry about Mel. I'll take care of her."

John looked at Erik over his shoulder. "Does this mean you don't want me coming back to your place tonight?"

Erik grinned. "Follow your instincts, Dad." Then he added more quietly, "Just remember what the doctor said."

Reba was back. She stopped short in the middle of the room at the sight of John with the pot of flowers. Her expression was cautious but pleased. "It's nice of you to help, John," she said, beckoning him to follow her. "My car's right out here."

As the two disappeared through the gallery doors, Erik intercepted Melanie trying to pull a slender vase of Queen Anne's lace off a table. Erik took it out of her hands and replaced it. "That's my father's job," he said. "He and Reba need to talk." He took her hand and pulled her to the painting of the sprig of mountain ash. "My father likes this. I'd like to buy it for him."

"No," Melanie said quietly. "Just wait until I come back to pick up what hasn't sold, and he can have it."

Erik wrapped his arms around her from behind, leaning down to kiss her ear. "Now that would be a fine contribution to Harvest House, wouldn't it? I insist. I'm buying it. I also bought the rose series and the iris. Even Bill bought something."

Melanie laughed, relaxing against him. She felt contented, tired, and lazily pleased with herself. "A rosebud for Jolene. He told me it was to remind her that her life was brand new."

Erik hugged her a little tighter. "He'll take good care of her. And I want to take care of you. Mel..."

The sudden urgency in his voice made her turn in his arms. She read the wish in his gray eyes before he spoke it. "Come home with me."

She leaned her forehead against his chin, sighing with acceptance. "Yes," she replied. Then she looked up and smiled. "But what about your bodyguards?"

"Bill and Jolene are going to Marco's, and your aunt and my father have a lot to talk about. Is there anything else you have to do for Maggie before you leave?"

That question was answered for him as Maggie joined them in a flutter of yellow. "Melanie, look!" she exclaimed, showing her the list of paintings. All but six had sold written beside them.

Erik pointed to the sprig of mountain ash. "List that with my others, please, Maggie."

Maggie found it on her list and scribbled beside it. "Out of fifty-two paintings!" She said in amazement. "It was a sellout. Melanie, you're a star!"

ERIK SAT IN THE WICKER CHAIR in the dark, watching Melanie pace the length of the veranda, thinking how apt Maggie's description was. Star. In the midnight darkness, Melanie's glittering ice-blue dress and her loose platinum hair sparkled like a light in the firmament. He felt like a lost sailor from long ago, with his first glimpse of the North Star. Now he could find his way home.

Melanie turned to him, leaning back against a column. "It's hard to believe that just a few hours ago this house was teeming with people." Perfect order had been restored and there wasn't a trace of the crowd that had packed Erik's home.

"All you have to do is employ a good housekeeper and use a clever caterer, and it makes people think you're brilliant."

Melanie smiled into his lazy expression. Reclining in the chair in his dress slacks with his white-on-white striped shirt open at the throat, he looked almost complacent. "I saw her in the kitchen feeding *hors d'oeuvres* and champagne to the man across the road. You'd better make sure she knows how much you appreciate her."

Erik extended a long arm, caught her wrist and pulled her onto his lap. "You can't stop love with a higher salary. I wouldn't want to."

She snuggled against him contentedly, Harvest Lake's unique perfume wafting along the veranda. Erik rested his cheek on her hair. "Well," he said softly. "Bill and Jolene seem happy together, and unless I miss my guess, my father and Reba will solve their differences tonight."

The knuckle of her index finger gently stroked the warm skin in the opening of his shirt. "Good. It's like Jolene's movie."

Erik leaned her back against his arm so he could look into her eyes. He put his hand on her forehead, pretending to test her for fever. "What?"

She laughed, caught his hand and kissed it. "Jo has this dream that she'll marry Bill, you and I will get married and we'll all live like a Fifties musical in Harvest Lake."

"Ah." He nodded. "Sort of a White Christmas in August."

"Exactly."

"I like it."

Common sense told Melanie things like that didn't happen, but such cynicism seemed frail stuff against the strong and tender arms that held her, the eyes that looked at her with a love so intense she felt no reason to doubt it. She stroked the side of his face, her own love swelling in her heart. "Me, too, Erik." She reached up to kiss his mouth and seal the promise she made yesterday.

Erik stood, easing her to her feet, then swept her into his arms. She laughed softly, nuzzling his neck. "Five bucks says you can't get me all the way up to the bedroom. I'm full of *hors d'oeuvres* and about a magnum of champagne."

"You're on."

He did it easily, dropping her into the middle of the bed with a bounce. Then he knelt astride her, unbuttoning his shirt. "All right, Quinn," he said. "Pay up."

"I don't think so." She nuzzled at his ear. "You were breathing heavily at the top of the stairs."

He tossed the shirt away, revealing a cotton, V-neck T-shirt molded to sturdy biceps and pectoral muscles. Then, he leaned over her to nibble at the small swell at the top of her dress. "It's wasn't the exertion."

The laughter went out of her in a rush and she lifted his head to look into his face. His eyes were filled with love and desire, and a tenderness that dissolved all her doubts about the future.

Erik saw the sudden change in her eyes and immediately understood it. Love between them was serious business. It meant compromise, stretching beyond what was easy to give. It meant passion that came from the same strong feelings with which each pursued life. Passions colliding could mean destruction—or a melding of feelings so strong, nothing could hold against them.

"We're going to be good for each other," he promised.

She pulled his head down and kissed his cheek, then his lips. "I know Erik. I'm not afraid. I think I'm a little—awed. Finding you after being alone for so many years has been like walking into a garden after wandering in a desert. It feels as though life is growing all around me."

Knowing how empty her father's death had left her, Erik could not have been more touched had she used words of adoration.

He laid her back again and slipped the dress off her. Her stockings and panties were next, joining the dress on the chair beside the bed. He pulled the blankets back on one side and lifted her onto the cool sheets. The silky chill felt delicious against her fevered skin.

Standing beside the bed, he began to pull his T-shirt off, but she reached out to stop him. She got to her knees on the mattress and reached under his shirt to push it up, planting kisses as she worked. Halfway up his rib cage, she encountered the scar and paused. Erik tensed, afraid his past had risen to frighten her again. But she put her lips against the scar and traced it from one end to the other with small, reverent kisses.

Emotion clogging his throat, Erik caught her face in his hands and said hoarsely, "I love you, Melanie. Our lives begin here and now—no ugly pasts, only tomorrow."

Melanie wrapped her arms around his waist and laid her cheek against his warm shoulder, chaotic emotion making her feel as though she might laugh or cry at any moment. "I love you, too," she whispered. "I'll make you the happiest man alive."

Erik tossed off his clothes and lay back against the pillows, pulling her down beside him. He could not imagine a man in the world happier than he was at this moment. He stroked a hand gently across her cheek and down her throat. "I've wanted to touch you for so long."

Melanie lay still as his hand moved down between her breasts, then cupped one with the same kind of wonder in his eyes that her body felt at the touch. She closed her eyes and savored his careful exploration. He circled the other breast with the same reverence, stroked across her ribs, then downward to rest his warm hand a moment on the concavity of her stomach. Then, his hand slid down along one thigh to her knee, along the other knee and up to her hipbone.

Melanie's body reacted as though it had been massaged, every muscle relaxed, heavy. He began again, with another purpose in mind. His hand on her breasts was imaginative, teasing—the thumb that stroked over her nipples causing a shock of sensation that shot out to every part of her body. She stirred and opened her eyes, and he lowered his head to kiss her.

His hand stroked in a circular motion down her ribs and stomach, and the calm of a moment ago was replaced by an exquisite tension. Melanie reached up for him, whispering his name.

But he pushed her back against the pillow, his mouth caressing her breasts, as his hand continued its downward path to the warm heart of her being. She shifted to allow him entrance.

She said his name again at his first teasing touch. The agonized tension began to mount immediately. It filled her from head to toe, then seemed to wind around her, immobilizing her, emptying her mind of everything but the tightening spiral of sensation inside her. The spiral unfurled with the suddenness of something long awaited but unexpected. Delicious spasms broke over her, taking control of all movement and all thought. She clung to Erik as eddies of pleasure ebbed and flowed along her body, lighting corners of it that had been dark for too long.

Before the last shudder passed, she began to explore Erik, forcing him gently onto his back.

This could kill a man, he thought, as her searching fingers followed the lines of his shoulder and chest, over his ribs, into the hollow at his waist and stomach. Thoughts of Melanie had haunted his nights for weeks, but they were like a shadow compared to this reality. She was stroking him, caressing him, driving him mad in a matter of seconds.

He felt her lips against his chest, trailing down—saw her hair following like a moonbeam, leaving a glowing warmth as it passed. Her fingernails gently combed along his thigh, then up the inside of his leg until he felt himself losing control. He took a handful of her hair, grasping to maintain sanity. He heard his own gasp of pleasure as though from far away. He sat up to take her shoulders and pull her down beside him. It felt as though he'd waited an eternity for her. He loved her so much, and the love in her eyes and her smile told him she understood.

Melanie took him into her with all the sweetness and startling power of new love. Pleasure filled her, rolled over her, absorbed her, then returned her to reality, forever changed, forever belonging to Erik.

Sheathed in Melanie, Erik thought distractedly that if the earlier pleasure he had felt could have brought him to death, then this was like being reborn. Feelings he'd never experienced, truths he'd never understood, promises he'd never thought he'd be able to make became as much a part of him as the cells that composed his body. In his arms, Melanie clung to him, whispered words of love to him, made promises to him. There were no more mysteries. Life was brand new and the future was an open road. Melanie was his.

They curled contentedly, facing the window that looked out onto the lake. The sky was bright with stars, and there was no sound but the faint lap of water against the bank of the lake. Melanie reached a hand back to touch his cheek and he planted a kiss in its palm.

"It's a crime that we waited this long to be together," Melanie said quietly.

He kissed her ear, then rested his cheek on hers. "It wasn't time lost, it was time learning. Like your efforts with the wild Iris. You couldn't understand it at first, and then you made a magnificent work of art out of it. Maybe that was us. We didn't understand that we had something beautiful but fragile, and we couldn't manipulate it to make it what we wanted it to be. It has to exist as it is, with its own needs and demands. We have to learn what they are and work with them."

Melanie turned to face him, enjoying the sensation of his muscled chest against her breasts. She smiled into his eyes in the darkness. "You've become such a philosopher."

He drew her closer, pulling the sheet up around them. "Suddenly I understand a lot of things I couldn't grasp before you walked into my life."

She kissed his collarbone, burrowed her nose into his neck and closed her eyes. "Things still confuse me," she said drowsily. "It just doesn't seem so important to have control of everything anymore."

He kissed her hair and held her close, smiling as she began to breathe evenly in sleep. "I love you, too, Mel," he whispered.

MELANIE SURFACED FROM a beautiful dream where everything she had ever wished for in life was hers—success, family, Erik. Someone was forcing clothes on her. She resisted, abandoning a halfhearted effort to open her eyes. "No," she said grumpily, slapping blindly at the hands working over her. "I want to sleep."

Laughing softly, Erik let her fall back against the mattress and leaned over her to knot the belt of the robe he'd put on her.

"Don't you want breakfast?" he coaxed, pulling her to a sitting position on the edge of the bed.

She pulled against him, hanging limply from his extended arm. "No. Sleep."

"I have something you'll like."

"Later."

He let her fall back and sat beside her, trying another tack. He kissed the hollow of her throat and nibbled at her jaw and her earlobe. "I have peaches," he crooned tauntingly, "and *brioches* from the bakery."

She made a fitful little sound, as though the temptation disturbed her effort to go back to sleep.

He kissed her mouth, long and lingeringly. "And Reba's strawberry butter," he added against her lips.

She smiled, her eyes still closed, and looped her arm around his neck. "Let me taste," she said.

He tried to use her arms around him as leverage to pull her up. "I set breakfast out on the veranda."

Then, she opened her eyes. Their soft brown was filled with the contented self-satisfaction of a well-loved woman, and a seed of desire that he watched flower as her gaze focused on him. "No," she corrected, her voice husky. "Let me taste you."

Whatever leverage he had gained, physically or emotionally, he gladly conceded when she opened her mouth on his and brought him back with her to the bed.

"WHAT TIME DO YOU HAVE TO BE at work?" Melanie popped the last of her *brioche* in her mouth, savoring the warmth of the delicious morning by closing her eyes and lifting her face to the sun. "And wouldn't it be nice if you didn't have to? You could come painting with me today, instead."

Erik looked at her, her wonderful hair hastily knotted on top of her head, trailing silver strands over her forehead and down her neck. His robe hung loosely on her, exposing her throat and most of one ivory shoulder. The temptation was almost more than he could resist. "An hour ago," he replied to her first question, "and yes, it would. Maybe after we've plumped up the college fund for our fourth child, we'll be in that position. Meanwhile..." He gestured with his coffee cup, leaving the obvious unsaid.

She opened her eyes and smiled at him, so filled with happiness she found it difficult to focus. Dreaming was so much more fun. "A girl?" she asked.

He put his cup down, arching an eyebrow in question. "Pardon me?"

"Our fourth child. A girl? If we're going to establish a fund, we'll have to know where to send this child. Harvard or Wellesley?"

"Doesn't matter. They're both coed now, I think."

"What about a dog."

"I don't think either accept dogs."

Melanie rolled her eyes at him. "I meant do you want a big dog or a little dog?"

Erik watched the lazy amusement in her eyes, enjoying this dreamy turn in her. She was usually so cautious, so precise. But, then, only yesterday afternoon he'd been a man in control. Now he felt like the helpless victim of this woman's body. Last night had changed everything.

"I suppose a big dog to protect our little girl."

Melanie leaned her chin on her hand. "Won't her big brothers do that?"

"When it comes to the crunch. Mostly, though, I think they'll tease and terrorize her."

She straightened resolutely. "Then let's have all girls."

Erik's smile softened and he reached for her hand, drawing her around the table and into his lap. He kissed her shoulder and reached a hand under the bottom of the robe. "If I had a house full of little girls who looked like you, I'd be afraid to leave for fear you'd all be stolen from me."

Melanie settled against him in helpless pleasure as his warm hand swept over her hip. "That would make it hard," she said, having difficulty concentrating on the thought, "to build the college funds."

The telephone rang shrilly from the bedroom. Erik growled over the intrusion, then grudgingly accepted that it was probably fortuitous. One more minute and he might never have made it to the office today. He swatted her lightly where his hand rested. "You can have the shower while I answer the phone."

Thinking that she was going to look pretty silly in her sequined evening dress on a Monday morning, Melanie gathered up her clothes and headed for the open door of the bathroom.

Erik picked up the receiver. "Hello," he said.

Melanie heard him say, "What do you mean, 'missing?'" She turned back to the doorway, her clothes over her arm, a little pulse of forboding ticking in her throat.

Erik glanced at Melanie with a reassuring expression. It didn't work. "You checked his apartment?" he asked into the phone. He waited while whoever was on the other end of the connection replied.

He listened for a long time, then said with studied calm, "Yes, I realize that. I will. I will. No, he can't move with all the kids there. Right. Thanks, Bill. I'm on my way to the office. Let me know what you find out."

Erik replaced the receiver and made a show of buttoning his shirt, reaching for his tie. "Speed it up, sweetheart," he said with a smiling glance at her. "I'm already two hours late."

"Are you going to tell me who that was?" she asked quietly.

He ran the tie back and forth under his collar, his expression guarded despite the smile. "Depends. Are you going to get upset?"

"Probably."

He turned to the mirror over the dresser. "Then maybe I'll keep it to myself. It's been such a beautiful morning."

Refusing to let her mind slip to memories of last night, the breakfast they'd just shared, and their teasing talk of children, she insisted, "Who's missing?"

He knotted his tie. "Bill's informant. But it isn't necessarily cause for concern. They'd agreed weeks ago that if he felt as though Finch was on to him, he had a way to disappear.''

Cold dread rose in Melanie's chest. ''Erik, if Finch knows about the informant, then he's no longer just suspicious of you, he's *sure* you know something. That isn't cause for concern?''

''No. It just means things are going according to plan.''

She tossed her clothes on the bed and moved to stand beside him so that they were reflected in his mirror together. ''Didn't we have an agreement that the moment you could prove something, you'd call in help?''

He turned away from the mirror to look down at her. The love and fear for him in her eyes made him almost willing to promise her anything. Then, he remembered that he had a lot to prove to himself with this case. He didn't think he could be any good to her if he didn't. ''Provided I had everything stacked against him. I don't.''

''A man has disappeared! How much proof do you need?''

''Melanie, we don't know that for certain.''

Melanie felt the beautiful future dissolve around her. ''You promised me,'' she said mercilessly.

''I promised conditionally,'' he corrected. ''I'm sorry, Mel. I know you're frightened. So am I. But I've got to do this. I was elected to do this. It's almost over, I promise.''

Her expression hardened and she turned away from him. ''You don't really think it'll be over with this, do you?''

He turned from the mirror to frown at her back in the oversize robe. ''What do you mean?''

She spun around, her brown eyes filled with anguish and anger. ''I mean that you stuck your neck out to investigate this case. You had your car bombed, a child you care about threatened and your informant has disappeared, and you *still* have more to prove.'' She advanced on him, her eyes steady. ''You'll always have more to prove because you just can't accept the fact that you're afraid. You'll have to prove your fearlessness to yourself over and over. This will go on through your entire life..." Her eyes seemed to lose focus suddenly and the anger softened, though the anguish compounded. "...and I won't live that way."

She turned away, but Erik caught her arm, pulling her around to face him. The robe slipped off her shoulder, but he didn't notice. He couldn't see anything but the expression of chilling finality in her eyes. Anger rose in him as well as heartache. "You're afraid of death," he said quietly, carefully. "I can understand that. But you're letting your fear take over. Now you're afraid of love as well."

"That's because to love you," she said evenly, "is to be afraid for you. I came this far with you, Erik. I did what I promised. You're the one who's welshing."

He dropped his hands, absorbing the pain of her accusation. "I've explained why I can't involve the police."

She nodded calmly. "I know. You always have a very good reason, and you probably always will. You're a lawyer—brilliant words are your stock-in-trade." She sighed, and it seemed to Erik that with her sigh, the life seemed to go out of her. "I haven't the verbal skills to fight you. But I hope that when you've finally got Finch behind bars and you're planning your next legal escapade, you'll remember what it was like to make love with me..." Her eyes filled and she swallowed hard, but her gaze remained steady. "...what it was like to have breakfast with me on the veranda on a sunny morning and talk about children. And I hope you'll be sorry that you let me get away."

She turned away from him, tears spilling over, and headed for the bathroom. But he caught her again, his hold more desperate this time, his gray eyes almost black. "You're not going to blame this on me, Mel. You're going to accept your part in it. *I'm* not letting you get away; *you're* running." She tried to pull away, but he held tighter, leaning over her to look into the misery in her eyes. "When you're hiding from the world on one of your mountain treks in search of flowers, I hope you remember what it was like to lie in my arms in this wonderful old house, wrapped in your childhood dreams." He paused while they stared at each other, love and despair alive in the look they shared. "And I hope you're sorry you couldn't muster the courage to hold on to those dreams."

Sobbing, Melanie tore away from him and ran into the bathroom, slamming the door behind her.

Erik watched her go, feeling pain claw inside him, wondering what good it did him to confront the past, if doing it destroyed the future.

WHEN MELANIE CAME OUT of the bathroom in the ice blue dress she'd worn the night before, she was coolly composed. She found calm easier to assume than she'd expected, because she'd forgotten that pain could deaden everything. She moved in a kind of fog, sharply aware of what she'd lost, but oblivious to what remained.

She found Erik waiting for her downstairs in the foyer, suit coat on, ankles crossed as he leaned against the door, reading the morning paper. He appeared calm as well, but when he raised his eyes to look at her, straightening and folding the paper, she knew that it was only because he, too, had shut off all his senses.

Suddenly, out of her fog came a swift and vivid image of the night before, complete with an emotional picture of how she'd felt—so new and hopeful, so much in love. She closed her eyes on it, then opened them to give Erik a vague smile. "I see we're going to remain civilized."

He tossed the paper on the hall table and opened the front door. "Of course. I'll take you home."

"That isn't necessary."

He raised an eyebrow and ushered her through the door. "You want to explain to the staid residents of Harvest Lake why you were seen walking home from my place in the dress you wore last night?"

She ignored the question and stepped aside as he opened the passenger door of his car. He pulled out of the driveway, maintaining a stoic silence as they covered the few blocks that led to the turnoff to town. When he didn't turn, she looked at him, and she saw the tightness of his profile as he looked in the rearview mirror.

"What's the matter?" she asked, turning in her seat to look over her shoulder. All she could see behind them were giant four-by-four tires and the bottom of the grill of a jacked-up truck. It seemed less than a foot away and closing in.

"He wouldn't slow down to let me turn," Erik said, accelerating. "You buckled in?"

Fear rippled up Melanie's spine. "Yes."

"All right. Hold on."

Melanie had no idea how fast they were going, but the passing scenery began to take on the surreal color and indistinguishable detail of a scary ride at an amusement park. Beyond the turnoff to town, Lakefront Road was sparsely populated and went inland from the lake, winding through a woods on one side and rambling hills on the other. The bulk of the oversize truck was so close that it cast a shadow inside the small Supra.

"Unbuckle and get down!" Erik ordered, pushing on her as she fumbled with her seat belt. She scrambled onto her knees, hiding her face in the seat.

The truck slammed into the left rear fender just as Erik put his foot to the floor. There was a loud thunk and the sound of scraping metal, but the force of the blow was diminished by Erik's burst of speed.

The truck had little trouble catching up, however, slamming into them just behind the door. Erik swore, but managed to keep the Supra on the road.

Anger was all he understood now. Fortunately, courtroom strategies had taught him to use anger to his advantage, to let it build, but to keep it cold and calculating. Finch and his friends were not getting him and they were not getting Melanie.

An old pickup loaded with hay and headed south forced the big truck back into its own lane for the precious few seconds Erik needed to think. When the truck pulled around again to renew its attack, Erik braked, slewing the rear end of the car sideways on the narrow road, while the truck shot ahead. Melanie screamed and fell over, and gravel flew as he turned south, struggling to regain control.

He gained a quarter of a mile before the truck was able to turn and follow, then lost the advantage again when he caught up with the overburdened hay truck. But it was going to work, he thought, trying to remain cool. The turn he wanted was just ahead.

He took Bick's Trestle Road with such speed that the dirt from its unpaved surface flew around them like a cloud, obscuring his vision and, he hoped, that of the pursuing truck.

"Where was the trestle?" he wondered, his foot still to the floor, his eyes trying to focus on something through the cloud of dust. As children, he and his friends walked its rails and took great pride in balancing on the planks of wood beside the rails that were all that stood between them and a drop to the road. Where was it?

Unable to see anything in his mirror but dust, he took the chance of slowing down, hoping to clear the road ahead. Maybe they'd torn it down, he thought desperately. The one-engine local hadn't run this way in fifteen years. He hadn't had a reason to come this way since he'd been home.

The bulk of the truck rose in his mirror as the dust cleared, and he let the anger roll over him, fighting to think in terms of satisfying retribution. Then he saw it—Bick's Trestle, running from the rim of one low hill on the right side of the road, to another hill on the left. Its complicated crisscross of peeling white beams and supports stretched across the road, one low arched opening in the center. It had been built in the days when nothing taller than a man on a horse passed under it.

Certain the driver of the truck was too intent on him to notice the cautioning sign, Erik sped through the small opening. Almost immediately, he heard the squeal of brakes, saw a cloud of dust in his mirror, then heard a crash, a splintering of wood, and the sound of glass breaking. Before he pulled Melanie off the floor, he smiled to himself at the image in his mind of the truck, now embedded in the trestle, or the trestle in the truck. Either way, he'd won another one over Finch.

GLADYS HANDED MELANIE two aspirins and a cup of coffee while Erik spoke to John on the phone.

"I want you to pick Reba up, then Jo, and ask her to bring some clothes for Melanie." His eyes went quickly over Melanie, still wearing last night's dress. "You're all staying with me for a few days. No, I'll explain when I see you. She's okay. Bill's coming by the office to pick her up. Do it quickly, Dad, and keep your eyes open."

He put the phone down and accepted a cup from Gladys. "Thanks." He looked at her sharply. "You're sworn to secrecy now. Not a word."

She looked at Melanie's white face and now mussy evening dress, to the angry glitter in Erik's eyes and shrugged. "I'm not sure I've got the picture, anyway. Except that your new car looks like you were hit by a log truck. You guys get into a bumper car thing after the show last night?"

He smiled grimly. "Close. I'm giving you the rest of the day off. Go home. Take a long weekend."

She looked doubtful and a little worried. "Maybe you should call the chief or the sheriff."

"I'll handle it," he said, giving her a gentle push in the direction of the door. "Go home."

Erik called his housekeeper, who apparently chose to argue over his suggestion that she stay home the following day.

"I know the barbecue's tomorrow," Erik said. He listened a moment. "Then if you've made the potato salad and bought the corn and hot dogs this morning, I can handle everything else."

He listened again. Mrs. Abbott seemed to be offering a barrage of objections. "I'm going to have a young lady with me for a few days," he said finally.

There was muted laughter on the other end of the line, then Erik said, "Right. You enjoy yourself, too, Mrs. Abbott. I'll call you next week."

Erik's office pulsed with quiet after he hung up the phone. He sat in the chair behind his desk, put his feet up on the corner and sipped his coffee.

Melanie sat in the chair facing him, his suit coat draped over her shoulders. "Did you get the license plate number?" she asked casually, although she felt very much as though she would be sick.

"He was smart enough not to have one," Erik replied.

"Did you see the driver's face?"

"I was too busy driving."

"In other words," she said with a sigh, "there's still nothing to take to the police."

"The guy in the truck planned it that way," he said. "I didn't. Anyway..." He hesitated, took another sip of coffee, and avoided looking at her. "You don't have to worry about that anymore. You're going back to Denver in the morning and taking Jo and Reba with you for a brief visit."

She lowered her cup to the corner of his desk. "What?" she asked quietly.

"You're going home." He glanced at her, seemingly more interested in his coffee. "That was what you wanted just an hour ago, wasn't it?"

"You're a fraud, Channing," she said, leaning her forearms on his desk with a knowing smile that had little to do with genuine amusement. "You're trying to get me out of harm's way."

He contemplated her for a moment, then shook his head. "You're not in danger."

"Really?" Her smile broadened. "That was quite a tea party this morning, then." She grew sober again, her eyes dark with anger. "I'm in danger when I'm with you because I'm important to you. Finch, naturally, doesn't know it's over between us, so he'd just as soon get both of us, because I'm sure he presumes I know what you know. Or maybe you're worried that he might try to get to me as a way of getting to you."

He struggled to keep that truth from registering in his eyes. But he knew that he'd failed when she raised an eyebrow.

"I think we're talking about a double standard, here," she said lightly. "I'm supposed to simply let you do whatever the hell it is you want to do, or heroically *have* to do, and not worry. When I find it difficult, you tell me I haven't got any guts. But when you find yourself worried about me, you simply take control of my life and send me off somewhere safe. And you don't have to explain yourself to anybody." She leaned back in her chair and folded her arms, her expression dead serious. "I'm not going to Denver unless you come with me."

Erik looked at her, her face as pale as her hair, her eyes so fiercely determined, he gave serious consideration to tossing her in his old seabag and mailing her home. "You know that's impossible," he said reasonably.

"Really? Then I'm afraid it's impossible for me, too. See you." She stood, snatched up her purse and headed for the door.

Erik reached it first, barring her way. "Mel," he said tightly, his patience slipping away, "you're being a brat."

She smiled blandly. "You've set such a fine example." Then, she pushed on him. "Now, get out of my way. You're not the only one in this world with things you *have* to do, you know."

"Mel," he warned, "I'm not in a great mood..."

"Well, pardon me!" she said with exaggerated graciousness. "But I've been wearing sequins for eighteen hours, been used in a back road demolition derby and learned I was a one-night stand. Don't tell me about bad moods!"

He shook her only once, but it was enough to make the sequins on her dress rattle. "You're on thin ice, woman," he said angrily.

The door burst open and Erik spun toward it, pushing Melanie behind him. He let his head fall back with the release of tension when he found himself face-to-face with Bill.

Bill looked from Erik to Melanie and said cautiously, "Hi?"

Erik pulled him into the office, closed the door and told him briefly what had happened. "Just in case Finch has any other ideas, I want the ladies with us." He reached for Melanie's arm and pulled her toward Bill. "She's in a difficult mood," he said, giving her a chastening glance. "Everyone is to stay in the house. If you have to lock her in a closet, you have my permission."

"Aren't you coming?" Bill asked.

"I'll be along in a couple of hours," Erik replied. "Watch yourself."

Melanie was halfway down the stairs with Bill when she dissolved into noisy tears.

Awkwardly, Bill put an arm around her shoulders. "Are you okay, Mel? Are you in pain?"

With dark humor she thought what a choice question that was. "Just reacting, I guess," she said, delving into her purse for a tissue. "It's been a lousy morning."

And that was a choice understatement. She couldn't live her life worried about Erik's safety; she'd made that decision, despite the painful consequences. She hadn't counted on having to know the outcome of his battle with Finch before she could hope for any peace of mind. It was just beginning to occur to her how little she'd gained.

"YOU CAN HAVE THE HOUSE," Melanie said. She and Jolene sat on the downstairs veranda, with John posted at the far end of it, watching the lake, his shotgun across his knees. "Looks as though you'll be needing a place to raise children."

Jolene, moving lazily back and forth in a caned rocker, frowned at her. She and Reba were taking their "incarceration" with an aplomb that Melanie found surprising and a little humbling. "Can't we just share it?" Jolene asked. "You'll want somewhere to come back to from time to time."

The visible difference in Jolene in the last few days was a positive result of this fateful summer. The desperation had been replaced by a comfortable calm. But her glow dipped a little when she studied Melanie. "You're sure you're doing the right thing?"

Melanie had explained her altercation with Erik and the basic difference in outlook that lay at the heart of it. "I'm doing the only thing I can. When this is over, I'm going back to Denver."

"Will that make you happy?"

"It'll give me peace of mind."

"Mel, would you be any more miserable married to Erik and worrying about him, than you would be having to live your life without him?"

Melanie looked up at her sister with a frown. Jolene had also found a new footing in their relationship. Finally made to feel like a true sister, she was less inclined to support Melanie unconditionally and more apt to act the devil's advocate.

"That's not the point," Melanie said, staring out at the lake. It was dusk and the North Star was visible.

"What is, then?" Jolene asked. "Can't you live with his work for two years if he's willing to give it up, or at least adjust it for you for the rest of his life?"

Melanie leaned back in her chair, crossing one foot over the other on the railing. "I want a husband, Jolene, not a dead crusader."

Jolene folded her arms and said quietly, "You want someone willing to hide out with you, Mel." That brutal truth delivered, she smiled gently. "You know what I think?"

Halfheartedly, Melanie raised an eyebrow in question. She wasn't sure she wanted to know.

"You're too afraid to do what you told me to do," Jolene said. "You're preventing yourself from enjoying the present with Erik, or having a future because of how you suffered when Dad died. That's wrong."

Melanie shook her head. "Jo, I'm just protecting myself."

"I know." Jolene stopped rocking to lean toward her. "But you can't love someone and protect yourself at the same time. I wanted Bill, but I couldn't let him hold me because of the memories it brought back. I had to get past that." She put a hand on Melanie's knee. "You made me move past that. Protection is a wall, Mel. A fence, a moat filled with alligators. Love can't get through it, can't survive it."

"Jolene?" Reba's head appeared around the door frame. "You said something earlier about baking brownies tonight, and I want you to know we're holding you to it." She turned her head toward John. "Honey, you want more coffee?"

"Not just yet, thanks. But call me when the brownies come out."

Jolene stood to follow Reba, then turned back to lean down and give Melanie a hug. "Even strong people have a right to be afraid," she said quietly. "But not forever."

Melanie watched her sister walk into the house, wondering wryly where she'd heard that before.

The moment the door closed behind Jolene, John moved to sit beside Melanie. Another bombardment, Melanie guessed, and gave him a wary smile.

"My kid and I have been through a lot together," John said candidly. "He's very unhappy now and that makes me unhappy."

Melanie closed her eyes and sighed. "That seems to be going around, John."

The chirp of crickets filtered up from the yard and there was the sound of laughter from the kitchen. "Do you know what happened in that alley in L.A.?" John asked.

Melanie replied stiffly. "The Mafia had him beaten up."

"He had three broken ribs," John said calmly. "A broken collarbone, a broken arm, a ruptured spleen and a detached retina."

Melanie felt the blood drain from her face and lowered her feet to the floor.

"He doesn't know that I know all that," John went on. "I also know that when they backed him up in that alley, they offered him $50,000 or the beating. I don't know if I'd have had enough guts to take the beating. That's a man, Melanie. Think about what you're giving up."

"I . . ." She had to try to find her voice. "I lost my father that way, John."

"I remember," he said, his voice suddenly gentle as he turned to smile at her. "He was a good man. Would you have left him because he took pride in being a cop?"

It wasn't simply the pride Erik took in his work, but Melanie was too weary to try to explain. She got to her feet, the small movement feeling like a great effort under the weight of her oppressive thoughts. She put an arm around a post and stared into the dark. "I respect and admire Erik's courage, John," she said. "But if the day comes when he dies for it, what will I have left?"

"What will you have left," John asked quietly, "if you leave him?"

ERIK SAT IN HIS OFFICE, staring at the blue-upholstered chaise near the fire, lost in images created by the memory of a conversation he'd once had with Melanie in this room. They'd been discussing the Victorian mood of the decor and he'd told her he envisaged a dainty woman at a spinet, singing a plaintive little song. She had laughingly denied any vocal ability, but had volunteered to paint like a true Victorian lady, and hum while she worked.

He could see her there, sketching on a pad in her lap and humming that classical tune that always came to her when she concentrated. He'd be sitting at his desk, working on a case or paying bills, and there's be laughter and children's footsteps upstairs. He would look up at her and find her watching him. They'd smile, secure in each other and their love.

Bill slammed into the room, and Erik's dream dissolved. "Want to talk business?" Bill asked, taking the small chair near the desk. Erik continue to stare at the chaise for another moment, reluctant to part with the remnants of his daydream. "Some time today would be preferable," Bill prodded.

Erik drew a long breath and tried to muster some enthusiasm. "Sure," he said. "What's up?"

Bill sighed. "You've been about as much fun lately as cold oatmeal."

Erik gave him a vague grin. "Apparently you've never flicked cold oatmeal with a spoon."

"Really?" Bill looked very interested. "Does it work? Isn't it too sticky?"

Erik's shadow of a grin was gone. "What have you got?"

Bill flipped through his notebook. "Remember that strange list of stuff? Needles and tractors? Well, I've spent a couple of days tracking them to the source, figuring it'd be impossible because they were stolen, or something. But they weren't." When Erik frowned and leaned forward, his elbows on his desk, Bill went on, "They're donations. Charitable institutions are sometimes assigned salvage rights for major companies. As a tax write-off, the companies give them leftover stuff, things that are out-of-date, even manufactured items that aren't quite up to snuff. You know, like seconds. Harvest House has had salvage rights to American Manufacturing for two years—they make everything on the list and more. Finch can either use the merchandise or sell it to a salvage dealer, and the charity gets to use the money."

Erik brightened. "And Finch has been lining his own pocket with the proceeds?"

"I'd lay you ten to one. And probably many other donations that go to Harvest House disappear. A little clever bookkeeping and no one would know the difference. Can you get him with this?"

Erik leaned back in his chair. "I can even tie him with a bow. Good work, Bill. You deserve a bonus."

"All right!"

"When this is over, I'll take you out for the biggest steak in Harvest Lake."

Bill's face fell dramatically. "I had a green bonus in mind."

Erik grinned. "All right. I'll take you for a salad." He felt the first trace of hope he'd felt all day. Once the initial pain of Melanie's decision had subsided, a pall had settled over him that he'd found impossible to shake. Nothing about his work or his life held any interest for him, or any appeal. He felt stalled, empty. But the knowledge that he could finally present a tight case against Finch before a jury made at least his professional life hold some promise.

"Ha, ha," Bill said. "More good news."

"What?"

"Brownies coming out of the kitchen, and I don't think any of the ladies thought to bring pajamas."

Chapter Thirteen

Melanie sat alone at the large round table in the dark sunroom. Reba and Jolene had gone to bed in the guest room, their safety the responsibility of Bill, who watched the lake from the upstairs veranda. John dozed in a recliner facing the front door, his shotgun across his lap. Erik had disappeared into his office after dinner and she hadn't seen him since.

The house made comforting night noises, small hums and creaks that Melanie couldn't think of as threatening, even considering their somewhat siegelike circumstances. This house seemed to embrace her, to love her as she had always loved it. She felt a brutal ache at the thought of leaving it. Images of the elegant but cozy front room formed in her mind, the wonderful kitchen, Erik's Victorian office, the turret room off his bedroom where they'd watched the ducks. It had almost been hers.

A swath of light fell across the floor at the other end of the room as the double doors opened. "Melanie?" Erik's voice called quietly.

She started guiltily. "Yes?"

He came toward the table without putting on the light. "What are you doing here alone in the dark?"

"Just sitting." She stood wearily and pushed her chair in. "Still getting your case together?"

"I'm finished for tonight," he said, stopping in the middle of the room and putting a hand out to her. "I'd rather you weren't in here. All the glass makes you too vulnerable."

She thought ironically that her vulnerability had nothing to do with glass. Loving Erik and this house had made her vulnerable. But even love and the Scofield house wouldn't make her risk the pain of losing a loved one to violence a second time.

Erik couldn't see her face in the shadows, only the pale aureole of her pulled back hair. But her features were imprinted in his mind and he guessed she'd be looking defiant, her soft brown eyes angry because he'd asked her to leave the room. To his surprise, she took his arm and let him lead her into the living room.

He closed and locked the sunroom doors, hating to disengage his arm to do so. He wanted more than anything to see her smile at him as she had last night and this morning over breakfast on the veranda.

"Cup of hot chocolate before you go to bed?" he asked. His voice was casual, but even he heard the edge of desperation in it.

Melanie wanted to linger a few moments with him, but that would serve no purpose, she knew, except to worsen a sense of loss that was already unbearable.

She smiled up at him—but it wasn't the smile he wanted. It was filled with sadness and a poignant courage that he'd seen in her this morning when she'd told him it was over. The look had haunted him all afternoon.

"Thanks anyway," she said. "But I should get to bed. We have a big day tomorrow with forty boys coming."

He nodded, but caught her arm to discourage her from walking away. She looked up at him expectantly and he sighed. "I'm sorry I accused you of being cowardly. I was hurt and angry. I know how profoundly your father's death affected you and I had no right to judge."

She looked wryly amused. "It's all right. I said a few unforgivable things myself. I guess it's hard to remain civilized when you have to accept that something beautiful just can't be." He put his hands to her face, guessing he was making a mistake, but not strong enough to stop himself. "Are we sure about that?"

"I am," she said with demoralizing swiftness.

"I'm not," he disputed as quickly.

She caught his wrists in her hands and leaned her head sideways to rub against his palm. A pleat appeared between her closed eyes as though she was in pain. "See?" she said. "We can't even agree that we disagree." She pulled away. "Good night, Erik."

"Mel..." He caught her arm again and she turned, almost afraid to look at him, fearful that one more glance of his loving gray eyes would shake her resolve. "Sleep in my bed," he offered softly. "I'll be down here all night. And check the tower room. There's something in there I didn't have the patience to show you last night." He released her and took a step back. "Good night, Mel," he said, and walked away.

HE HAD BUILT A WINDOW SEAT. It followed the quadrangle of the window and was covered with a collection of plump, colorful cushions. More than any words of love he'd ever spoken, this revealed his feelings eloquently, tenderly. Pain raked at her.

She sat among the pillows and looked out into the night, seeing a sunny afternoon, a small boat, her father concentrating on his fishing line, and herself, about fourteen, looking up at this house and dreaming. In those days, she'd thought that all she'd have to be was rich to live in it. She hadn't known she'd have to be brave, as well.

Melanie leaned forward, buried her face in the pillows, and cried her heart out.

ERIK CROSSED THE LIVING ROOM toward his office and stopped at the sound of a car in the driveway. Bill was down the stairs and John was on his feet before Erik could turn toward the door.

The knock was swift and authoritative.

John, standing behind the door, shotgun ready, pulled it open. Bill waited on the other side, revolver drawn.

David Olson, Harvest Lake's chief of police, walked into the room out of uniform. He looked from Bill to Erik, then to John who'd come out from behind the door.

Olson was a tall, slender man who had an untarnished but unremarkable career. Had he decided to tie in with Finch as part of a personal retirement plan more adequate than what the city provided, Erik wondered, or was it all more innocent than it appeared?

Olson reached inside his jacket. John pumped the shotgun and Bill drew the hammer back with a loud click. Olson froze, a dry smile forming. "I know what's going on, and I'm here to help."

"Prove it," Erik said.

Olson sighed. "Then tell your Rent-a-cops to let me get this report on Finch out of my pocket."

"MELANIE?" Erik's voice penetrated her fitful sleep and she sat up, her hair tousled, her eyes wide and bleary.

"What?" she asked, alarmed. "Is it Finch?"

He laughed softly, sinking to the edge of the bed. "No, it's breakfast. I brought you a tray so you could have it on the veranda."

Melanie finally focused on his face and saw the sadness behind the smile. She propped up her pillow and leaned back, trying to ignore the little race of feeling caused by his hip so close to her leg. "Thank you. Was it a quiet night? I didn't hear anything."

"Very quiet. I suspect our friend Finch has more important matters on his mind right now than us." He handed her the glass of juice from the tray.

"What would that be?"

"Destroying evidence. Covering his tracks."

She looked Erik in the eye. "Are you planning to rush in, single-handed, and stop him?"

He placed a hand on the mattress on the other side of her hip and returned her level gaze. "That would be foolish," he said, his tone softly scolding. "But I do have it handled." Then, his focus shifted from her eyes to her mouth, and he leaned forward to put a gentle but thorough kiss there.

He pulled away with great effort and got to his feet. "And when you're finished with breakfast," he said, "we could use your help in the kitchen. Mrs. Abbott had everything ready but the melon ball salad." He went to the door and turned to look at her one more time, as though he might be memorizing her there. Then, he closed the door behind him.

Melanie sipped the juice, then put it aside, finding herself unable to swallow.

THE KITCHEN WAS PANDEMONIUM. The doors were open onto the patio, and John worked over the briquettes in one of two long barbecues, while Bill and Erik placed folding chairs around the pool, insults and laughter flying between them.

Melanie watched them greedily.

"Darling, will you help me with this?"

Melanie turned at Reba's call to find her trying to shake out a large white cloth over an enormous table. Melanie caught the ends and pulled them out, smoothing the cloth in place.

"Good morning, Reba." She forced a smile across the broad expanse of white. "Sleep well?"

"Surprisingly, yes." She came to put an arm around Melanie's shoulder and led her back into the kitchen. "All this excitement seems to be rejuvenating me."

Melanie asked quietly, "You're sure it isn't John?"

Reba stopped in the middle of the kitchen, her eyes suddenly serious. "We're getting married, Melanie."

That shouldn't hurt, Melanie thought, but it did. It was the kind of pain curiously associated with happiness—the bittersweetness of being removed from it. She wrapped Reba in a hug. "That's wonderful," she said. "I'm so happy for you."

"We're supposed to be bridesmaids." Jolene joined their little circle, a checked bib-apron over her white blouse and jeans, a melon baller in her hand. Her expression was sad and concerned. "If you can stay long enough."

"You know I wouldn't miss it." Melanie pulled her sister into her free arm. "And what about you and Bill?"

Happiness lit Jolene's dark blue eyes. She looked renewed, Melanie saw with satisfaction. She hugged her, determined to remain controlled. "See? You got your Rosemary Clooney--Vera Ellen movie. It's just that you'll have to launch your sister act with your aunt instead. Now..." She pulled back from them and pushed her sleeves up. "Give me something to do."

"Okay." Reba folded her arms, apparently accepting the challenge. "Accept that life is never perfect, that any sensible woman will take on hell itself for the sake of a good man, and ask Erik to marry you."

Melanie gave Reba a scolding frown. "I meant something to do in the kitchen."

Jolene hooked her arm in Melanie's and led her toward the counter where a watermelon had been halved and hollowed. "Come on. You can help me."

MELANIE PUT A FIVE-AND-A-HALF gallon bowl of potato salad on an end of one of three long picnic tables Erik had set up near the pool. By the time she walked to the other end of the table to check the pitcher of lemonade, the bowl was handed back to her—empty.

The boys had been swimming for two hours, the noise was enough to draw response from another galaxy, and food was being consumed at such an alarming rate that she wondered if someone would have to make an emergency run to the grocery store. But everyone appeared to be having a wonderful time.

Erik passed among the tables with an ice-filled cooler containing cans of pop, Greg holding the handle on the other end of the cooler. Melanie had to smile at the boy's slightly self-important air. She knew he was enjoying his status as Erik's friend in front of the other boys. And Erik seemed to be doing his best to make a subtle point of their relationship. He sent Greg back to the house for things that only someone familiar with it could find. He asked him to answer the phone, to help Bill bring out more chairs, to get his camera from the den.

Jerry Finch made a quick appearance toward evening, talking with the boys and staff members, formally and icily making a show of shaking Erik's hand and thanking him for hosting the party. Melanie saw John and Bill close in on them, pretending to wipe off the table only several feet from the conversation.

Maggie was visibly changed from the effusive woman who had hosted Melanie's show. Though she managed to look everyone in the eye, her expression was withdrawn and remote. Melanie had no idea what she knew, but found it easy to give her the benefit of the doubt and assume that whatever her involvement was in Jerry's dealings, it had happened against her will.

Melanie had almost no opportunity to talk to Erik. She served, cleaned up, arbitrated squabbles, played hackey sack and nursed several severe cases of indigestion.

"Erik says you're going back to Denver."

She looked up from a cup of coffee at the kitchen table to see Greg, in shorts and a tank top, silhouetted against the double glass doors and the dusk beyond. The outside lights had gone on, and the level of activity on the patio was finally beginning to quiet.

"Pretty soon," she said, her voice a little strained. She'd come inside thinking a few minutes alone might help her fight off an encroaching depression. It wasn't working.

Greg took the chair nearest her. His eyes were large and troubled. "I thought you were his lady."

Her throat was closing. It was just because it was dusk. It was a melancholy time, a letting go of sunshine while still waiting for the moon. "No," she said.

"He says you are," Greg insisted. "He says he loves you but you can't stay because your dad was a cop and he got killed. And you're afraid the same thing might happen to him because of his job."

Greg folded his arms on the table, his expression grave. "My dad died, you know."

Melanie smiled sympathetically. "I know."

"We had a little grocery store. Gang members used to come in and take stuff without paying for it. It was broken into so many times, we couldn't afford insurance. But my father loved the store. He used to tell me he'd wanted one since he was a little kid. He worked hard."

Melanie shook her head. "It must have been very difficult for him."

"It really was, when he got sick." Greg's eyes filled. "He used to ask me to help and I'd get mad because I thought it was stupid. Then he died."

Melanie put her hand over his on the table. "I'm sorry, Greg," she said.

He shrugged, and it was such a telling gesture, Melanie thought. It didn't mean that he didn't care, but that he was powerless to do anything about it, or about the loneliness and poverty into which his father's death must have placed him and his mother. "It was just a little store. I was telling Erik about it one day and he explained to me that all somebody really has in life is the love of his family and his friends, and honor in the way he lives. He says all the other stuff—cars, money, babes..." He glanced at her and explained seriously, "Not ladies but babes, you know?"

She nodded. "Babes. Yes."

"Well, they don't mean anything because, when it's all over, it's not what you've got, but what you did. For my dad, the store was important and everything in it was good stuff that he took care of and sold for a fair price." He shook his head. "I didn't understand that for a long time. But then I got to thinking. My dad had a lot of friends, and my mom still loves him and misses him even though he's been dead for two years." He looked into Melanie's eyes, his own eyes dark and brimming with tears. "I try not to think about it, but I miss him, too. I guess I know how you feel, sort of."

Melanie reached over to wrap her arms around him. "Things will work out for you," she said with conviction. "I know they will. You're very special, Greg. Just remember what Erik said."

"Greg, come on!" two boys shouted, sliding the door half-open. "We need another man for one last game of pool tag! Miss Quinn, could you referee?"

DARKNESS HAD FALLEN when the party moved indoors—and Melanie noticed that Erik was missing. She wasn't concerned until she realized that Finch was also absent. She approached John who was pulling nachos out of the oven. "Where's Erik?" she asked.

He glanced around, putting the pan down on a cutting board. "He was outside a few minutes ago."

She'd just come in from the patio, but she didn't want to alarm John. "I'm sure Bill will know." She started off in the direction of the game room, where she'd last seen him.

"Bill got a call from his office," Jolene said, pouring popcorn from a popper into a large bowl. "He left about fifteen minutes ago."

Boys swarmed into the kitchen in search of more food, and Melanie escaped to the pool area for a moment of solitude. She didn't like this—she didn't like it at all. She recalled a snatch of Erik's telephone conversation with Bill the morning of her quarrel with him. "He can't move with everyone at Harvest House..." But tonight, everyone at Harvest House was here—except Finch and Erik. She knew with chilling certainty that their showdown was tonight.

She paced, fighting the instinct to run to his rescue. She'd decided she couldn't live with the worry, she reminded herself, and Erik knew that. This was the point at which she simply walked away. He knew what he was doing—and if he didn't, it was no longer her concern. She'd made her choice, and he'd made his.

Dread swelled inside her, filling every corner of her being. She stopped still in the cool moonlight, understanding with sudden clarity that there was a grave difference between making a decision and living with it.

She turned to continue pacing and collided with Greg.

"I know where he is," he said quietly, apparently understanding her concern. "I heard him on the phone. He went to Harvest House."

When Melanie said nothing, he went on urgently. "He set this up. He told me to tell Finch he was asking me about the storage building. He wanted him to know he knew about him. He's gone there all alone, Melanie."

"I know. That's what he wanted, Greg."

Greg stared at her. Sounds of rowdy laughter were coming from the house. "Would you want to be? I mean, if you didn't have to be?"

Something about that question clattered in her brain, but she didn't have time to think about it. She headed for the house.

"Are we going to go after him?" Greg asked, following her.

"No." She stopped to take him by the shoulders. "*We* are not. You are going to stay here and enjoy the party. Promise me?"

He looked reluctant, then agreed grimly, "All right."

Melanie ran into the house, pulled Jolene away from the popcorn popper, and dragged her upstairs to the bedroom. While she routed in her purse for her keys, she explained what she suspected.

"You can't go there, Melanie!" Jolene reasoned. "Call Bill."

"There isn't time." Melanie pulled out her keys and shouldered her purse. "You call Bill. He'll know whether to call the police or not."

"Maybe the call from Bill's office was something he and Erik had planned," Jolene suggested hopefully, "and he's with Erik right now."

"Or maybe it's something Finch planned, to get Bill out of the way and give him a clear shot at Erik."

Jolene held her back as she tried to hurry from the room. "Let's get John."

"No," Melanie said patiently. "He'll try to stop me. Then, he'll want to go himself and, with his heart, that would be dangerous."

"All right, then," Jolene said. "I'm coming with you."

"No. You have to stay and help John and Reba with the boys. Try not to alarm him, okay?"

Jolene followed her through the house to the door. "How am I going to do that?" she whispered. "His son's missing, you're off to rescue him..."

Melanie gave her a quick wry grin over her shoulder. "Let's hope the situation isn't half that dramatic." She glanced at her watch. "If you don't hear from me in an hour you can assume there's a problem and call the police." She leaned forward to give her a quick hug. "Bye."

THE LAKESHORE ROAD to Harvest House was narrow and dark. Dense forest rose up on either side of it, and Melanie concentrated on watching the center line in her headlights, trying not to wonder where Erik was at this moment, or what could be happening to him. But the knowledge that Finch would kill him without a second thought filled her awareness.

"Please let him be all right," she prayed quietly as she drove. "Please."

"If you want him to be all right," a voice said in her ear, "you'd better park the car in the bushes by the turnoff."

Melanie gasped in alarm, turning to glance at the young man leaning over the back of the front seat. "Greg!" She turned back to the road just in time to avoid blazing a new trail into the woods. "You promised me!"

"Pull in right here. I know, I'm sorry." His eager tone belied the sincerity of his apology.

Melanie did as he directed, nosing the car into a thick clump of bushes. She turned to Greg, her eyes blazing in the darkness. "You are *not* coming with me, do you understand? If anything happened to you..."

"If you go alone," the boy replied calmly, "something could happen to Erik. I know where everything is in the compound, but you've only been there once."

For a moment, that made sense. And Melanie would have liked the company. The night was very dark, and the lights around the compound in the small valley would make approaching it without being seen difficult. Then, common sense reminded her that Greg was just a boy. "You don't know where he went, either," she reminded him.

"Yes, I do," he corrected calmly. "The dorms."

"I know where the dorms are."

"You don't know how to get into them through the woods."

"Greg..."

"If you go in on the road, they'll see you coming. Are we gonna sit here and argue, or save Erik?" The boy sounded mature, but looked frightened.

"All right," Melanie said finally, "but I'm in charge. Is that clear?"

Greg smiled. "Yes, ma'am."

Her leadership was immediately compromised by a need to ask Greg to point the way through the woods. He led Melanie down a path, assuring her the boys used it all the time. It rose and dipped, was sometimes wide enough for two to walk abreast, but usually so narrow that pine boughs scraped Melanie's bare arms and pulled at her hair. Greg raced along it with stealthy ease, and she had to caution him more than once not to get too far ahead.

After what seemed an eternity, they reached a clearing. Thirty or forty feet separated them from the back of the dormitories. Greg looked carefully to the left and right.

"Do you hear anything?" Melanie whispered.

"No," he whispered back. "But that doesn't mean nobody's here. Now we're going to run to the back door. Stay low." He frowned at her hair. "Your hair sticks out like a flashlight. Don't you have something to put over it?"

Melanie rolled her eyes. "This isn't a guerilla raid. Just lead the way, and I'll be as invisible as you are."

Melanie followed him across the open stretch of grass to the building. Distractedly, she noticed that the night smelled of pine and was eerily silent. Greg went inside and Melanie followed him.

The dormitory smelled pungently of boys. Greg went across the room to two wide windows and peered out. "Finch's car is here," he reported, "but I don't see Erik's."

Melanie ran to look over his shoulder. There were lights on in the administrative building, and Finch's sedan was parked in front. She tried to console herself with the thought that, if Erik had come to look around, he'd have hidden his car as she had hidden hers.

Greg pulled the drapes closed, then removed a flashlight from his pocket.

"Where did you get that?" she asked.

"Erik keeps it in the bottom drawer of the kitchen cabinet." He quickly picked out each corner of the room. Melanie noticed a general untidiness that could simply be attributed to boys being boys, but there was no sign of Erik.

"Why are you so sure he'll be in one of the dorms?" she whispered.

"Because they've got the best view of the storage building. Come on. Let's try the next dorm."

Erik wasn't there, either. Greg looked around the third dorm in frustration. Then he went to the window and peeked around the curtain. "I'll bet Finch has got him. I'm going to the administration building."

"No, you're not!" Melanie whispered harshly, grabbing his arm as he moved toward the door. "I'm . . ."

"Ssh!" Greg ran back to the window. "Look!"

Looking over his head, Melanie saw a large tractor-trailer rig pull into the compound and back up to the storage building.

As they watched, Finch and one of the burly men Melanie remembered from her afternoon of spying with Erik, came out of the administration building and went to greet the driver of the truck. An envelope changed hands.

"They're going to move the stuff!" Greg whispered.

But Melanie was less interested in that than in whether or not Erik was in the administration building. She pulled Greg away from the window and shook her finger at him. "Now, you listen to me, Butler," she said firmly. "I'm going across the compound to see if they've got Erik in the administration building. If you take one step out of this dorm before I get back, I'll personally take a ruler to your backside."

"It's all open space!" Greg protested. "They'll see you!"

Melanie sighed. "You've been leading this operation, Greg, because you knew the trail through the woods. But I'm not a total incompetent, you know. I'll go to the other end of the compound and cross around the back."

"You do that," a male voice said behind her, "and the ruler finds your backside before Greg's."

Melanie and Greg spun around in surprise. "Erik!" Greg exclaimed and ran into his arms.

Melanie looked at him over Greg's head, her heart thumping with relief. He wore black jeans and a black turtleneck, obviously dressed for stealth. The color made his gray eyes look dramatically darker. He was obviously in good health and suddenly she had an impulse to shout at him or hit him. With Finch beyond the window, and Greg in Erik's arms, she could do neither. So, she whispered harshly and kept her distance.

"Where *were* you?" she demanded.

Erik pointed to the open door through which he'd apparently just emerged. "Great pair of detectives," he said dryly. "You don't even check the closet."

"We didn't expect you to be hiding from us!"

"I didn't know it was you, did I?" He moved Greg aside and went to peer cautiously out the window. "They're going to be loading that for a while," he said, then turned to give them his full attention once again. "So what in the hell are you doing here?"

Melanie folded her arms. "We came to rescue you. What does it look like?"

"What made you think I was in danger?"

"When I noticed you were gone, I also noticed Finch was gone, too."

Erik nodded. "I followed him."

"She thought he mighta followed you," Greg said, apparently intending to defend her. "And that you'd get caught."

Erik nodded again. "Now that I'm being followed by a woman and a child, I probably will get caught."

"Don't blame us," Melanie said indignantly. "You want to get caught! You want to stretch your courage so far it'll kill you!" She jabbed a finger toward the window. "They're moving something illegal, and you probably still haven't called the police."

Greg put an arm around her shoulders. "Melanie," he said consolingly. He turned to Erik, with a worried expression on his face. "My mom always sounds like that before she starts crying."

I'm going to lose it, Erik thought. I had the situation under control, my courage in hand, and now... He looked at the two pairs of eyes staring at him, one wanting him to say something reassuring, the other filled with messages he was probably misunderstanding because of the circumstances. He wanted nothing more than to take them both back to his house—maybe even keep them there. But Greg had a mother who needed him, and Melanie had said goodbye.

Unfortunately, now they would have to see this through with him. He couldn't send them away, with Finch and his friends milling around outside. He had to wait around to make sure the truck really did contain the donated items, and then he had to implement his plan. Melanie and Greg would have to wait with him, then he could send them off when it was time to follow the truck.

Melanie looked as though she was on the brink of tears. Considering how she felt about this sort of thing, she was probably scared to death. He couldn't speculate now about her reasons for coming. He had other things to think about.

He put an arm around each of them and held them to him, indulging himself for just a moment. Then, he pushed them down on the edge of one of the beds. "Stay there and please be quiet," he said. He went to the window and watched the truck. The way it was positioned, he couldn't see what was being loaded.

It was half an hour before Finch, his henchman, and the driver walked into the office, talking and laughing.

"I'm going to run out to check the truck," he said, glancing out the window again to make sure the office door had closed behind them. He frowned at Melanie and Greg. "I want your promise that you'll wait here for me."

Greg and Melanie looked at each other, but said nothing. Melanie was too annoyed to be cooperative, but she had even less confidence in Greg's motives for remaining silent. With a last warning glance at them, Erik disappeared into the darkness.

Greg peered through the curtain for several minutes, then began to shift nervously. "Where is he?" he asked anxiously.

Melanie looked through the other side of the curtain, straining to see through the shadows. It was hopeless. "I don't know," she said with unconvincing bravado, "but if we can't see him, nobody else can, either."

The faint creak of the dorm door made Melanie emerge from the curtain with a start. Greg was gone.

"You little monster!" she whispered to the open doorway. With a groan and a prayer, she followed him outside. He had almost reached the truck before she caught up with him. She grabbed a fistful of the back of his jacket and spun him around. "What do you think you're doing!" she demanded in a harsh undertone.

He tried to shake her off. "I'm going to help Erik! Go back to the dorm!"

"You are not. You're coming back with—"

Her orders were interrupted by the sound of the door opening in the administration building. A wedge of light began to form, and Melanie grabbed Greg's arm, running around to the other side of the truck, flattening herself and him against it. Their return route to the dorm was cut off, and she saw no sign of Erik. She heard voices and footsteps across the compound.

She was considering several not very promising options, when a long arm reached out of the back of the truck, grabbed the shoulder of Greg's jacket and pulled him up. She grabbed futilely for the boy's leg, when the same hand reached down for her. Just as she opened her mouth to scream, Erik's face appeared out of the shadows of the truck. "Don't you dare!" he whispered sharply. The voices and footsteps grew closer. She let herself be hauled into the truck and wondered, after her glance into Erik's face, if she wouldn't have a better chance of surviving this night at the hands of Finch and his crew.

Erik pushed her and Greg into the dark interior of the truck. She collided with something and uttered a small gasp of alarm. Erik shushed her, taking hold of her shoulders and guiding her in a straight line, then pulling her down beside him behind a stack of wooden crates. Greg pressed in on her from the other side, as the voices sounded clearly from the open truck.

"Who's meeting us at Portland Airport?" The voice was high and raspy.

"Abernathy," Finch replied.

"So when do we divvy up?"

"Soon as I get my money, Harper," Finch snapped. "You'll get yours. Now get this..."

The sound of a powerful motor suddenly filled the night, followed almost immediately by a screech of brakes.

A woman's voice, loud and shrill followed the slam of a door. "You sleazy, ignorant, two-timing, hen-witted idiot!" It was Maggie. "You can get me into trouble with the law, clean out our bank account, threaten to drown me in the lake and leave me without a word..." Her voice dropped ominously low. "But don't think for one minute that you can clean out my gallery and get away with it."

"Now, Maggie. Would you rather see me in cement overshoes for nonpayment of a substantial debt?"

"Jerry Finch, if you don't take every last painting out of that truck, I'll call Channing and sing so loud you'll be able to hear me in South America! I was almost glad to get rid of you, until I realized you'd cleaned out my gallery." There was a pause. "What the hell's in the truck, anyway? Isn't this semi a little overkill for sixty paintings?"

"It's none of your business, Maggie."

"I want to..." There was a sound of a scuffle, then Finch said in a bored tone, "It's the salvage stuff from American Manufacturing. And now that you know that..." His voice became hard and flat. "Harper, tie her up in the office and pull the phone out of the wall. It's been fun, Maggie. On to greener pastures."

"They'll find you, Jerry. *I'll* find you! I'll tell them about the city hall pay-offs, the..." Her voice faded away.

"Lock the trailer and move!" Finch ordered. "We've got two hours to get to the airport."

The loud clang of closing metal doors was followed by complete darkness. Melanie felt Greg clutch her arm. She reached instinctively for Erik's.

"It's all right," he whispered. "Keep still until we're under way."

Sure, Melanie thought bleakly. I'm locked in the back of a truck with a ton of stolen merchandise, a boy who stowed away in the back of my car, and the man I love who—the last time I could see his face—didn't look at all as though he felt the same way. And I'm on my way to South America. But Erik says it's all right. Uh, huh. That's the kind of summer it's been.

As they drove off, Melanie discovered that riding in the trailer of a truck was not at all like riding in a well-sprung luxury car. In the small pool of light from Greg's flashlight, Erik took the blanket that was draped over an elegant desk chair and folded it into a pad for Melanie and Greg to sit on. Then, he took the light and checked the contents of the truck. Everything mentioned on the list, except the tractor, was accounted for. Finch had stolen from his wife and the children he was supposed to be protecting.

Erik went back to their little shelter between the cartons of syringes and propped the flashlight against one of the boxes. Greg looked bright and excited. In typical adolescent fashion he was aware only of the adventure and not the danger. Erik wanted to shake him.

If everything went according to plan, he could get Greg and Melanie out of this unscathed. If there was a hitch in anything—if they lost Bill on the road, if the police weren't waiting at the airport—it could be over for all of them.

"It'll be all right, won't it?" Greg asked quietly. Erik knew the boy had been watching his face and probably mistrusted the frown.

"I don't know," he said frankly, sitting down across the narrow space from him. He had to turn sideways to find room for his legs. "My plan didn't take you and Melanie into account. What are you doing here?"

Greg looked at him, wide-eyed. "Like Melanie said. We came to rescue you."

"That's why Melanie's here." Greg returned his look without softening his expression. "But I know she wouldn't have willingly brought you with her."

Greg glanced at Melanie, then shook his head at Erik. "She didn't. I hid in the back of her car. I didn't think you'd want her to come alone. She could have gotten hurt."

"I didn't know he was there until the turnoff to Harvest House," Melanie explained.

"You should have taken him back," Erik said.

Melanie rubbed her bare arms against the chill. "We were both very concerned about you. You have my permission to sue us, if we live."

"Don't be smart," he warned.

"And don't you be smug!" she shouted, forgetting their perilous circumstances. Erik shushed her, and they all sat in silence for a moment, waiting for evidence that they'd been heard. But the drone of the motor continued.

"I'm sorry if our presence botches up your moment of glory!" Melanie went on in a harsh whisper. "We were worried about you! I forgot that this was probably the opportunity you've been waiting for all along. Your chance to risk..."

Suddenly, she was on her knees and he had a biting grip on her shoulders. "This is not my 'moment of glory.'" He repeated her words with distaste. "It's an opportunity to finally put away a royal scum. And as much as I want that and have worked for it, my concern at the moment is for you and that child—"

"Hey!" Greg interrupted indignantly. "Who are you calling a child?"

Erik spared him a quick glance. "*You* are a child. And you're in enough trouble already, so I'd keep it down if I were you." Erik turned his attention back to Melanie as though he suddenly couldn't understand her. "You're usually so sensible. If I had been in trouble, what did you think your hundred and ten pounds could have done for me?"

"I didn't think that far ahead," Melanie admitted defensively. "Bill was gone and I didn't want to risk upsetting your father. You weren't sure you could trust the police, and there wasn't time to plan a brilliant scheme."

Erik looked into her tired, frightened eyes and believed her. His mind leaped immediately to what that meant in relation to her decision to leave him, but he was afraid to analyze it too closely for fear of being wrong.

"All I knew for certain," she said quietly, shivering as she spoke, "was that I didn't want you to find yourself cornered in some alley... alone... again."

Erik took off his sweater and pulled it over her head. "You understand what that means?" he asked quietly.

She angled her chin out of the high neck. "No, I don't. And if I don't, you can't possibly."

He gave her a long look before sitting back against the boxes. "If you're comfortable believing that..." He pulled her down beside him and settled her in the crook of his arm. "You okay, Greg?" He nudged the heavy-eyed boy with the toe of his shoe.

Greg sat up with a start. "Hm? Yeah."

Erik smiled at him. "Lie down. Try to get a little sleep. I'll wake you when I need you."

The boy's eyes widened for a moment. "Will you? Promise?"

"Promise."

Satisfied, Greg curled onto the blanket, and Erik reached across him to tug the other end over his shoulders. Then, he settled Melanie against him again. "Rest," he ordered gently.

Melanie didn't want to rest. She didn't want to think. She wanted to be back to yesterday morning, when she'd felt so in love and understood exactly what she wanted.

"I wish you had called the police," she said stubbornly.

"I didn't have to," he said. "The chief came to me last night. He was developing a few suspicions himself about Finch and began investigating on his own. He's wanted in three provinces in Canada for various embezzlement schemes."

"No one thought to check his credentials when he started the home?"

"Superficially, he looks qualified. He has teaching credentials, experience as a counselor at a detention home for boys in Washington. That's probably where he learned he could make that salvage rights business work for him. He found a wealthy woman, convinced her his dream to open a home for boys was noble, got her to marry him and bankroll him. Finch was a hometown boy, the community immediately took to his outgoing, talented wife. Who would bother to ask questions?"

Melanie sat up to look into his eyes, forgetting about Finch. She suddenly realized what the chief's visit to Erik meant. "You mean the police are going to help you?" she asked.

He cleared his throat. "Well, the plan was that I was to find out what was in the truck. If it was the salvage goods, I was supposed to let Finch catch me, get him to admit he was selling it off for himself because of a debt to Abernathy, that he's done other 'favors' for Abernathy while in office, then the police were going to close in."

Melanie realized she and Greg had ruined his plan. She let her head fall against his shoulder with a groan. "I'm sorry."

He kissed her hair. "No problem. We move to Plan B."

"What's that?"

He hesitated a moment. "Ah . . . I'm making it up as I go along."

THE SUDDEN CESSATION of movement awoke Melanie with a start. Greg was still fast asleep on the blanket, but Erik was not beside her. She felt a moment of panic. Had something happened to him while she was asleep? She sprang to her feet, whispering desperately, "Erik!"

"Here!" he called quickly.

She followed his voice to the back of the trailer, where he was moving two large crates apart.

"What are you doing?" she asked.

"When they open the doors," he said, dusting his hands off, "I'm going to be up here, and you and Greg are going to stay back where we were hiding."

"Why?"

He knew she'd ask. "Because," he replied calmly, "your responsibility is to the boy. If something goes wrong and I get caught, stay hidden until the last possible moment."

Greg suddenly appeared between them. "No," he said.

"Now, look . . ." Erik began darkly, but the sound of someone unlocking the trailer door stopped him. He pushed Greg and Melanie. "Get back!" he ordered in a harsh whisper. They scurried to their haven, and Erik sank into the dark shadows behind the crates.

A big man in a suit climbed laboriously up the extended ramp into the trailer. Erik watched, his breath suspended, while the man moved among the boxes, puffing on a cigar. He felt reasonably sure the man was Abernathy. He might have been any well-dressed executive—except for the bulge under his coat near his armpit. He moved farther into the truck, and Erik prayed that Melanie and Greg were well concealed. Abernathy turned abruptly and asked from the rear door of the trailer, "Where's the tractor?"

"Coming on a flatbed," Finch's voice replied.

"All right. Looks like we're square." Then, there was the sound of Abernathy grunting as he got down from the truck. "Where'll you be if I need to get in touch with you again?"

"Colombia." There was a snicker. "I hear you can buy D.A.s there."

Paper rustled and there was a sound like that of cards being shuffled—or cash. Erik waited for sirens, the sounds of running, booted feet, a corny but satisfying, "All right, the jig is up. Drop 'em." Nothing. Surely, the chief had alerted the Portland Metro division. Surely, Bill had followed the truck to the airport. Or did they lose him? Was he really here alone with a woman and a child, about to walk into a situation reminiscent of the one in the alley on Spring Street? He smiled wryly to himself. Why was he even wondering? From the outset, this plan had run according to Murphy's law.

With a little jolt of surprise, he noticed that the fear was gone. Not the fear of how this predicament would end—as Melanie had said, he'd have to be crazy not to be afraid. But the long-abiding fear of the fear was gone. He let his brain turn off for a moment to enjoy the feeling.

He'd had to live with phantoms every day to realize that he wasn't invincible. He'd had to lose the woman he loved, to realize that what she wanted had to be as important to him as what he wanted. Courage wasn't reckless daring and the stoic acceptance of pain. It was the acceptance that he was not alone, could not function alone, and didn't want to. It was reaching out to pull someone else close enough so that she, too, could see how truly vulnerable he was.

He came back to awareness with a start when crates began to move around him. Abernathy's men were unloading the truck. His heart thudded. As the men rolled a full dolly down, Erik circled the last crate between him and them. When they started up the ramp again, he sent up one last prayer that, while his unexpected presence would cause a commotion, Melanie could get Greg out of the truck and run to safety. The chance was slim, but it was the only one they had.

Hands grabbed the crate, and not giving himself time to think about it, Erik shoved it with all his strength. The crate and the two men tumbled out of the truck. There was a shout of alarm, the beginning of a curse. Erik hit the ramp at a run and hurled his body at Abernathy, who stood at the end. Erik struck him with a teeth-jarring impact, noting with satisfaction that Finch was coming toward him, drawing a gun out of his jacket. "Run, Melanie!" he willed desperately.

Erik made sure Abernathy was out cold and sprang to his feet, determined to keep Finch and his man busy while Melanie and Greg made their escape, even if that meant being a target. Finch kept coming at him; he cocked his pistol. Melanie and Greg were crouched at the top of the ramp, and for an instant it seemed that the diversion would succeed. Triumph turned to terror when Melanie leaped—not away from the truck, but at Finch.

Erik ran the few yards that separated them with a desperation that made the distance seem like the breadth of the Grand Canyon. He watched the gun point awkwardly at the sky as Finch took the impact of Melanie's body against his chest, then sideways, then at her as she wrapped her arms and legs around him. Finch stumbled backward, and his henchman moved in to try to pry Melanie off him. With a deftness Erik had to admire, Greg kicked Finch's man brutally in the backside. When he cried out in surprise and pain and turned toward the source of the attack, Greg kicked him in the groin. The man doubled over, helpless. Greg moved toward Finch and the wildly arcing pistol, but Erik shoved him out of the way.

Melanie had two fistfuls of Finch's hair and Finch began firing, his aim desperate and indiscriminate. Erik manacled the man's wrist above his head, peeled Melanie from him and landed a fist in his face. Finch sank to the asphalt and Erik took the gun.

He looked up to discover they were surrounded by police. Bill loped toward him, glancing toward Melanie and Greg. "You guys okay? When did they become part of the plan?"

Erik gave each of them a forbidding glance that promised retribution. "They never were. The police get everything we need out of Finch's office?"

"Everything. Enough incriminating correspondence and memos to tie him to Abernathy and the mob, and send him up for twenty or thirty years. What about the truck?"

"Just what we thought."

A tall, thickly-built man in a suit approached Erik, his hand extended. "Channing, I presume. I'm Billings with Portland Metro Police. Sorry we were late coming in. Dispatch gave us the wrong end of the freight terminal. Good work. We've got more than we need."

"Good."

The man frowned suddenly. "I got a call that your police suspected Miss Quinn might be with you, and that a boy is missing from your party."

Erik swept a hand toward where Melanie and Greg waited arm in arm. "Safe and sound—through no fault of their own. Do you need them tonight?"

Billings shook his head. "We need you to identify this stuff, but they can go. Want me to send them home in a patrol car?"

"Thanks, but I'll send them with Curtis. Be with you in a minute."

Billings returned to the hub of activity around the truck where Abernathy, Finch and their crew were being read their rights and eased into police cars. Erik went in search of Bill. He found him in the truck, matching its contents with the list from Finch's office. He grinned at Erik as he approached. "Everything's here except the tractor. You did good, Channing."

Erik nodded, returning his grin. "Yeah, we did. You want to take Mel and Greg home for me? I'll have to stick around for a while."

"Sure. Right now?"

"I'm going to chew them out for a few minutes," Erik replied, "then they're yours."

"Go easy," Bill cautioned. "They both look a little done in."

They were standing arm in arm, Greg leaning wearily against Melanie's shoulder. The kid's upside-down world had just been turned inside out as well. He was probably wondering what would happen to him now that Harvest House's director was being carted off to jail. For one angry moment, Erik hated Finch with a murderous fury. The man was a great example for kids he'd supposedly been teaching to straighten out their lives.

Melanie looked pale and tired. Her eyes watched Erik with uncertainty as he took Greg's arm, then hers, and pulled them toward Bill's car. He backed them up against the passenger-side door and tried to look severe. When he remembered the sight of Melanie leaping onto the gun-wielding Finch, it wasn't difficult. "I told you to run," he reminded her.

She looked at him steadily. "I'm tired of running from you."

The self-righteous anger went out of him in a rush. He looked into her soft brown eyes and saw everything he'd ever wanted, all he'd become so sure he'd never have. His heart turned over. He tried to remember that she'd risked her life in spite of his instructions, that she'd allowed the boy to risk his life . . .

Unable to deal with her for the moment, he turned to Greg. "And you . . ."

Greg shrugged. "You still owe me ten bucks from the last poker game. I couldn't let them shoot you."

Erik grabbed a fistful of the boy's collar and pulled him closer, intending to lay out in specific detail all the things that could happen to him in life if he continued to flaunt authority. Then, he looked into the fearlessness in the boy's eyes, the complete trust, and understood that Greg hadn't flaunted authority, he'd simply exercised his right to love.

Erik looked up at Melanie, saw her watching him with the same look in her eyes and realized that what he'd learned in the truck was confirmed. Courage was letting yourself be loved. He held Greg close with one arm and reached for Melanie with the other. "Thank you both," he said, his voice thick with emotion, "for caring that much."

"We ready?" Bill asked. Then, more quietly, as Melanie and Greg climbed into the car, "Where do you want me to take the kid? Harvest House? I think they sent for his mom when he turned up missing."

"Take them both to my place."

"Right."

"Incidentally. Any news from your informant?"

Bill smiled. "Yeah. Called me from his sister's in Sacramento."

Erik sighed, relieved. "Good." Then, he leaned into the window to look at Greg and Melanie. "See you guys later. Try to stay out of trouble."

Chapter Fourteen

Melanie awoke to a broad stripe of sunlight falling across her face. Still drowsy, she wasn't interested in opening her eyes. Every muscle ached like the morning after a first aerobics class. She couldn't remember why she should feel that way, but trying to figure it out was too much trouble.

She felt happy. Eyes still closed, she smiled at nothing and decided the reason for it might be worth thinking about. She remembered a hug had generated that feeling—a hug from Erik. "Thank you." A snatch of conversation began to drift across her mind. "Thank you both for . . . caring so much."

She sat up with a start, suddenly remembering everything. The flight in her car to find Erik, the stealthy search of Harvest House, the long ride in the back of the truck and, finally, Erik flinging himself at Abernathy. The terror she'd felt at that moment came back sharply, and she closed her eyes against it.

But it was diluted almost immediately by the sound of laughter from downstairs. Melanie picked out Jolene's voice, Bill's, Greg's, and a woman's voice that she couldn't identify. She heard John and Reba, then Erik. The happy feeling with which she'd awakened rolled over and over inside her. She threw the covers back and ran into the bathroom to splash water on her face and comb her hair. She still wore Erik's black sweater, but she was too eager to see him to take the time to tie back her hair or to change clothes. She hurried down the stairs to find everyone in the living room, except Erik, whom she could see on the telephone in the kitchen.

"Melanie!" Greg, looking fresh and smiling, ran to meet her at the bottom of the stairs. But behind the smile, she could see sadness. Before she could wonder about it, Greg turned to the sofa. "Mom, this is Melanie!"

A small dark-haired woman put a cup on the coffee table and rose from between Jolene and Reba to greet Melanie. She wore a plain black skirt and a white blouse, like the uniform of a waitress, as though she'd come directly from work. She was probably in her midthirties, Melanie guessed. She wore lines of grief, strain and worry around her eyes and mouth, but her smile was warm and genuine. "I'm Ellen Butler," she said, taking Melanie's hands. Hers were dry and strong. "The police brought me," she said in a shy voice. "When they told me Greg was missing, I was wild with worry. They thought he might have gone with you, but no one was sure where you were, so they brought me here. By that time, it was all over and you were asleep upstairs. I wanted to stay to thank you for taking care of Greg."

Greg swallowed audibly, the adventurer of several hours ago lost in the loneliness of a young boy. "I wish you could stay longer, Mom."

Ellen Butler hugged her son fiercely. "I have to go back to work, Greg. Just two more months and you'll be home. That's . . . not very long."

Melanie felt her throat close when the woman's voice faltered. She put an arm around her as Erik walked back into the room.

"I should go," Ellen said. "There's a police officer waiting outside to take me home. Thank you all for . . ." She offered her hand to Erik, who took it and pulled her toward the kitchen.

"Could we talk for a few minutes, Mrs. Butler?" he asked.

She looked uncertainly from Melanie to Erik. "Well, of course . . ."

Erik pushed Greg toward her and took Melanie's hand. He glanced at the other two couples. "Excuse us for a few minutes."

Over her shoulder, Melanie saw Bill give him a "thumbs-up."

"What...?" Melanie began to ask, but he simply pushed her ahead of him into the kitchen.

With all of them finally seated around the table, Melanie, Greg and his mother looking at one another in confusion, Erik crossed his arms on it and leaned toward Ellen Butler. "The judge has agreed," he said quietly, "to suspend the rest of Greg's time in a juvenile facility, if they can feel reasonably sure that his delinquency won't be repeated. He was pretty brave last night."

Greg stared at him. Joy leaped in his mother's eyes. "You mean he can come home with me?"

"I won't get into trouble again," Greg promised fervently. He raised a hand solemnly. "Swear to God! I promise."

Erik nodded. "I know you mean that now," he said.

Greg looked affronted, "I mean it now. I'll mean it tomorrow. I thought you knew that."

Erik smiled. "I do. But I'm still going to be around once a week to hold you to it."

Greg looked at him in pleased surprise. "You're gonna come to Portland?"

"You got a problem with that?"

"No." Greg laughed, then became suddenly serious, his brow darkening as he came around the table, arms open. Erik stood up to hold him close. "It'll be scary," Greg admitted, "to know that you're a hundred miles away."

"I can be in Portland in a couple of hours if you need me." Erik held him away and smiled down at him. "Otherwise, you have everything a man needs to stand on his own. You're smart and you've got guts. All you're lacking is experience, and that's why you have a mother. If you keep up your grades, we'll talk about a loan when it comes time for college."

Ellen Butler, sobbing, came to put her arms around Erik, sandwiching her son between them.

There were hugs and tearful goodbyes as Greg and Ellen were put in the police car that would take them home.

Everyone waved until they were out of sight. Reba, dabbing at her eyes, turned to the group assembled on the sidewalk. "What does everybody want for lunch?"

"Blockheaded son," John said with a dark glance at Erik, "on rye."

Erik rolled his eyes and caught Bill's arm as his friend tried to back away. "Stick around. You're as much to blame as I am." He smiled placatingly at his father. "Dad, we've been all over this. We didn't tell you it was going down last night because—"

"I'm good enough to hold a shotgun at a window," John interrupted aggressively, "But too *old* to be trusted in the crunch."

"I didn't want you to get hurt."

"So you leave me behind to worry myself into a coronary! And you!" John jabbed a finger at Bill, who hid behind Erik. "I thought you and I were a team! When he doesn't think straight..." He pointed at Erik. "...*we* think for him. I..."

"John, it's over!" Reba took hold of his arm and tugged him toward the house. "They were only trying to keep you safe for me. Come inside," she crooned sweetly, "and I'll tell you my plans for later."

John looked at Erik and Bill, then at Reba, obviously undecided whether to pursue love or war.

"You're never watching my swimsuit video again," he threatened, his voice quieter as Reba pulled him away. "And you can find another source for chili . . ."

Bill moved out cautiously from behind Erik. "He has the swimsuit video?" he demanded of his friend. "You never told me. John? John!" Bill took off after the older man. "Erik *made* me do it! I *wanted* to include you . . ."

Jolene watched him lope into the house, with an indulgent shake of her head. Then, she turned to her companions. "I know you two have things to talk about." She smiled from one to the other. "Intelligent compromises to make, sensible conclusions to reach." She shooed them toward the lake as she backed up the walk. "Go ahead. Take your time. I'll save you some lunch." She went into the house, leaving them standing alone in the sunny morning.

"Is she getting a little pushy?" Erik asked.

Melanie smiled after her. "That's confidence," she said, "coupled with every sweetheart's earnest wish to see everyone else as happy as she is." She looked up at him, her eyes vaguely uncertain. "So, are you feeling up to intelligent compromise?"

He wore a thoughtful look that made her feel tense with concern. He was a man very sure of what he had to do. Perhaps compromise was out of the question. Perhaps, in her querulous refusal to see things his way, she'd ceased to be an important element in his life.

Erik watched her expression change from uncertain hopefulness to worry. He wondered if the past few days hadn't simply swamped whatever hope he'd entertained that he could change her mind and make her stay.

But she'd come running to his rescue like the cavalry. Certainly that meant—no, he couldn't presume anything.

"Come on." He put his hand at the back of her neck, needing to touch her. "I know where we can talk."

He walked her through the garage to the boathouse, helped her into the boat and pushed off.

The morning air was perfumed and breezy, the lake calm and laced with sunlight. Erik guided the boat to the middle of the lake, turned in a wide circle and cut the motor. They bobbed at anchor, the residential side of the shoreline stretched like a ribbon into the blinding sun. The Scofield house stood out like a jewel. Four hands waved from the downstairs veranda.

Erik and Melanie laughed, then waved back. There was a small commotion as the figures disappeared inside.

Melanie continued to stare at the house, a painful catch in her throat. She felt clearly, suddenly, the girl of long ago who had sat out here with her father and fished. She felt all her hopes and dreams—and her painful loss. But, only for an instant. Her heart was so full of love, her life so full of special people, who cared about her and whom she cared about, that her grief receded, and she felt as excited about the future as she had when the Scofield house had been only a cherished fancy.

Erik saw tears well in her eyes, guessed she was remembering her father and her pain and moved carefully to sit beside her. He put an arm around her and she leaned into him, drawing a ragged breath.

"I bought one of your paintings of the iris," he said, leaning his cheek against her hair.

"You did?"

"Yes. I hung it next to the goldenrod in the sunroom. Remember when you told me that the goldenrod exemplified what it felt like when we kissed?"

"Yes."

"You're right. Touching you, holding you, making love to you is like that—gold stacked upon itself until it's one quaking pyramid of beauty."

She felt precisely that. "Yes," she repeated.

"But *real* love," he went on gently, "is more complicated. It's composed of what we give and take from each other. It's the iris you found so hard to commit to paper. It's elegant, complex—an evolutionary masterpiece that didn't achieve its status by starting out as a daisy. I think an iris is love in a flower. Do you know what I'm saying?"

She straightened to look into his eyes, understanding his metaphor, but not its conclusion. "You're saying loving each other will be difficult."

He smiled softly. "Loving each other will be easy. Always understanding each other will be difficult." He hesitated. "But my mind is made up. Whether you're here or three thousand miles away, I'm still going to love you. I know time and distance can't change what I feel."

He wrapped his arms around her, holding her tightly. "If you stay, I'll go into private practice when my term is up. I'll even specialize in corporate law, or something equally dull, if that would make you happy. I don't have anything else to prove. I learned in the back of the truck that loving someone takes as much courage as anything I've ever done before. I still have two years to serve, though. I suppose..." His voice quieted, becoming edged with emotion. "I could accept your going home to Denver for that time, and coming back to me when I'm free to..."

Melanie leaned back against his shoulder to kiss his chin, all the tension and uncertainty leaving her. "No," she said. "I'm not leaving for even two minutes. I guess I just had to come to terms with the truth that you can live a life of peace and quiet, and have only that—or you can love and fight and care. You can get hurt, lose people that are important to you, but in the end you gain more than you could ever lose because you're not hoarding—you're investing in the process."

Erik looked into her face, saw love and excitement and eagerness there, and was afraid to let himself believe that the prospect of sharing her life with him had prompted those emotions.

Melanie watched astonishment, then disbelief play across his face, and wrapped her arms around his neck, hating herself for making it so difficult for him to trust her capitulation.

"Anyway," she said, giving him a quick kiss, "I think I have a definite talent for the work. For the rest of your term, I can follow you around as a sort of henchman—henchwoman?"

"No," he said. He caught the flyaway tendrils of hair at her cheek and smoothed them back, his heart weak with tenderness. "You're going to be home taking care of our little girls and teaching them all about flowers."

"Okay." She leaned into him, smiling, as though she were enjoying that thought. "Then we should get the dog right away."

He lost the thread for a moment. "Dog?"

She snuggled closer and leaned her head back to look up at him. "You remember. We decided on a big dog to protect our little girls. We should pick it out now, because training a puppy and a baby at the same time could be pretty awful, don't you think? And we'll want to start working on having a baby right away. Won't we?"

Erik looked deep into her eyes, unable to find the grief there that always lay like a shadow beneath the surface. Love and excitement went deep. He let himself believe that God had reached down and handed him a wild iris. "Yes." He kissed her. "We will."

Epilogue

"No one," Erik said feelingly, leaning into the mirror over the dresser to knot a sedately patterned blue tie, "celebrates their first anniversary with six other people."

Melanie stood beside him in a black slip, adjusting diamond earrings. A lanky, half-grown Great Dane the color of coal slept on the carpet at the foot of the bed. "If they were part of a triple wedding, they do. And Ellen and Greg are such an important part of our lives, we couldn't leave them out."

Erik pulled the end of his tie through and slipped the knot into place. "I can't believe I let you talk me into that. It was like something from a Gilbert and Sullivan operetta."

She turned abruptly to put her arms around his waist. "You aren't really upset that Jo and Reba and I thought it would be fun to celebrate together?"

He couldn't maintain the pretense any longer. Smiling, he pulled her close. "Of course not. I was just thinking that if there was no one else involved in our plans..." His hand wandered over her silk-clad hip, bringing the material of her slip up as his fingers retraced their path. "I could take this off you..."

Melanie sighed and leaned her weight against him, protesting halfheartedly, "Erik, we've been late for everything this year."

He nibbled on her ear, nipped at her shoulder. "That's what you get for being so desirable."

"I'm not desirable. You just have too much energy. Erik!" Feeling herself succumbing to the sensations he so easily aroused in her, Melanie wedged a space between them. "You promised me dinner and dancing at Marco's," she said firmly. "And I'm holding you to it. Now, finish dressing. Everyone will be here in ten minutes for cocktails."

Erik frowned and, with a deft yank, pushed her backwards onto the bed. He trapped her there with one knee between hers and a hand on either side of her. "Do you know what happens to bossy wives?" he demanded.

The dog was between them in an instant, not planning to stop the roughhousing, but to join in.

"Sasha!" Erik said, pushing her aside. She took that as an invitation to play, and leaped on Melanie.

Erik pushed her firmly aside. "Stay!" he ordered. Whimpering, she sat up in the middle of the bed, looking worried and hurt.

Melanie laughed. "I don't know what happens to bossy wives, but bossy husbands are eaten by their wives' dogs."

"Some are abandoned," Erik said ominously, ignoring her threat. "Some are spanked." He leaned a little closer, the threat in his eyes not quite concealing the humor. Sasha whined. "And some get presents."

She laughed throatily. "If you're offering me a choice, I'll take the present."

Erik stood and pulled her up into a sitting position. "You're so predictable," he said. From the drawer of his bedside table, he extracted a jeweler's box. "I knew that would be your answer." He handed it to her and sat beside her. "Happy Anniversary, darling."

Out of a velvet nest, Melanie pulled a pin in the shape of an iris, made of amethyst and gold. Sasha's large black nose threatened to inhale it. Erik pulled the dog aside, rubbing between her ears.

"Oh, Erik," Melanie whispered. She held it to her and wrapped her free arm around his neck. He'd already given her so much—the comfort and protection he'd promised, and such warmth and fun that fear had receded from her life completely. "Thank you. I love it." She kissed him, nestling against him as his arms encircled her. If there was one small cloud on her horizon, it was the office he'd just leased in a new building still under construction downtown. It would be ready to occupy about the time his term was up as district attorney.

She lifted her head to look into his eyes. "Erik, are you sure about the office?"

"Melanie, I'm sure." He spoke with the bemused impatience of a man who'd answered the question many times before. "And if you ask me one more time, I'll take the pin back and you'll be left with only the other two choices."

She put her cheek against his. "I just want you to be sure."

She'd been as loving, devoted and supportive a wife as any man could hope for. He wanted to do this for her and he was beginning to realize that he wanted to do it for himself. "I'm sure," he insisted, caressing her back. "I'm looking forward to working for myself, setting my own schedule, making more time for you. Now..." He pulled her away and folded his arms, feigning seriousness. "I presume you've bought me something."

He was surprised when she lowered her eyes and soft pink color rose from her neck to her cheekbones.

"Not exactly," she said.

"What?" He threw her back against the mattress again. Sasha barked and wagged her tail. "The treatment for bossy wives who forget to buy their husbands an anniversary present is even worse!"

She laughed, pushing at his chest. "I do have something for you."

"That's more like it." He braced himself over her, feigning severity. "It better be good."

She sobered suddenly, her eyes deepening. She ran her hands up his chest and over his shoulders. "I can't offer you a choice, just two possibilities," she said quietly. "Son or daughter."

He stared at her, images flooding his mind, emotions filling his chest.

A daughter, Erik thought in wonder, with Melanie's platinum hair, a son with those wide brown eyes, a child that was part of her and part of himself—proof that they finally understood the miracle of their love for each other.

Still speechless, he rolled onto his back and pulled her over him, holding his wife and the bud of their child with a fierce possessiveness that astounded even him. Sasha forced her large black snout between them.

Melanie laughed and kissed him, then the dog. "I take it then, that you're pleased?"

"I am ecstatic," he whispered, his voice thick with emotion. "I am . . . overwhelmed."

Melanie leaned her forearms on his chest and smiled into his eyes. "Is it right to be this happy?"

Erik held her hair back from her face and kissed her reverently. "Sure feels right to me," he said.

PASSPORT TO ROMANCE VACATION SWEEPSTAKES

OFFICIAL RULES

SWEEPSTAKES RULES AND REGULATIONS. NO PURCHASE NECESSARY.

HOW TO ENTER:

1. To enter, complete this official entry form and return with your invoice in the envelope provided, or print your name, address, telephone number and age on a plain piece of paper and mail to: Passport to Romance, P.O. Box #1397, Buffalo, N.Y. 14269-1397. No mechanically reproduced entries accepted.
2. All entries must be received by the Contest Closing Date, midnight, December 31, 1990 to be eligible.
3. Prizes: There will be ten (10) Grand Prizes awarded, each consisting of a choice of a trip for two people to: i) London, England (approximate retail value $5,050 U.S.); ii) England, Wales and Scotland (approximate retail value $6,400 U.S.); iii) Caribbean Cruise (approximate retail value $7,300 U.S.); iv) Hawaii (approximate retail value $ 9,550 U.S.); v) Greek Island Cruise in the Mediterranean (approximate retail value $12,250 U.S.); vi) France (approximate retail value $7,300 U.S.).
4. Any winner may choose to receive any trip or a cash alternative prize of $5,000.00 U.S. in lieu of the trip.
5. Odds of winning depend on number of entries received.
6. A random draw will be made by Nielsen Promotion Services, an independent judging organization on January 29, 1991, in Buffalo, N.Y., at 11:30 a.m. from all eligible entries received on or before the Contest Closing Date. Any Canadian entrants who are selected must correctly answer a time-limited, mathematical skill-testing question in order to win. Quebec residents may submit any litigation respecting the conduct and awarding of a prize in this contest to the Régie des loteries et courses du Quebec.
7. Full contest rules may be obtained by sending a stamped, self-addressed envelope to: "Passport to Romance Rules Request", P.O. Box 9998, Saint John, New Brunswick, E2L 4N4.
8. Payment of taxes other than air and hotel taxes is the sole responsibility of the winner.
9. Void where prohibited by law.

- -

PASSPORT TO ROMANCE VACATION SWEEPSTAKES

OFFICIAL RULES

SWEEPSTAKES RULES AND REGULATIONS. NO PURCHASE NECESSARY.

HOW TO ENTER:

1. To enter, complete this official entry form and return with your invoice in the envelope provided, or print your name, address, telephone number and age on a plain piece of paper and mail to: Passport to Romance, P.O. Box #1397, Buffalo, N.Y. 14269-1397. No mechanically reproduced entries accepted.
2. All entries must be received by the Contest Closing Date, midnight, December 31, 1990 to be eligible.
3. Prizes: There will be ten (10) Grand Prizes awarded, each consisting of a choice of a trip for two people to: i) London, England (approximate retail value $5,050 U.S.); ii) England, Wales and Scotland (approximate retail value $6,400 U.S.); iii) Caribbean Cruise (approximate retail value $7,300 U.S.); iv) Hawaii (approximate retail value $ 9,550 U.S.); v) Greek Island Cruise in the Mediterranean (approximate retail value $12,250 U.S.); vi) France (approximate retail value $7,300 U.S.).
4. Any winner may choose to receive any trip or a cash alternative prize of $5,000.00 U.S. in lieu of the trip.
5. Odds of winning depend on number of entries received.
6. A random draw will be made by Nielsen Promotion Services, an independent judging organization on January 29, 1991, in Buffalo, N.Y., at 11:30 a.m. from all eligible entries received on or before the Contest Closing Date. Any Canadian entrants who are selected must correctly answer a time-limited, mathematical skill-testing question in order to win. Quebec residents may submit any litigation respecting the conduct and awarding of a prize in this contest to the Régie des loteries et courses du Quebec.
7. Full contest rules may be obtained by sending a stamped, self-addressed envelope to: "Passport to Romance Rules Request", P.O. Box 9998, Saint John, New Brunswick, E2L 4N4.
8. Payment of taxes other than air and hotel taxes is the sole responsibility of the winner.
9. Void where prohibited by law.

 RLS-DIR

PASSPORT WIN 1 of 10 Vacations SEE INSIDE TO ROMANCE

VACATION SWEEPSTAKES

MONTH 1 ENTRY

Official Entry Form

Yes, enter me in the drawing for one of ten Vacations-for-Two! If I'm a winner, I'll get my choice of any of the six different destinations being offered — and I won't have to decide until after I'm notified!

Return entries with invoice in envelope provided along with Daily Travel Allowance Voucher. Each book in your shipment has two entry forms — and the more you enter, the better your chance of winning!

Name ______________________________

Address ______________________________ Apt. ______

City ______________ State/Prov. ______________ Zip/Postal Code ______________

Daytime phone number ______________________________
Area Code

☐ I am enclosing a Daily Travel Allowance Voucher in the amount of $__________ Write in amount revealed beneath scratch-off

- -

VACATION SWEEPSTAKES

MONTH 1 ENTRY

Official Entry Form

Yes, enter me in the drawing for one of ten Vacations-for-Two! If I'm a winner, I'll get my choice of any of the six different destinations being offered — and I won't have to decide until after I'm notified!

Return entries with invoice in envelope provided along with Daily Travel Allowance Voucher. Each book in your shipment has two entry forms — and the more you enter, the better your chance of winning!

Name ______________________________

Address ______________________________ Apt. ______

City ______________ State/Prov. ______________ Zip/Postal Code ______________

Daytime phone number ______________________________
Area Code

☐ I am enclosing a Daily Travel Allowance Voucher in the amount of $__________ Write in amount revealed beneath scratch-off

CPS-ONE